CW01208550

The Fall Guys

Gerry Rose

authorHOUSE

AuthorHouse™ UK Ltd.
500 Avebury Boulevard
Central Milton Keynes, MK9 2BE
www.authorhouse.co.uk
Phone: 08001974150

© 2009 Gerry Rose. All rights reserved.

No part of this book may be reproduced, stored in a retrieval system, or transmitted by any means without the written permission of the author.

First published by AuthorHouse 7/27/2009

ISBN: 978-1-4389-6094-4 (sc)

This book is printed on acid-free paper.

In this novel, references are made to a number of historical facts. However, in the time-honoured fictional tradition, the actual story is, of course, entirely made up.

To Lesley

On Saturday 2 October 1981, the Hunger Strike by Irish Republican prisoners in the Maze Prison Belfast was called off. The Hunger Strike had begun at eight o'clock on 1 March 1981 and was to see the deaths of ten men, men who gave their lives for a lost cause.

For many Republicans the campaign, known throughout the world as the H-Block campaign, was seen as a great propaganda victory. To other hardliners however, it was seen as a comprehensive defeat. The anticipated wide-scale carnage threatened by the IRA as hunger striker after hunger striker died never came. The British Prime Minister had merely called their bluff.

With the ending of the campaign came the inevitable volley of suggestions, arguments and questions as to what would happen next. This is the story of an attempt by two renegade Republicans to redeem the lost cause. If successful it would have altered the face of British, Irish and even world political history for years.

Friday 22 January 1982

Prologue

The wizened grey haired old man had been calling the dog for some time and there was still no sign of the spaniel. Carefully, he clambered over the small wire fence that separated the road from the sand dunes and the beach.

Suddenly, he could hear the dog barking above the frightening roar of the wind and sea, and with a hint of apprehension in his large stride, he moved slowly over the wet sand in the general direction of the sound. Then, he could see the dog amongst some rocks, foam swirling about its paws, its floppy ears dripping wet.

As the old man approached, he could see that the dog was standing over what appeared to be a body. Racing to where the dog stood, he pushed it away without looking at his canine companion, unable to take his eyes away from what lay in the water before him.

It was a body all right, and despite having no experience of such things, the old man guessed that the dead man had been in the sea for some considerable time. Leaning over the body, the old man grabbed it by the shoulders, noticing as he touched the slimy texture of the cashmere sweater the man had been wearing when he had met his doom. Laboriously, he dragged the corpse up the beach, the cocker spaniel still barking continuously by his side.

It took him all of ten minutes to reach the grass verge beside the road and, dropping the body, the old man slumped on his backside on to the wet ground panting heavily for breath.

After a few minutes rest, he called the dog and returned to the road. Considering it highly unlikely that anyone would be driving along the quiet old coast road in such terrible weather conditions, he decided to hurry back to his own cottage and telephone the police from there. Setting off at a brisk pace, no longer feeling the cold, he thought hopefully that he had found fame at last and day-dreamed as he walked of having his picture in the newspapers, perhaps even being interviewed for the television.

Below, London Transport's world famous red buses vied with the equally familiar black taxicabs and throngs of other vehicles for acceleration space on the infamously busy streets of the city. John Birbeck watched from his office window without much comprehension, a heavy heart having diverted his eyes from the office he had been clearing of personal belongings for the last few days.

In truth, he also felt slightly tipsy from the champagne that had been served at his retirement party and drink had always had a melancholy effect on him. The door of his long departed assistant's office opened and his successor and friend Ian Maitland entered the office and sat down in one of the visitors chairs in front of the outgoing Birbeck's desk, the desk that would officially be his own in the morning.

'How does it feel then John?' he asked as Birbeck turned away from the window for the last time and sat down behind his desk to face Maitland.
'Ask me that one again in a month or two Ian. At the moment, I don't know what I feel. One half of me shouts three cheers, and the other half tells me that it is one foot in the grave time.' replied Birbeck honestly.
'Come on John, you're a very fit fifty-five, another good thirty years to go.' countered Maitland sincerely.
'The thing I've been asking myself Ian is what have I really achieved? Terrorists still bomb innocents in our cities, top politicians, Royalty and the famous still need constant protection and I've come

and gone and nothing has really changed. Probably got worse, if we were being brutally honest about it.'

'Notched up a few good results though, haven't we?' suggested Maitland, unhappy to see Birbeck depart in such a depressed frame of mind.

'You make it sound like a game Ian and I can't accept that it's as trivial as that, it can't be.'

'More of a complex jigsaw puzzle with all the pieces spread all over a ten acre grassy field, some even lost.' Maitland continued the theme 'But we can't be expected to put society back on the rails, never could. That's not our role. If life was a great bed of roses, we'd all be out of a job.' offered Maitland reassuringly.

'I am out of a bloody job,' countered Birbeck in a quiet, friendly manner.

'Christ John, we'd better stop or you'll have me convinced that I should retire too. What good would that do?'

'It would do no good at all Ian. As I said, ask me how I feel in a month or two. Today has been very difficult.' Maitland nodded that he understood and just then, the telephone on Birbeck's desk interrupted them ringing three times before he picked up the receiver. Silently, he listened to the caller before giving his thanks and disconnecting.

'That was Jamieson. Do you want the good news or the fucking fantastic news?' he asked suddenly lighthearted.

'I'll have the good news thanks.' Replied Maitland expectantly.

'Well, my car is ready and I must take my leave. The show is therefore, all yours.' He rose and walked around the desk and shook hands firmly with Maitland.

'All the very best Ian, and believe me, you are going to need it. And, any time you feel like you need some professional advice, please hesitate before calling.' The two men stood smiling at each other, a sad parting of men who had been through hell together.

At the door Birbeck looked back.

' By the way, the fucking fantastic news is that Liam Blaney's body has been washed up on a remote beach on the west coast of Scotland.' He smiled and turned to leave.

'One more jigsaw nearer completion,' replied Maitland ' I told you we hadn't done too badly.'

The news of Liam Blaney's death lifted John Birbeck's spirits as his driver Jordan whisked him, for the last time, through the streets of London to Waterloo station.

Having slipped into a first class compartment and found a seat, he recalled the details of the dangerous jigsaw of which Blaney had been an important component part, and was saddened by the knowledge that there still remained a missing piece.

As the train rolled out of Waterloo, he closed his eyes and brought his superb memory to bear as he pieced together the events, events that could so easily have resulted in his early and disgraceful retirement from the force he had served with great pride for more than thirty years.

It had all started on a farm in Ulster in October 1981….

Friday 16 October 1981

1

The metallic blue Jaguar XJ-6 sped across the border that separates the six counties in the north from those in the south of Ireland. The small, well-dressed handsome man sitting in the front passenger seat looked at his watch. It was eighteen minutes to midnight. Smiling, he lit another king size cigarette happy, in the knowledge that he would be there on time.

Looking out of the smoked glass windows he realized for the first time what a beautiful night it was, full moon with the stars shining like the diamonds clustered in the Rolex watch that he wore on his left wrist. As they drove no words were uttered, Liam Blaney did not believe in wasting conversation with his employees.

Blaney sat back in the bucket seat and closed his dark brown eyes. As he did so, his photographic memory brought instant images of the four men he and his partner were about to meet. He recalled every known fact about their careers to date and wondered momentarily if they would all turn up. Deep down however, he knew that they would. After all, he had been the master who had chosen them.

Eleven months he had spent gathering together the evidence required to convince his partner that the Frenchman was the man to co-ordinate the expedition; eight more months to track down the Englishman; six months just to find the American and eight long years of hard input to train their own man for the forthcoming exercise. Opening his eyes, Blaney stubbed out his cigarette and leaned back in his seat to enjoy the remainder of the journey.

Just then however, he felt a sudden pang of deceleration before seeing the lights and the large red and white barrier slung across the road in front of them. Blaney glanced at Cotton, his driver, who was showing no sign of tension. Mildly annoyed, he slipped his hand into the pocket of his cashmere cardigan and felt for the note.

A young army Corporal approached and Cotton leaned forward and flicked a switch. The window to his right lowered gracefully and the soldier placed his rifle in the open window and spoke with a deep Scottish accent.

'Evening gents, bit late to be out for a pleasure cruise it is not?' he began, looking into the car.

'Not a pleasure trip son, going to Belfast on a business trip, early morning start,' explained Blaney casually leaning over his driver and pressing, without difficulty, a twenty-pound note into the soldier's hand.

'Very good sir, have a good trip.' Smiled the young corrupt member of the British security force as he crushed the note tightly into the palm of his hand to avoid detection by his colleagues. Straightening up, the Corporal waved for the barrier to be raised. It was lifted immediately and the XJ-6 accelerated through, reaching 60mph in no more than eight seconds.

Blaney sat back and afforded himself a wry smile. Three times he had crossed the border at that spot and three times the same Corporal had accepted a bribe. His father had always told him that money could speak louder than words. Blaney checked his watch again, it was midnight and he would be there on time.

Earlier that day, Hovercraft flight number 082 from Calais arrived at Ramsgate Hoverport. Jacque DeVille drove his large Citroen saloon down the ramp and onto the wet concrete. It was a beautiful morning and the crossing had been very calm. In his car and hidden behind the rear passenger seats, he had a suitcase containing amongst other items of false identification, a secondary passport.

At passport control, DeVille had his passport checked by a friendly young man who merely noted that the face on the photograph matched that of the small black man smiling back at him before waving DeVille through saying as he did that he hoped DeVille would enjoy his stay in the United Kingdom. At Customs, he passed through the 'Nothing to Declare' section and was not stopped.

Five minutes later, the Frenchman was driving his Citroen up the slope that led from the Hoverport to join the early morning traffic and head for London. He felt very relaxed and in no hurry. After all, although he was due to catch the 20.30 flight that evening from London Heathrow to Antrim in Ulster, he had all day to keep his other appointment, which was simply to check into the Hilton Hotel in London's famous Park Lane.

As the traffic wound its way towards London, the beautiful morning turned into a beautiful autumnal afternoon. Leaves were falling in abundance from the trees allowing shafts of glorious sunlight to stream between the newly created spaces. DeVille loved England in the early fall and was gladdened by the fact that things were pointing towards a reasonably long stay in the country.

Later that afternoon at the Hilton, a Commissionaire took his car keys and a Pageboy carried the suitcases containing his stylish clothes to his fourth floor room. DeVille tipped the Page five pounds and when he had left, emptied the contents of the suitcases into a large wardrobe. He then stripped and put on a silk dressing gown. Crossing the room to the windows, he looked down on Park Lane with its hustle and bustle of non-stop traffic. Turning away, he shook his head. Nothing could shock the British out of their routines. DeVille headed for the bathroom with a ribald smile on his face.

After showering and shaving, he spent some time placing and brushing his jet-black hair into place. Splashing some Christian Dior aftershave on his face, he dressed in a Dior suit and checked his image in a large full scale mirror, slipped his wallet into an inside pocket, left his room and took an elevator to the ground floor where he refused the offer of a taxi and left on foot for Knightsbridge.

At five pm, DeVille clambered from a London taxicab laden with green Harrods bags stamped proudly in gold with the name of the world famous store and climbed the few steps to the Hilton Hotel. Another Pageboy was on hand to carry his new purchases to his room and again DeVille gave five pounds for the service thus ensuring that he would never have to look very far for a Page in the London Hilton.

After an early meal, which he ate alone in the vast dining room, DeVille again went to his room and showered and shaved. Dressed more casually in a cashmere roll neck sweater, plain slacks and a suede jacket that matched his shoes, DeVille telephoned reception and asked for his car to be brought to the main entrance. At six fifteen he left the Hilton and drove to Heathrow Airport where he caught his scheduled flight to Antrim in Northern Ireland.

There, he joined a small queue at the Hertz Car Rental booth.

The beautiful young woman rolled off her lover, satisfied with her efforts. As he lay on his back breathing heavily from their joint orgasmic pursuits, she viewed him with great satisfaction. A total satisfaction that always overcame her after spending time in bed with Paul. Raising her hand, she ran it through his dark red hair, down his slightly hooked Roman nose, down through the fair fuzz on his broad chest to his navel and finally arrived at his limp, wet lower regions. Her long slim fingers brought his limp organ slowly back to life. Chuckling, she reached across him and gently nibbled his left ear.

Suddenly however, he threw back the silk sheets and leapt from the bed, telling her that he had to go out. Rolling onto her back to reveal her perfectly shaped large breasts, she sighed heavily, she had been hoping for more sex. However, recognizing his mood, she pulled the sheets back over her naked body.

It was their unwritten rule that she never asked him about his work and he in turn never volunteered any information. Whatever his work was, she knew it had to pay well if the house in which he lived was anything to go by. Hearing the shower spring to life, she decided to join him. The least she could do was scrub his back.

When he had dressed he checked his time, kissed the girl, who was again tucked up in the large bed, and left the house. His small red sports car was parked in the garage and it sprang to life the instant he turned the ignition key. He admired beautiful things and looked lovingly at the sheer lines of his car as he climbed out of the low seats to close the garage door behind him. Pulling the garage door closed, he jumped athletically into his much loved vehicle and slammed the door. Driving away, he listened to the affluent sound of tyre on gravel and, as he guided the car along the narrow tree lined drive; he checked his watch before turning into the main road and speeding off towards the farm.

Paul O'Neil was twenty-five years old with exceptional good looks and physique. The house that he had just left had belonged to his beloved parents, both doctors, who had been shot dead by the British troops in an ambush that had gone so tragically wrong some eight years previous. His terrorist work had begun then as he was taken under the wing of the Provisional Irish Republican Army and trained with great care for their major projects, projects like the one that he was about to begin.

Feeling apprehensive as he sped through the night, he thought of the parents he had loved so much, of the plans he had held for following them into the medical profession, of their happy home in which he still lived, of their lives wasted at the hands of the British enemy. Such thoughts eased his apprehensions and he looked forward to playing his part in achieving the unification of Ireland. The woman who shared his house knew nothing of this unquenchable ambition.

Nearing the farm he parked the car in an old farm lane and

walked across wet fields for nearly a mile to the farmhouse. Paul O'Neil trusted nobody, which explained why he was the Provisional's top man and completely unknown to the security forces and, more importantly for O'Neil, still alive.

While Jacque DeVille was spending a small fortune in Harrods that afternoon, Jonathan Miller was driving off from the eighteenth tee at his local golf club in Wentworth, Surrey. He needed a par five for a round of seventy-four and his drive sailed straight down the centre of the fairway and came to rest amongst some fallen leaves. His opponent, an attractive professional golfer from Los Angeles hit her shot to the left of the fairway causing her ball to come to rest some forty yards behind Miller's.

'You'll be okay there Paula,' he called, deliberately taking his time to replace his club in his bag to enable him to follow behind her and watch her magnificent ass roll in her tight fitting grey golf slacks as she marched down the fairway in front of him.

She was in England on vacation to visit her sister and had been talked into a round of golf by the handsome man she had met at a party in her honour the previous evening. Had she known then what she now knew of his considerable golfing prowess, she would have refused his challenge. However, the golf was almost over, her defeat confirmed on the previous green, and she was increasingly excited at the prospect of spending the remainder of the day with her conqueror. Briefly, she thought of her husband at home in California, but knew that Miller was the man who could help her get off for the first time in a month, and duly dismissed her husband from her thoughts.

Miller made a short putt on the eighteenth green for his seventy-four while Paula missed from eight feet thus emphasizing the scale of her defeat. After congratulating her victor and accepting his invitation for a drink in the bar, they walked to the clubhouse laughing together in a fine mood. The clubhouse, a converted mansion, was deserted but for two old chaps sitting in the corner drinking Gin and reading through the day's newspapers.

Paula sat watching Miller as he stood at the bar and could not help but notice the curt way in which he spoke to the barman. Perhaps, she thought, there is a dark side to Jonathan Miller. Dismissing this, she looked forward to the possibility of enjoying his magnificent body.

After a couple of drinks Miller suggested that they go back to his place for a swim to freshen up. Paula heard herself asking if he had a spare swimsuit knowing full well that even if he had said no she would have gone with him anyway. Miller told her that he was sure to have a costume to fit her and they left the clubhouse hand in hand.

Jonathan had been correct and Paula soon found a revealing bikini that fitted her like a glove. When Miller arrived in navy swim shorts, the very sight of him sent shivers down her spine and she was certain that they would become lovers that afternoon.

Later, the alarm clock burst into its noisy purr and Miller leapt cat-like to switch it off. Paula sat up quickly trying to remember where she was and on seeing Jonathan's muscular suntanned frame, lay back in the bed, smiling at the happy memory.
'I am afraid I must go out tonight Paula, I've got to go over to Ireland for a meeting first thing tomorrow morning.' He was standing under the shower and switched it on.
'Would you mind dropping me off at my sisters on your way?' she asked relaxing in the mess that earlier had been an immaculately made bed.
'Of course not.' he replied scrubbing himself vigorously, his mind already straying from his latest sexual conquest.
As requested, Miller drove Paula to her sisters before driving his Mercedes to Heathrow Airport where he caught the same flight as Jacque DeVille to Antrim.

After passing through the arrivals gate, Miller made his way to the car rental booth where he joined a queue behind a smartly dressed dark haired black man who, from the sound of his accent, was French. The cars were parked in a corner of the highly fenced car park and Miller drove his hired Ford over the security ramps and out of the car park behind the foreigner.

An hour later, he was aware of the fact that the same car was still in front of him. Ten minutes later however, the Frenchman drew into a lay by and Miller overtook him. He was not to see the car again until after the meeting at the farm.

The two men stood waiting in silence. They had been right and the plane was on time. Then they saw the flashing lights on the aircraft's under carriage. Separating, one of the men ran along the left hand side of the large field setting alight the torches while his partner lit those on the right. With the torches lit, the men ran back to where the two cars were parked and switched on both sets of headlights. The light aircraft circled once before beginning its approach to the makeshift runway.

Sitting on the bonnet of one of the cars, the men watched with interest as the small single engine aircraft bumped down onto the grass field. The pilot taxied the plane to the end of the runway and stopped. The two men watched as the door opened and a tall blond man carrying a small overnight bag jumped to the grass. Walking to the edge of the torch-lit runway, the man watched as the pilot realigned the airplane before speeding along the field and taking off again into the clear night sky.

One of the two men opened a car door and flashed the headlights and the new arrival ran, fleet of foot, down the field to where the cars were parked.

Their instructions had been quite clear, hand over the keys to one of the cars and do not converse in any way. They obeyed their instructions to the letter and watched the man get into the car and drive off. When he was out of sight, they began gathering together the torches. The arrival had certainly stirred their curiosity although they would never see him again.

Outside the field the man stopped the car for a few minutes to ensure that he was not being followed. Satisfied, he looked at his watch. It was five minutes to midnight and he calculated that he would be there on time. Crawford Spencer had arrived in trouble torn Ulster and enjoyed the feeling as adrenalin pumped through his veins.

A large grandfather clock struck once at twelve fifteen causing John McCormack to lift his weary body from a deep Chesterfield and stretch his aching arms above his head. He crossed the room to one of the large French windows and pulled back one of the heavy velvet drapes. It was totally dark outside with only the sound of a hooting barn owl to break the silence. Letting the drape fall back across the window, McCormack went to a drinks tray where he pulled the top from a decanter and poured himself a large measure of fine Cragganmore malt whisky. It was miraculous, he thought to himself, how the whisky could help relieve his pain. Carrying the glass, he went to his writing desk and pulled a chair under him as he sat down.

He was a small man of sixty-seven years with grey hair and extremely thin. Sitting back for a moment to let the whisky take effect, he held his chest as the pain flashed over him in crushing spasms. Slugging from the whisky glass he extracted a blue folder from a secret compartment in the desk. They would be arriving in fifteen minutes and he decided to skip read the details once more, details so meticulously compiled by Liam Blaney his colleague on this awe-inspiring venture. Taking another large gulp of the whisky, he opened the folder and concentrated on the details of the four killers, scanning their photographs, as he read:

Jacque DeVille
Born:Paris, France in 1945;
Height:Five feet eight inches;
Colour:Black, black hair, brown eyes;
Record:Came to the attention of the Provisionals in May

1974 following his killing in Paris of the Israeli ambassador.
Cost:One million French francs.

Jonathan Miller
Born:London, England in 1953;
Height:Five feet eleven inches;
Colour:White, blond hair brown eyes
Record:Large number of killings attributed to him as the 'Blond Anglo' including the killing in Bilbao of a Spanish army general.
Cost:Seventy five thousand pounds sterling.

Crawford Spencer
Born:Long Island, New York, USA in 1949;
Height:Six feet four inches;
Colour:White, blond hair blue eyes;
Record:Claims, and can substantiate, fifteen successful operations in the States and Canada.
Cost:One hundred thousand American dollars.

Paul O'Neil
Born:Ballymoney, Co Antrim, Ireland in 1956;
Height:Five feet nine inches;
Colour:White, dark red hair, brown eyes;
Record:Provisionals top man since 1977.

 McCormack drained his glass, pushed back his chair and went to the drinks tray and poured himself another large malt. Glancing at the clock, it was twelve twenty five; he again went to the windows and looked out. Again, there was only the sound of the barn owl and he wished to God that they would hurry up.
 Treeacre Farm is set in some two hundred acres of rolling Ulster countryside with some thirty acres rising onto a large gentle hillside making it perfect sheep farming country. McCormack had inherited

the place from his father and had turned it into a good profit making concern. The large farmhouse set in an acre of woodland in the centre of the farm, gave the place its name. The main building was Georgian in style and was superbly furnished and the outbuildings, which numbered six in all, were in excellent condition.

McCormack who had been reading in the library slipped the folder behind some papers in the secret compartment and locked the desk. Pocketing the key, he left the library and walked across the marble floored hall and entered the dining room. In the centre of the room stood a large mahogany table, which was set out like a boardroom. Six places were set; all with yellow folders lying unopened and blue pencils sitting equi-distant from the folders awaiting the arrival of their users. McCormack surveyed the scene with a critical eye. A perfectionist, he thought somewhat sadly, right to the very end. Holding his chest again he cursed the fact that no one had turned up on time.

Just then however, he heard the sound of a car drawing up and moments later the doorbell rang. McCormack hurried to the door and opened it to cast a strong shaft of light onto the face of his friend and colleague Liam Blaney.

McCormack was delighted to see him and although Blaney was shocked at his friend's appearance, there was no doubting the fact that Blaney was also happy to see his old sparring partner.
'You're the first one here Liam. I was beginning to think that I had got the frigging date wrong.' He took his friend's arm and led him into the library where they both agreed on a whisky.

It was twelve thirty eight before the six men took their places around the large table in the Georgian house on Treeacre Farm. Liam Blaney sat at the head of the table with his ill friend to his right. They had decided that given McCormack's state of health, Blaney should do most of the talking. He looked with a degree of self-satisfaction at the super fit killers in front of him and began.
'Well gentlemen, I would like to begin by thanking you, on

behalf of the Irish Republican movement for making the journey here tonight,' he smiled at the four newcomers and the atmosphere relaxed noticeably before he continued ' I would like to state that your attendance is greatly appreciated.'

'Let me do some introductions because apart from McCormack and myself, I assume that you are total strangers to one another.' The four men nodded although Blaney noticed Miller and DeVille eyeing each other carefully.

Blaney stood and walked around the table rather slower than the others liked before stopping behind DeVille and tapping the Frenchman's left shoulder.

'This is Jacque DeVille from Paris and you will be interested to know that he was the man responsible for the death of a certain Israeli ambassador in Paris in 1974.' DeVille remained expressionless as Blaney walked behind the tall American.

'Crawford Spencer here, is from the United States and I have no doubt that you have all heard of the Harvard Mechanic.' Spencer appeared to enjoy the fact that the others nodded an acquaintance with his notoriety.

'Jonathan Miller is the Blond Anglo.' Nothing further needed to be said about Miller, the others had heard of him also.

'Finally, I come to Paul O'Neil and let me say that within the Irish Republican movement, Paul is considered, by far, to be our best man in your field. The death of an English Member of Parliament within the confines of the English Parliamentary complex is not beyond this man as he has already proved.' Blaney returned to his seat aware of the fact that the others were eyeing O'Neil in a different light than they had eyed each other and concluded that they had identified O'Neil as having a different remit from their own.

The introductions complete, Blaney allowed a momentary silence allowing the others to ponder over the fact that collected around the table were perhaps the most successful professionals assassins currently active in the western world.

Breaking the reflective silence, Blaney began to speak in a quiet, controlled voice and continued to do so without interruption for the next twenty-five minutes outlining the plan the four men had been commissioned to implement. When he had finished, he asked the group if they had any questions and for some time no one spoke as they gathered their thoughts on the scheme they had just heard. Quite simply, if successful it would at least equal the significance of Oswald's killing of John F Kennedy in 1963.

Finally, DeVille broke the silence, speaking in his heavily accentuated English.
'Let me just get all this clear Monsieur Blaney,' he paused to stand and move away from the table. Moving his hands in front of him as if carrying a football, he continued 'What you say is that you want us to go into England and bring down the British Government by systematically killing each member of the Prime Minister's Cabinet?' He shook his head and threw his hands in the air as if to rid him of the imaginary football and sat down.
'I find such a scheme how you say, comprendre?'
'Comprehend,' suggested Miller rather quietly.
'Yes, impossible to comprehend.' concluded the black Frenchman.

Blaney smiled impatiently before responding, 'You have, my friend, a comprehensive grasp of the operation, but let me stress that McCormack and I both believe that once the initial blows are struck and your first victims are dead, then those bastards in Westminster will be willing to start negotiating with the Irish government with a view to the unification of Ireland in accordance with the wishes of true Irishmen throughout the entire world.'

'Jesus H Christ, you guys better have a couple of million bucks to fund this operation,' began Spencer smiling his willingness to participate without further discussion.
'Spencer,' began Blaney opening the folder in front of him 'You need not worry yourself about such matters. Yesterday, I returned from Switzerland where I had been to set up the formalities for the transfer of up to half a million pounds sterling into your personal accounts.' Blaney then proceeded to pass around the table a photocopy of the transaction and the killers knew enough about

Swiss banking to recognize the genuine article. Blaney continued after another suitable pause.

'I have told our bank to credit your personal accounts with one quarter of a million pounds on my instruction and such an instruction will be given upon the reported death of each cabinet minister.'

'Well,' began Miller rubbing his chin with his thumb 'It certainly is one hell of an offer, but what I would like to ask is when we know to stop the killing and what are the arrangements for aborting the mission? Thus far you have not mentioned any exit clause in the contract.' He looked directly at Blaney with his penetrating brown eyes and Liam realized for the first time that of all the killers in the room, Miller was the most dangerous. Suppressing any anger or anxiety, he replied in a quiet but firm voice.

'That is because there is no escape clause. Only when both governments begin the formal process of unification will we consider this mission complete.'

Looking around for reaction, he was surprised when it was Paul O'Neil who spoke. 'That's all very well for me Liam, but these guys are probably the best and most successful professional killers in the business, they won't accept this mission without a decent contract, why the hell should they?'

'Because you will be there to make fucking sure that they do complete the job.' stormed McCormack before falling into a short coughing fit. Recovered, he rose to his feet holding his chest and began walking around the table as he did so. The hired killers realized for the first time that there was in fact no contract to negotiate, their very presence in that room meant that if they were to get out of this mission alive, they would have to go through with the crazy scheme. For the first time, they were united as a team.

McCormack continued. 'You will all be paid very large sums of money, so everything must be planned with meticulous thought given to every detail. Of course, the British Prime Minister will come to know of our plans but not until it is too late for her to do anything about it. This is a battle she can't win, she will have no option but to open negotiations.' McCormack returned to his seat.

Holding his chest again he nodded to Liam, his contribution for the moment, made. Blaney attempted to retrieve the situation.

'Going back to the point Miller made about abortion, let me emphasize what my friend McCormack has said, by making it quite clear that any order for aborting this mission will come from us through O'Neil. Of course, we shall consider your interests as best we can, but you must appreciate our position. We simply can't afford to hand over large sums of money to the assassins benevolent society.' There was a general rumble of muted laughter around the table before Blaney continued.

'But, you better believe me when I say that if any of you gentlemen quit this operation without permission, then you will be signing your own death warrants.' He looked around the table defying anyone to prolong the discussion, but the others had heard enough to believe that Blaney truly meant what he was saying, even if they seriously doubted if he could carry out his threat.

That matter settled to a degree of satisfaction, Blaney went on to explain that in the folders in front of them they would find a list of dates, telephone numbers and other information, which was self-explanatory. McCormack was obviously in some considerable discomfort and asked with some irritation if there were any more questions.

'I've got one or two,' interjected Miller again.

'What would they be?' snapped McCormack.

'First is simple, how many people know of this plan?'

'Only the six people in the room at present,' answered Blaney patiently.

'What do you mean "at present"?' asked Spencer and Blaney replied with a considerable degree of sarcasm. 'Obviously, the British government are going to find out pretty soon mister Spencer. Your next question Miller?'

'How long have we got?'

'The information in the folders sets out a clear timetable.' Replied Blaney knowing well that Miller had been subtly referring to McCormack's state of health.

'Three months at most.' stormed McCormack confirming that

despite the fact that he was a dying man, he was committed to this mission.

'Well then,' Miller concluded with a smile ' we had better get to work.' Everyone in the room nodded their agreement. The mission was on, the contracts accepted.

When the four killers had left Treeacre Farm, McCormack and Blaney went to the library and enjoyed another whisky. McCormack, obviously in considerable pain, it was who spoke first.

'Well Liam what do you think?' He asked gulping at his drink.

'Oh. I think we sold it to them alright, although I think Miller took some convincing.'

'He'll be no problem, too much money at stake for him to back out.'

'Yes, although the sad thing about all this, is the risk to young O'Neil.' reflected Blaney looking into his glass.

'I know, but we agreed it was absolutely necessary if we were going to convince the others that our intentions are serious.' McCormack reminded him.

'Indeed,' agreed Blaney finishing his whisky ' and it will soon be time to make contact with our man in London.'

'Yes, there is no going back now.' Concluded McCormack and Blaney knew that it was time he left his sick friend.

Amongst the trees at Treeacre Farm could hardly be described as the best place to spend an evening, but for Colm Elliot, it was not his own choice of nocturnal entertainment. Hearing some bushes rustle behind him, he turned swiftly to see his colleague Jim Anderson coming towards him carrying a large Thermos flask and two black plastic mugs.

'That old shit not gone to bed yet?' asked Anderson crouching down beside his sergeant and handing Elliot one of the mugs.

'Has he frig. You know Jim; I think he's waiting for someone. He's been at those bloody curtains three times now.' Anderson poured some piping hot tea into Elliot's mug. 'Christ that's boiling!'

'What did you want, cold tea?'

'Point taken smart ass.'

'Do you think that we should set the cameras up just in case?' asked Anderson suddenly serious.

'Yeah I do,' replied Elliot thoughtfully as he sipped his tea. 'You never know with this little bastard.'

The British security forces had put McCormack's home under constant surveillance some six weeks earlier due to his known association with the Dublin based ship-owners Joseph and Liam Blaney. It was widely anticipated within political and security circles that the ending of the Maze prison hunger strike would mean a hardening of the extremist resolve for a violent solution to the Irish problem. McCormack's known extremism coupled with the Blaney involvement in the arms trade presented itself as the obvious reason for the surveillance although Elliot had argued vehemently that McCormack's cancerous state made him an unlikely candidate for terrorist of the year. His superiors however, had overruled him and had appointed him to night duty for his troubles.

They both saw the headlamps as the car entered the driveway to the house and Elliot with his Canon AE1 at the ready scrambled forward in the bushes to get a better view of the arrival. The Jaguar stopped and Elliot and Anderson clicked incessantly as a man, who they both recognized, climbed from the passenger seat and walked to the main door and rang the doorbell. Seconds later, the large door opened throwing light onto the faces of the men as they greeted each other, totally unaware of the fact that less than a hundred yards away they were being photographed.

The next five minutes saw the arrival of three more cars and these men also had their faces committed to celluloid by Elliot and Anderson. When the arrivals were all in the farmhouse, Elliot crawled back to where Anderson sat in the trees.

'Did you recognize any of them?' asked the young sergeant.

'The first one was Liam Blaney but I've never seem any of the others before. What about you?'

'Only Blaney.'

According to the log taken by Jim Anderson, the three strangers left the farmhouse at exactly 1.22am. Liam Blaney departed some fifteen minutes later in his Jaguar and as they had done with the other cars, Elliot and Anderson photographed the vehicle and recorded the number on the registration plate. No record or photograph was taken of Paul O'Neil, who had arrived and sloped off into the night after the meeting via a dark entrance at the side of the house.

Half an hour later, the large house was thrown into darkness when the dying McCormack went to bed. Elliot and Anderson remained on duty in shifts during the remainder of what had been an unusually eventful watch.

Saturday 17 October 1981

2

Typewriter keys clashed loudly, telephones rang continuously and teleprinters pumped out endless sheets of information. What a bloody racket thought Mac Bradley as he pushed shut the glass door to his office. The noise dimmed instantly and he crossed the room stopping for a moment to look at the framed photograph of the idealistic young graduate he had been twelve years earlier. Rolling his eyes, they fixed on the picture below and smiled with real joy, at Marie and the kids. At his desk he lifted the telephone as he sat down in his imitation leather swivel chair.

'Is Elliot in yet?' he barked. 'Well tell him to get his arse in here, I've been waiting for a bloody half hour.' He was almost shouting. It was a habit he had acquired over the years, bawling out his subordinates.

Elliot knocked on the glass door and entered. Bradley looked up and muttered something about Elliot needing a haircut. Ignoring this comment Elliot, dropped four large photographs onto his Chief Inspector's desk, sat down in the visitors chair and awaited Mac Bradley's reaction.

Bradley sifted through them carefully before throwing the photographs down on his desk and asking 'Anything on these bastards yet?' He clasped his hands together and was unhappy with Elliot's hesitancy. 'Well?'

'Top one as you know is Liam Blaney, but the other three are totally new to us I am afraid,' offered the sergeant.

'What about the car number plates?'

'The Jag is registered to the Blaney business, the other three were either hired or stolen.'

'Hired from where?'

'The airport at Antrim, two of them.'

'Anybody remember these faces?'

'A girl with the car hire firm seems to think that the black one was French.' Bradley looked at DeVille's photograph while Elliot continued. 'Airline records support this, the other man filled his in with a false address, we've checked it out.'

'Ok. What about the other car?' asked Bradley confident in Elliot's ability to be as thorough as was possible.

'Driven by this one,' began Elliot pointing to the photograph of Spencer. 'It was stolen in Belfast three days ago but hasn't been traced since last night.'

'Keep on that. Anything else we know about this little gathering?'

'Not yet although a Land Rover patrol recorded the number plate of a Fiat sports car in a farm lane quite near the farm just after midnight.'

'Has the owner been traced yet?'

'Yes but there is nothing to connect the owner with any terrorist faction and he was not seen entering the farm.'

Bradley sat silent for a few moments drumming his fingers on the desk.

'You know Colm; this French guy annoys the hell out of me. Why go to the bother of putting on an act when you've nothing to hide.' He thought for a moment before asking Elliot if he wanted a coffee.

Elliot nodded and Mac Bradley re-entered the main office with its continuous noise and crossed to the hot drinks machine. Waiting for the coffee to filter into the plastic cups he stood surveying the scene totally unaware of what was going on around him. Returning to his office he kicked the door shut behind him.

'That's professional behavior Colm,' he began passing Elliot his coffee and returning to his seat. Elliot accepted the coffee in silence well aware of the fact that some very useful information could come from Mac Bradley once his thought patterns began to flow. 'He's a real smart bastard is Blaney. I'd give my bloody eyeteeth just to get him into our interview room for twenty-four hours. But what have we got on him? Bloody zero.' He sipped at his coffee.

'You think they're up to something?'

'That's for you and Anderson to discover. I was thinking of pulling you off the McCormack detail but now I want the two of you to watch that old rat morning noon and night. Work only as a pair, report directly to me and I want no cock-ups. Do what you feel is needed, I am trusting your judgment on this one Colm but be careful, this could turn nasty, the boys are really pissed at the failure of the hunger strike.' Elliot finished his coffee and threw the empty carton into the waste paper bin beside Bradley's desk.

'Anything else that I need to know?' Asked Elliot and Bradley laughed.

'Well, we also know that Joseph Blaney left Greece yesterday morning on a Blaney Bros cargo ship. Check with Lloyds, there might just be a connection between our little clandestine gathering and a tip off we have received that Joseph Blaney is gun running again.'

'I hope the tip off is right this time.'

'So do I Colm, so do I.'

Thursday 22 October 1981

3

It was a cold wet evening and the rain poured from the bleak dark sky, running in thick rivers along gutters to converge on helpless drains and cause dreadful overflows. Trees and bushes shook furiously in the wind that was attempting to clear away the last of 1981's leaves. Dustbin lids crashed to the ground causing stray cats to cry in the night while less adventurous dogs barked from within warm houses at the strange but frequent noises.

Barry Piers slammed his car door shut and put the bag of drinks on to the passenger seat beside him. Slipping his MG sports into gear, he headed for home. It has been an exhaustingly boring day and with the rain coming, all he longed for was a quiet night at home with his wife Ann. Sighing gently, he knew that his wishes were not possible, it was his father's birthday and Ann had insisted on inviting Lady and Sir Peter Piers for a celebratory meal.

Ten minutes later, he turned the car into the small drive that led to his house. It was a fine Scandinavian type building with large open aspect solar paneled windows and an interior that was furnished with tasteful simplicity in pine.

Closing the garage door he ran to the house. He was a tall wiry man of twenty-nine years with neatly cut jet-black hair. Entering the hallway, Ann walked to where he was standing shaking the rain from his heavy Barbour jacket and put her arms around him before kissing him gently on the check.
'Busy day?' she asked rubbing his slightly damp hair.

'Quiet,' he replied 'What about you?' he took Ann by the arm and led her through to the kitchen where he found a towel and began drying his hair.

'I'm always busy, you should know that,' she answered crossing the room to the large window where she pressed a button and watched the blinds swish shut and close out the cold wet night. 'Get much done?' she continued returning her attention back to her husband.

'Not bad really, spend most of the time verifying the schedules and travelling times.'

'Mmm, sounds tedious.'

'It was. God, I could do with an early night.'

'Perhaps your father and Elizabeth will leave early,' suggested Ann doubtfully. 'Meantime, you go get washed while I finish preparing the meal.'

'We could pretend we're not in when they come.'

'Go and get washed.'

'It was worth a try.' Barry smiled and headed upstairs.

'Yeah, ten out of ten for effort Mister Piers.' Laughed Ann turning her focus back to the various pots and pans on the hob.

It is an understatement to describe Ann Stuart-Piers as merely beautiful, her exceptional features, dark eyes, long dark hair and perfect white teeth complimenting her stunning figure. She had married Barry two years earlier after a three-year live-in engagement. Their current home had been a wedding gift from their parents who had been life-long friends and were obviously delighted at the match of their only children. Barry, since leaving Oxford, had worked as an investigative journalist before publishing a well-received first novel, and was now working on his second book. Ann worked for a trendy woman's magazine where she was building a considerable reputation as a feature writer. By any standards, they were combining very well, successful careers with a happy marriage.

Sir Peter Piers was a tall silver haired man of fifty-nine, an architect and Cabinet Minister in the Conservative government. It was also rumored that he was one of the wealthiest men in politics, having inherited a small fortune from his industrialist father. His wife Elizabeth was the second Lady Piers, Barry's mother having been tragically killed in an airplane crash when he was an infant. They were ten minutes late and Barry met them at the door.

Their greetings and birthday congratulations over, they were seated in the drawing room while Barry served drinks and Sir Peter admired with a respectable degree of jealousy, his daughter-in-law's stunning beauty.

' I must say Ann; you get lovelier each time I see you. ' Ann blushed rather obviously, her father-in-law's alleged reputation as an occasional womanizer embarrassing her considerably.

'It's living with me that does it.' Interjected Barry as he took a seat beside his father. 'So, what's new in the government?'

'Oh this and that although I must say that I find the run up to the Queen's speech something of a bore, all the media is after is hints and clues as to what is likely to be in it.'

'Well, someone must be making a fortune,' continued Barry sipping his favourite drink of vodka neat. 'The newspapers are full of leaks and suggestions.'

'Speculation, I'm afraid, old chap,' replied Sir Peter.

'So, there will not be new proposed legislation to limit the powers of the Trade Unions, or rebellious Local Governments, or young offenders?'

'That's already part of our remit as you know; it was in our election manifesto. Some of it must be included. One must admit to having jolly fun with the press though,' chuckled Sir Peter sampling his Glenmorangie. 'This is rather fine Barry.'

'Do you deny then, that the government are intending to kick the shit out of the Trade Unions?' Barry persisted. Having been a staunch socialist since his early days at Oxford, Barry loved a debate with his father whom he admired and respected despite the fact that he was a Tory.

'Surely you are not advocating that we protect those people?'

'Those people?' Mocked Barry.

'You know perfectly well that we, as a government, are totally opposed to the hooligans and thugs like those at Grunwick. They simply can't be allowed to operate outside the law.'

'But that is only a small minority.'

'Now, now Barry, we all know that millions of law abiding trade unionists in this country are fed up with the bully boys and went to the ballot box and voted Conservative, hoping that we would deal with the problem.'

'Don't bullshit me father, the Tories have wanted to divide and rule the trade unions since they defeated the Heath government in the early seventies.' Barry was realizing that he was losing the debate, there was no way of winning against his father, who Barry thought, was just having fun at his expense anyway.

'I can assure you Barry, we've wanted to divide and rule the trade unions for a lot longer than that,' smiled Sir Peter.

'There will be trouble, real violence. You do realize that?'

'We are paying the police handsomely, they will cope.'

'But it doesn't concerns you?' Asked Barry becoming angry.

'Of course it does, but if we are going to make real progress in this country, we are going to have to get away from this old thinking.'

'Good job its Tebbit's law and not yours father. You lot are going to come unstuck.' Concluded the young Piers with a slightly raised voice.

'You must be losing Barry if you are raising you voice so soon.' Interrupted Ann, who had been discussing other matters with Elizabeth.

'It's a good job it's father's birthday. Normally I would not let him off quite as lightly.' He smiled, crossed the room and carried a small neatly wrapped package back to his father. Sir Peter carefully unwrapped the golden paper to reveal a small dark green box, which had "To the man who likes a good screw", printed in gold letters on the top of the box. Sir Peter cautiously removed the lid to discover a small gold plated screwdriver. It was, Elizabeth concluded, a point's victory to Barry.

Ann then produced the real present, which was a leather bound volume with embossed gold lettering of Barry's first novel. Sir Peter fondled the book with great care, so glad to be able to add the volume to the priceless collection held in his library at Piers House. This volume however, would take pride of place.

The meal was up to Ann's usual high standards and after a couple of after dinner drinks Sir Peter and Elizabeth announced their early departure explaining that the politician had some papers to read prior to his attendance at a Cabinet meeting at 10 Downing Street the next morning.

An hour later Sir Peter drove his Rolls Royce Silver Shadow up the long drive to Piers House. Elizabeth, after a glass of piping hot milk, went straight to bed. It was four hours before her husband climbed the stairs from his study to join her there.

Friday 23 October 1981

4

A few hours after Sir Peter Piers had eventually gone to bed in Piers House, DeVille finished his breakfast in his room at the Hilton Hotel. He then called room service and had the dishes removed, then washed, shaved and dressed. Picking up the previous day's Evening Standard, he opened the newspaper at the Accommodation to Let pages and jotted down the three addresses of the houses he had ringed in pencil the evening before. With the aid of an A-Z London street map, he then made three telephone calls and arranged times for inspection visits to the properties for later that day.

His appointments made, he crossed the room to the windows and peered out. It was still raining, so he chose a raincoat from his wardrobe, made sure that he looked fine in the mirror and left. Minutes later, he was guiding his car carefully into the heavy Park Lane traffic.

The rain never stopped all morning and in turn, he was shown around the first two houses on his list. To his disappointment, neither of the houses met his required standards and he left the respective owners saying that he would call back that afternoon. DeVille was adamant that the house he eventually rented met his listed prerequisites.

Closing the door of the Citroen after his second visit DeVille once again consulted his A-Z. The next house on his list was in Kenton, Middlesex and he estimated that it would take him an hour to get there, which afforded him an hour or so for lunch. He found a small bistro and ordered a simple meal of scampi washed down with a single glass of fine French wine. When he left the restaurant it was still raining heavily and he cursed quietly to himself as he ran to the car.

The house in Kenton turned out to be just what he was searching for. It stood in a large garden completely surrounded by twenty-foot high conifers and was set back some twenty-five yards from the quiet street in which it sat. Ensuring that his appearance was satisfactory, DeVille rang the doorbell and waited a few moments before a small man answered and Deville introduced himself.

Although it was not a prerequisite, DeVille could not help admiring the pale green walls, the well polished parquet flooring and the superbly framed watercolour paintings of butterflies in the entrance hall. The rest of the house was just as aesthetically pleasing to the French man and when the house owner suggested an inspection of the rear garden, DeVille took one look at the slanting rain and decided that he had in fact seen enough.

'I think not in this weather but I would very much like to rent your lovely house, if that is acceptable to you.' He offered.

'Indeed.' Replied the man. 'Can I get you a cup of tea and we can sign the necessary papers,' he suggested, leading DeVille into the dining room, which adjoined the kitchen via a breakfast bar.

'I would much prefer coffee if that is possible?'

'Of course,' smiled the man 'We English expect everyone to be tea drinkers like ourselves.'

Over coffee, the house owner explained to DeVille that he had recently been divorced and that he was a botanist due to leave the following week on a short field trip to southern Cyprus, but that on his return he would be living in accommodation at his college.

'How long will you be wanting the house?' He asked finally.

'For the full three months, I think.' Replied DeVille knowing from the newspaper advertisement that the house was to be let for a maximum three months. They agreed on the details and DeVille told the man that he would be back in an hour's time with the cash for three months advance rent along with a returnable deposit against the valuables in the house.

Leaving the owner to prepare the necessary documentation, DeVille drove around the local streets to fully familiarize himself with the area. He then parked his car in nearby Preston Road and entered the underground station where he bought a ticket and caught the next Metropolitan line train to Baker Street. Thirty-five minutes later, he climbed the stairs from the platform handed the remainder of his ticket to the attendant and stepped from the protection of the station into a wet Preston Road. Back in his car, he considered the location of the house to be ideal for purpose before heading back to complete the arrangements on the rental.

Later that afternoon and with the rental formalities complete, he drove back to the Hilton Hotel to pack his things, stopping on the way to purchase a suitcase in which to carry the clothes he had bought in Harrods a week earlier. Happy with the way things had gone, he decided to take in a show and with the aid of hotel staff, managed to obtain a ticket for the musical Cats. When he went to his room to wash and change, it was four thirty and still raining.

Commander John Birbeck OBE QPM stepped into the heavy rain. Pulling the collar up on his navy blue cashmere coat, he rushed across the sidewalk to where his car was parked. Opening the rear passenger door he jumped in and told his driver Jordan to take him to Waterloo. The streets were jam packed as usual and he sat in silence as he was driven through the busy London traffic.

For once, his thoughts were not of terrorism and crime but of the happy prospect of spending the next seven days on vacation with his wife Sara and their children Mark and John. Please God, he prayed silently, let me get my vacation without interruption.

John Birbeck was head of Scotland Yard's Anti-terrorist Brigade. It was a post he was sure he had attained because nobody else had really been silly enough to want it. Amongst police jobs, the Anti-terrorist squad with cases of Irish Republican bombings, middle-east assassinations and iron-curtain subterfuge, was one of the most exacting. Birbeck thought with some comfort of his fast approaching retirement and once again hoped for his week in peace with his family.

Jordan dropped him at Waterloo and said that he hoped the Commander would have a good vacation. Birbeck replied that seven days away from the place would do him good.

Standing in his Saville Row suit under his elegantly cut coat as he watched the departures and arrivals flickering on to and from the large black electronic board at the head of the platforms, Birbeck could have passed for a merchant banker or senior civil servant instead of the head of one of the most successful anti-terrorist organisations in the world. Despite the obvious security risks to both himself and his family, Birbeck had been determined to lead his life as normally as possible, refusing twenty-four hour cover. Alone, he caught the Shepperton train and in just under an hour was leaving the small Shepperton platform as the train was readied for its return journey.

Outside the station, he turned left to where a small number of cars were parked and opened his own Mercedes and slipped in out of the rain. He drove slowly through the town and along the Thames, so beautiful in the summer, to his house. Turning into his short drive, he guided the car straight into the open garage beside his wife's Mini Cooper.

As he sat in the car for a few minutes, it never failed to amaze him how the clouds of stress and frustration that surrounded his work began drifting away the instant he arrived home. He smiled at the thought of Sara, climbed with newfound energy from the Mercedes, ran to the side door of the house and stepped into the kitchen where the smell of cooking welcomed him home. Upstairs he could hear Sara running his bath and taking off his coat he climbed the stairs to join her.

An hour later the boys returned from boarding school and the Birbecks' had their first family meal together for eight weeks. For the next week however, they hoped to be inseparable.

Opening his wallet, Miller extracted ten ten-pound notes and handed them to the old farmer. He in turn counted them again before rolling the cash in half and stuffing it into the right hand back pocket of his dirty old Levi's. Miller watched his actions as he handed over the keys and concluded that the miserly old bastard was highly unlikely to tell another living soul that he had rented the mobile home.

'You'll need to go down to the village to buy yourself a gas cylinder, but that won't cost you much.' The old man said finally before starting off down the track. Miller merely shook his head and smiled at the confirmation of his assessment of the old man. Perhaps he could get even with the old sod later.

Walking across the muddy track to his car, Miller opened the boot and took out two suitcases, one of which was empty and a briefcase and carried them up the three slippery wooden steps, which led into the damp smelling mobile home. Dropping his luggage on a bed come sofa, he pulled back all the curtains and pushed open all the small windows stopping only to watch the old farmer disappear down the lane recounting his money. Thieving little shit, thought Miller, a hundred pounds for two weeks and no bloody gas.

His anger worsened when he then discovered that there were no sheets or blankets for the beds. Storming from the caravan, he locked the door and drove back down the track in his hired Ford.

As Miller passed, the old man had to jump off the track to avoid being knocked over. He might have stopped, he thought to himself, not very mannerly for a bloody writer but he had heard that those types were always a little bit on the peculiar side. His manners however were unimportant, what did matter was the fact that he had got another customer; the van had been there since late spring and had been unused since early August. He had thought it the ideal place for it, what with the well-stocked river and the wooded walks. Lucky thing, he thought considering his change of fortune, keeping that advertisement in the local paper. It had cost him a few bob all right but now he was being rewarded for his entrepreneurial spirit. He tapped his back pocket as he walked and hoped his wife would have his dinner ready.

Miller drove through the village heading for central London. His caravan home was well out in the country yet only an hour's fast drive from London and the action zone. Seeing a public telephone booth as he drove through the next village, Miller stopped and reversed the car. Jumping from the car he pulled open the heavy door and took a note of the number. It would be his contact phone as long as it remained in working order and some skinny longhaired vandal did not rip open the coin box for the few pence it would contain.

In London, he bought the items he required to make his stay in the mobile home as comfortable as possible. From a drugstore in Kensington he bought razors and shaving soap, a toothbrush and paste. From an Army and Navy Surplus store he bought a large sleeping bag, Army sweater, roll neck sweater, thick denims, a woolen hat and strong gloves. From a Safeway food store he purchased various items of instant fast food and some fruit. On his way back to his hired car, he stopped at an electrical goods store and purchased a small radio. He left the gas cylinders to last, buying two large canisters and heaving them to the car.

On his journey back to his new home he recalled that he had forgotten to buy some reading material and stopped at a small bookshop to purchase a large selection of thrillers. He was ready but had a full day to spare, 24 hours in which to relax and read before the real action started.

Liam Blaney stood with a glass of whisky in hand looking out over the River Liffey from his panoramic penthouse flat. He had tried the number twice, had failed to get a reply and was not amused.

Stepping back from the window, he sat down in one of the large white leather chairs and lifted a copy of the Lloyds shipping list from a chrome and glass table in front of him. According to the list, Joseph would be back in Dublin on Monday. Blaney hoped that Joe would be careful, it was not the time to be dragged into the bloody courts on an arms smuggling charge.

Rising again, he crossed the room to the telephone and once again dialed the number. It rang a number of times before being answered.

'John Mayo.' came the reply.

'Where the fuck have you been?' stormed Blaney 'I've been calling all afternoon.'

'Sorry about that Mister Blaney, I've been out visiting a sick aunt.'

'I'll give you a bloody sick aunt Mayo. You are now on standby.' He paused for a second to take a sip of his whisky. 'That means, as you well know, that I expect you to take the girl tomorrow. Understand?'

'But Mister Blaney she will not be at school tomorrow.' Mayo sounded mildly panic stricken.

'I told you to prepare for such an event.'

'I did Mister Blaney, it would just be much easier on Monday.'

'Telephone me tomorrow at one pm. Say nothing but "Secured".'

'But Mister Blaney ...' pleaded Mayo.

'What have you to say?' Interrupted Blaney; suddenly calm.

'Secured Mister Blaney.'

Liam Blaney smiled and put the telephone down. He had every confidence in his man Mayo.

It had been three years since Susan Lamont had walked out of her marriage. Three years of hard toil during which she had discovered the harsh realities of life, realities she had never imagined possible. She had been so desperate, she had even considered suicide; a notion she had carried with her for some months. Courage and not fear had won her through, courage to fight on; courage to help her gain back her self respect after the shock of losing her husband to another man; courage, and the determination to be strong for her daughter Laura, who was now five and had just started school. Slowly, she had come back from the very edge of personal disaster and now with her new flat, rewarding job and most importantly a new love in her life, she was glad to be alive.

Walking from Wembley Park station, she decided to catch a taxi to her parents home to pick up Laura. They had invited her to stay for tea, but she had declined, preferring to get back home to Northwood and spend the evening with her daughter. At a pelican crossing, she crossed the street to the taxi rank where she joined a queue of four. As she waited, she recalled the time in her young life when black people had been uncommon in Wembley. Now, she thought, she was the uncommon sight, although the changes to the ethnic population in London didn't really bother her.

Her parents were happy with their lot. Both were retired civil servants who thanked God for their health and civil service pensions. Susan was pleased with how well they both looked after their recent trip to the Canaries, but was glad to have them home to help with her child minding.

After a brief catch up with her Mum and Dad; her father who noticed, as they walked, the new spring in the step of his daughter, accompanied Susan and Laura back to Wembley Park station. He was happy that she had come through her terrible tunnel of despair and was quietly hopeful that she had a new man in her life.

Later, with Laura asleep in her room, and as she sat by the drawing board in the study of her flat, the telephone bleeped in the sitting room. Rushing through from the study she sat down and lifted the receiver and was absolutely delighted to hear the voice of her new lover, Sir Peter Piers.

Surveying the room, Spencer thought it satisfactory. From

around his neck he took the Nikon camera and slung it onto the small bed. Amateur photographer, he laughed, Jesus H Christ, he had used that one a few times. Kicking off his shoes he lay down on the bed in need of a light sleep, the hotel was quiet and remote with a small staff and suited his needs perfectly.

As always, he found it difficult to sleep, never in any of his many assignments did his thoughts alter, they always returned to his days at Harvard and the events which led him up his particular path in life. It was all because of the lousy no good son of a bitch Rodgers and even after all the years that had passed, he still hated the bastard.

They had shared rooms since their initial introduction during their fresher year and had played on the basketball squad together. Gradually they became inseparable and even on dates they made up foursomes with the girls lucky enough to be in their company. That those early times were good there was no doubt and the problems only really started when Spencer met and began to date Linda Tomlin. They fell in love very quickly and became lovers that Christmas eve and were very happy together. At least Spencer thought them very happy together.

One evening after a late lecture, a friend came to tell Spencer that Rodgers had been in an automobile accident and that his female passenger had been killed. The fact that Rodgers had a female passenger in his car had surprised Spencer because Rodgers was supposed to be going home for the weekend to visit his parents. The dead female passenger turned out to be Linda Tomlin.

Spencer never discovered what Linda had been doing in his friend's car; he simply went into a deep fit of depression and began to meticulously plan the death of Rodgers. Spencer was particularly surprised how simple it all was and one afternoon while Rodgers was in basketball practice, he simply made slight adjustments to the brakes on Rodgers open topped Maserati.

Never in his life would he be able to forget the tremendous feeling of joy and revenge when later that day the police arrived on campus with the sad news that Rodgers had been killed in a second tragic road accident. Later, at the fatal accident enquiry it was decided that Rodgers had simply been a foolhardy speed merchant who had paid the ultimate penalty for his tragic foolishness.

Lying in the small English hotel room, he thought again of his lovely Linda. Why had she been in the car with Rodgers? It was something he had asked himself a million times and something he would never be able to answer. One thing he did know was that he had never stopped loving her, perhaps he would never get her out of his twisted system, she was his non-healing wound and every job he completed merely helped to avenge her untimely death and kick the scab from that wound.

Hearing a female voice, he began to wake. He could see no face through the blurry sleep in his eyes. Linda? No, it was a strange face to him, a face he had never seen before and she was saying his name. He rubbed his eyes and tried to recall where he was.
'Mister Spencer?'
Suddenly he remembered where he was, the hotel in Kent, and this lovely creature in his hotel room?
'Sorry, I must have fallen asleep.' He heard himself say as he took stock of the tall pretty blond standing before him.
'I just came to tell you that dinner will be ready in half an hour, father says he forgot to tell you." Explained the girl retreating from the room.
Spencer darted a glance at the telephone beside his bed.
'That's not working I'm afraid, father is waiting for the engineer to call and fix it.' Smiled the girl perceptively.

Spencer spent the half hour before dinner getting washed and shaved. He then dressed casually and dined alone in the small dining room before watching the excellent television offered by the BBC in the empty television room. Despite the quality of the output from the television however, Spencer felt the need for a drink and went in search of the bar.

To his dismay, the bar was empty also and he was looking around for some service when the girl who had disturbed his sleep earlier lifted her head from below the bar. Smiling, he sat himself down on a bar stool and ordered himself a beer. As the girl busied herself with his pint tumbler, Spencer admired her superb young figure, a sudden desire growing in his groin.

'Why don't you pour yourself one and join me.' He suggested accepting his large beer glass.

'I don't mind if I do mister Spencer, looks like it is going to be a long night.' The girl smiled her captivating smile and revealed brilliant white teeth before pouring herself a gin and tonic.

'Is it always this quiet?' Asked Spencer.

'Gosh no. You should see this place in the middle of August, three or four deep at the bar with tourists.'

'I suppose this is not the tourist season.' Smiled Spencer.

'You could say that.' Laughed the girl and raising her glass she added

'Cheers mister Spencer.'

'Call me Crawford please.'

'Okay Crawford, I'm Kathy, Kathy Drinkwater.'

'Pleased to meet you Kathy Drinkwater.' Smiled Spencer and they both laughed a hearty ice-breaking laugh.

That evening at 10 Downing Street, the Prime Minister and most of her cabinet met in the cabinet room to finalize the details of the speech Her Majesty Queen Elizabeth II would give to the nation during the forthcoming State Opening of Parliament.

Normally, Britain's first lady Prime Minister was a patiently persistent woman. However, that night many of her colleagues thought the strain of office was beginning to show for the first time and after minimal debate, her cabinet filtered out of number 10 on their way to a hopefully quiet weekend at home with their families and friends.

When they had all gone, the Prime Minister wearily climbed

the stairs to her sitting room where she kicked off her shoes onto a superb Persian rug, curled her legs up onto the floral sofa, opened her Prime Ministerial briefcase and began pouring over various reports. The large black carriage clock on the table announced 10pm. The Prime Minister would still be working there in three hours.

At the exact moment the Prime Minister was opening her briefcase in 10 Downing Street, O'Neil paid his entrance money and entered the small Soho club. Alone, he found a place at the bar and watched as he waited to be served as an enormously big-breasted girl performed to the latest batch of disco records on a small stage in the middle of the room.

A topless barmaid approached and he ordered a beer despite the fact that he was unable to take his eyes away from her great tits with extra large nipples.
'Not very busy in here tonight.' She said to pass the time as she poured his drink. 'A girl can get very bored on a night like this.'
'Oh,' mused O'Neil. 'I rather like it quiet.'
'I like it anyway.' Laughed the girl eyeing the handsome O'Neil who had got the message.
'What time do you finish?' he asked unable to believe his good fortune.
'Two.' She replied handing him his beer. 'That will be a pound.'
O'Neil handed the girl a five pound note and pocketed his change.
'See you at two then?' She asked.
'Bet your boots on it.' Winked O'Neil noticing that above her breasts she had a very pretty face.
Leaving the bar, O'Neil found another room in which a blue movie was being shown on a large video screen. He found a seat without difficulty and sat down to kill time until two when he hoped to get his hands on the girl's superb breasts. On the screen, two blond studs were doing what he had always thought impossible to a girl who at least sounded like she was enjoying the experience. O'Neil looked forward to two o'clock with growing anticipation.

He had arrived in London two days after the meeting at Treeacre Farm and had traced an associate who had rented him a flat the last time he had lived in London. With a down payment of one thousand pounds, he had received the keys to a neat flat in the centre of Soho. O'Neil preferred to stay in busy over-populated areas and the flat which nestled amongst pubs, cafes, cinemas and strip-clubs was ideal for someone wishing to go about their business unnoticed.

He had spent the first day getting familiar with the area, the rooftops, alleyways, backstreets and rat runs, times of police patrols, all of which might be essential information should an emergency exit be necessary. What he discovered from these checks was to his liking, his associate certainly had an eye for a good property and if anything, the flat was better than the one he had masterminded the 1973 bombing campaign from.

He then spend time stock-piling the flat for a long stay and collecting train timetables, times of flights out of the United Kingdom to Paris, New York, Dublin and the many other cities worldwide in which he held bank accounts. To O'Neil these were mainly precautions because failure was not a subject normally etched on his brain although survival was and his current campaign seemed to offer above average risks.

Finishing his drink, another topless delight appeared to take his order while on the screen the two studs were taking turns in servicing each other while the girl merely encouraged them with her tongue. Two o'clock thought O'Neil, was not coming fast enough.

Saturday 24 October 1981

5

Strong shafts of autumnal sun glinted in through the kitchen windows as Anna O'Grady stood watching the children playing in the garden. She enjoyed having young Patricia's friends playing with her, it compensated for her own loneliness. It was not Raymond's fault that he was away from home so much; he was after all, the Private Secretary to the Prime Minister of the Irish Republic and with the economy in the state it was, coupled with the constant strife north of the border, they certainly needed to put in extremely long hours.

Crossing the kitchen, Anna opened the fridge and extracted some eggs. She always made the kids eggs on toast on Saturdays; it was their favourite. Opening the bread bin she groaned at the fact that it was almost empty, she had forgotten to collect it from Langan's that morning. Opening the door she called her daughter who came at once.

'Patsy, be a pet and jump on your bicycle and go over to Langan's, I forgot to get the bread order.'

Patricia smiled silently, took the bread money from her mother and ran to the garage to get her bicycle. It would only take her ten minutes to get to Langan's and back.

The O'Grady home stood in its own extensive grounds some fifteen miles outside Dublin. The family had moved there when Ray had been appointed to his present civil service post and they had settled well into the local community. Patricia still attended Royal Dublin School for Dumb Children during the week, but that did not affect her relationships with the local children and accordingly she enjoyed her weekends at home.

She cycled out of the drive and along the narrow tree-lined road towards the market cross and the shops. Behind her, Mayo started the Volvo estate in which he was sitting and began following her along the avenue totally surprised at his good fortune. At the cross roads Patricia stopped and waited for a car to pass before carrying on. When she reached the shop, she stood her bicycle against an old fence and ran up the sidewalk to the shop.

Mayo pulled the Volvo up behind the bicycle and ran over the rear wheel. Getting out of the car he stood waiting for Patricia to reappear. When she came out holding the bread, she was very upset about what had happened but was pleased when Mayo apologized and offered to run her home. Opening the rear door, Mayo pushed the tangled bicycle into the estate and helped the girl into the passenger seat and as they drove off, she was pointing in the direction of home.

At the cross roads Patricia began gesticulating with sudden panic when the man ignored her mimed pleas and turned left and away from her home. Fifty yards along the road, Mayo stopped the car as Patricia watched and he took a handkerchief from his jacket pocket and slipped it over her mouth. She scratched at his face in desperation before feeling the energy drain from her body.

An hour later, an anxious Anna O'Grady left the house and walked to the Langan's shop, seeing no trace of her daughter en route. The old shopkeeper could only confirm that Patsy had collected the bread.

When she arrived home in a state of extreme panic, the telephone was ringing in the hall. Lifting the receiver, her worst fears were confirmed; Patricia had been kidnapped.

After a late breakfast McCormack lay relaxing in his large bath for half an hour. He then dressed in preparation for the arrival of his doctor who came at ten thirty and as usual prescribed painkillers. McCormack had long since given up caring what the doctors gave him, it alleviated the pain and that was all that mattered. There had been times when he had considered emptying a bottle and ending his misery but the thought of his coming glory soon put an end to such thoughts. The very idea that he, a sick and dying man, would be instrumental in the final downfall of the great British Empire was powerful enough to encourage him through the agony and the endless sleepless nights. Yes, the dream was far too great to be destroyed by mere pain.

When the doctor had gone, McCormack went to his study where he pulled the drapes to allow the sun to penetrate the dingy cigarette smelling room. Lighting another cancer stick, he went to his desk and opened it. For a few moments he stared at the folder without opening it and then carried it to the wall safe, which was situated behind an oil painting of the most famous of all Irish racehorses Arkle, and locked the folder safely away.

At the drinks tray he poured himself a large Scotch, which he finished in one swift drink. Leaving the study for the hall, he pulled on a sheepskin jacket that once had fitted him but was now far too large and went out into the bright autumn sunshine.

He needed to stop at the drugstore for his medicine but that would not take long and he would then be free to drive to the telephone booth and receive the calls from the men in London. The mere thought of the four killers made his heart flutter.

Just before mid-day, he arrived at Ballymena railway station. Parking his car he entered the station and walked along the near deserted main platform to a public telephone booth. Pulling the heavy door open with some difficulty, he entered the booth and tested that the phone was in order by lifting the receiver and dialing the special engineers number and replacing the receiver. Moments later the telephone began to ring and he killed the reply, checked with his watch and awaited the first call.

Miller had risen at first light and had gone for a long run in the heavy woods to the north of the caravan. On his return, he washed quickly before driving to a nearby village where he bought a number of newspapers and some milk and rolls for his breakfast.

After breakfast he sat in front of the fire and read his way through the newspapers underlining anything of significance which related to any of the cabinet ministers familiar to him via Blaney's folder.

Jonathan Miller had spent the majority of his childhood alternating between his aunt's house in Cambridge and his boarding school in Wiltshire. His parents had separated shortly after his birth, both had emigrated to far and opposite sides of the world and he had not heard of them since. His aunt had cared for him well, but he had always been a distant child and difficult to communicate with. At school he excelled in physics, sport and self defence, the latter of which was a great commodity at a school over-flowing with bullyboys and homosexuals.

After school he went to Oxford University, having considered Cambridge too near to his aunt. There, he gained a blue in soccer and a first class in physics and fell in love with a beautiful fine arts student. Following the easy going cloistered atmosphere of university life, he found great difficulty settling into the working life so he and his girl spent the next two years living in Biot in southern France. During the long summer months while the girl painted, Miller spend his days hiring out sailing equipment on the beaches of Juan Les Pins where he enjoyed the company of the beautiful girls who holidayed in an area frequented by the rich and famous.

One evening as he returned to their apartment in the ancient town of Biot in his old Citroen Dianne, he saw a police car and ambulance parked among a crowd outside the apartment building. Miller was arrested and questioned for three days about the rape and murder of his lover. Miller knew that the girl had been expecting a Parisian art dealer that day to look over her excellent work but for some strange reason kept the information to himself.

Six days later, Jonathan Miller committed his first murder. On a dark evening, the Parisian art dealer left his plush gallery, which contained one of Miller's girlfriend's paintings and walked towards his car. Miller pounced from behind and whispered the girl's name constantly to the small Frenchman as he repeatedly stabbed him.

The next day Miller returned to England and was not to hear again of his terrible crime. His mood surprised him, for the first time he had felt real passion and to his surprise the passion was for his crime and not for his dead lover. The sudden realization of this fact was to determine his future as hired assassin for some of the best known terrorist groups in the world, the PLO, the OAS, Black September, the Red Brigade and now the Provisional IRA.

At twenty minutes to twelve, he pulled on his recently acquired duffle coat and woolen hat and drove to the nearby village and stopped at the telephone booth he had noticed the day before. Meticulously he dialed the first of the numbers given in Blaney's folder, the time by his Rolex was twenty seconds to twelve. The line clicked and the telephone rang twice, as expected, before being answered.
'Number please.' It was the voice and code he had anticipated so he slowly read the number and was told curtly 'Six thirty tonight.' The line went dead.

Miller hung up, pushed the heavy door open and walked quickly to his hired Ford. Six and a half hours, he mused, he had time to read a good book.

Spencer had spent the morning riding in a meadow near the hotel with Kathy Drinkwater and was now helping the girl dismount at the stables door. Looking at his watch, it was mid-day and he needed to get to a telephone by twelve fifteen. He waited, as Kathy made sure that the horses were safely stabled and as they walked towards her car she asked.
'How about you taking me for a nice cool drink?' She offered her hand, a gesture he found easy to accept.
'Sure honey, but I've got to get to a telephone by twelve fifteen to

make an important business call.' He replied hoping that she would not ask any questions.

'I know just the place.' Replied Kathy releasing his hand and skipping round to the driver's side of her small car.

Spencer was happy with the way things were developing with the girl. She was a mathematics student at London University and had an apartment in town. He also had a strong physical desire for the girl but wanted to play her along carefully, he might be grateful for a good friend in England before his adventure was over.

She drove the car as if it was her ambition to emulate Jackie Stewart and ten minutes later they were driving into the car park of what Spencer could only describe as a typical English pub. They walked into the lounge bar holding hands and she informed him that there was a telephone in the hall and that she would buy the drinks.

Spencer left her and walked through a double glass fire door to the hall and found the public telephone. Dipping to get under the acoustic hood above the telephone, he extracted some coins from his pocket and dialed the number from memory. It took a few moments for the connection to be made and when it finally was, he pushed a coin into the slot and was greeted with the unhealthy sound of John McCormack's voice. Spencer gave the number of the public callbox at the hotel and was told "six-forty-five tonight." Breaking the connection, Spencer went back to the bar to concentrate on Kathy Drinkwater.

DeVille had breakfast in the dining room at the Hilton Hotel. Afterwards, dressed in suede jacket, cashmere roll neck and slacks, he left the hotel and walked briskly to Baker Street station. The walk took him twenty minutes. From Baker Street, he caught a Metropolitan line train to Preston Road, arriving shortly before eleven thirty.

From a greengrocer in Preston Road he bought some fresh

fruit and in an off license up the street he bought two bottles of his favorite brandy. He then walked through a small playing field to the house he had rented, arriving at twelve ten. Switching on the large colour television, he watched the remainder of the lunchtime news taking notes of anything of interest to him or his group. At twelve-thirty he dialed the same number that Miller and Spencer had dialed before him. The difference between DeVille and the other two was the fact that he was given two times, namely six and seven o'clock that evening.

After making the call, DeVille spent the remainder of the afternoon sifting through Blaney's folder in an attempt to choose the first suitable candidates with which to begin their task. He was searching for targets that would provide his newfound colleagues with minimum danger and difficulty.

Standing in the familiar trees at Treeacre Farm, Elliot and Anderson watched McCormack drive away from the large house. They waited for a few minutes until a walky-talky that Elliot was holding told them that the sick farmer had headed away from the farm at speed.

Elliot told the walky-talky man to follow McCormack and turned and waved the telecom engineer from behind a cluster of thick bushes some thirty yards to the rear of their vantage point. When the engineer had joined them, Elliot walked with the man towards the farmhouse, briefing him as they went.
'Okay McGlynn, you know the score?' He asked when finished. McGlynn merely nodded, he was well used to this sort of subterfuge, it had been his reward for topping his class at college. Elliot turned to his partner.
'Soon as you hear anything, get us out of there. Okay?' Anderson, who had caught the bug that he and Elliot laughingly referred to as the McGlynn Syndrome, merely nodded.

Elliot and McGlynn made their way along the perimeter fence to the rear of the house, climbed over the fence and made their way up a narrow path to the back door. Elliot took out a small bunch of keys from his pocket and began trying them in the lock. By chance, McGlynn turned the door handle and to their surprise the door into the large kitchen opened gently.

'Be Jesus, the old shit's not even locked the door. I think we had better be quick.' Oddly enough, McGlynn nodded his agreement.

Inside, the silent engineer went about his work with absolute efficiency while Elliot roamed throughout the many rooms hoping for a deeper insight into the character of John McCormack. The dining room with its boardroom sobriety would have been where the meeting had taken place but there was nothing of interest to Elliot. The study he found more appealing and he soon discovered the safe, which he unfortunately had neither the time nor the aptitude to crack open. The desk he opened with ease, but as he had expected, it contained nothing of importance. Upstairs was just as fruitless although the overall state of order and cleanliness helped him to realize that perhaps there was more to the sick mind of McCormack than he had thought. Descending the stairs, he found McGlynn sitting in the marble hall, his work complete. Elliot pointed to the kitchen and they left the house by the route they had entered it.

Nothing to write home about, thought Elliot as he and McGlynn re-joined Anderson in the trees although he would appreciate a good look inside John McCormack's safe.

Anderson waited until McGlynn had gone before asking 'Any luck?'

'Not a bloody thing, but he has a handy looking safe I would like to get into.' Elliot stopped and looked back momentarily at the house before continuing 'Let's go and have some lunch, I'm fucking starving.' Anderson followed Elliot to their van also thinking of the safe. After all, that was his specialty.

Mayo had found the place by accident while out walking with his dog to check rabbit snares he had set the previous week. It was situated in dense woodland south of Dublin and was surprisingly in excellent condition. It had obviously been a railway workers' hut, but with the railway long gone, there was only the slightest trace of where the track had once been.

The girl had angered him when she had scratched his face although her action had wiped any doubts he had held about putting her into the canvas bag clean from his mind. Driving, he was still furious, with the girl and with Liam Blaney for making him risk all by taking the girl at a weekend. The bastard would have no hold on him when this job was over.

Stopping on the way to the place, he called Liam Blaney as instructed and waited anxiously for the reply. When it came, he said 'Secured.' And put the receiver down as instructed.

It took him another half an hour to reach the hut. He had made it as comfortable as possible for the girl. After all, she was only a child. Emptying her out of the bag, she was still drowsy with the morphine and he slowly undressed her, noticing her budding breasts and sprouting pubic hair. These things distracted him and other thoughts ran through his vile mind. Sweating, he was suddenly aware of the fact that he was in danger of losing control and he quickly wrapped her in a large army sleeping bag and zipped up the sides. Throwing her onto the small camp bed he had provided, Patricia coiled away from him like a frightened animal.
'If you are a good girl, you will come to no harm. If you are a bad girl, you will never see your mother and father again. Do you understand?' Patricia nodded, tears forming in her pathetic little eyes.

Leaving the hut, Mayo locked the door securely and carried the canvas bag containing the girl's clothes back to the car and drove back to Dublin.

Paul O'Neil ejaculated into the moist womanhood of the girl he had met in the Soho club the previous evening. As he pumped the remnants of his joy into her, she squirmed with orgasmic delight beneath him. Was there no way in which he could satisfy her endless thirst?

'That was lovely.' She smiled at him as he rolled panting from her onto the crumpled bed.

'Mm not bad.' He replied, content with his efforts.

Ten minutes later, O'Neil entered the small kitchen, opened the refrigerator and took out a carton of fresh orange juice and began drinking from it. He was glad that Pauline had her own flat; he would certainly have been unwilling to take her back to his own hide-away.

A pine clock above the cooker told him that it was twelve-thirty. He had half an hour before he was due to contact McCormack, enough time for a quick shower. The girl joined him in the bathroom dressed only in a large tee shirt and sat down on the toilet seat, crossed her long legs and watched O'Neil as he washed quickly.

'I hope that you don't think that I'm that easy all the time.' She began.

'Of course not.' Smiled O'Neil.

'You don't disrespect me for what happened then?'

O'Neil stepped from the shower and kissed her forehead gently 'Don't be so silly, of course I don't.'

'That's good.' she smiled before asking 'Will I see you again?'

'The way that you make love Pauline, you will be sick of the sight of me.'

He rubbed himself vigorously with one of Pauline's soft pink towels.

'That's something to look forward to then.'

'I'll pick you up at the club tonight.' He said starting to pull his clothes on.

'Can't we meet earlier? I thought we might spend the day together.'

'Sorry love, I've got some business that I must attend to today.'

O'Neil said goodbye and made his way back to a Soho bustling with life which of course meant that he had some difficulty finding a public telephone. When he eventually did, he phoned McCormack at once, annoyed at the fact that he was three minutes late.

'You're bloody late Paul.' came the reply.
'Sorry John.' He began ' I take it that the others have contacted you.' O'Neil opened his diary and pulled the accompanying pencil from the spine and began jotting down the numbers as McCormack read them out.
'Okay, that's the last time you will be in touch with me so I'd like to take this opportunity to wish you well and give you a word of warning.'
'Thanks for the luck John, but I don't need any warnings.' interjected O'Neil.
'Okay, but watch your bloody back I do not think you can trust your new colleagues.' McCormack warned anyway.
'I can look after myself John, but thanks anyway.'
'I know you can, but can you look after the other three as well?'
'Bit late to be thinking that now John.' The pips went before O'Neil continued 'don't worry yourself. I'll be in touch with Blaney. Up the Republic!'
'Aye, up the Republic.' replied McCormack before the line went quiet.

O'Neil left the telephone booth and found himself a café where he ordered breakfast, or was it lunch?

Blaney waited patiently for a reply and when it came it was the voice of an extremely anxious woman.
'Mrs. O'Grady?' He asked anxiously.
'Yes.' She stuttered breathlessly.
'Do not say another word, just listen to what I've got to say and your wee girl will come to no harm.' He had rehearsed this role for some weeks and was enjoying it considerably.
'I have Patricia and want you to know that if you and your husband follow these instructions to the letter, then no harm will come to her.'
'How much do you want?' Demanded Anna O'Grady, totally desperate.

'I told you not to speak Mrs. O'Grady' he stated calmly.

'Sorry.' offered Anna quietly.

'I want you to contact your husband and tell him to return home. Do not tell him why you are making the request or what has happened. I must also stress that if you contact the Garda, then you will get your Patricia home in a box.' Blaney hesitated to allow what he had just said to penetrate Anna O'Grady's numb brain. 'I will call your husband at your home in three hours time and shall give further instructions then. Do you understand what I have said Mrs. O'Grady?'

Anna was unsure if she was being invited to talk and as she considered this, there was a click and the line went dead.

Anna sat stunned for a few moments before lifting the receiver and calling her husband who was in the Prime Minister's office.

At that moment, John McCormack was parking his car at the main entrance to his house on Treeacre Farm. Entering the house, he went straight to the kitchen where he ran a quick check on the door from the rear garden. Chuckling to himself, he went into his study where he poured himself his usual scotch whisky. He was delighted, it was as he had suspected.

'I have a call for you Sir Peter.' Piers looked across his desk at his son. The call could only be from Susan, so he asked his secretary to take the number and to say that he would call back. Pressing the intercom off, he spoke to Barry who was sitting in a comfortable green leather visitor's chair opposite him.

'I simply do not think that it is fair of you to ask me to arrange a guided tour around the PM's private suite at number ten, it would be a rude invasion of their privacy.'

'Come on father, I am quite sure that the Prime Minister would willingly oblige an old friend. After all, I did go to school with her son.' The young author was not used to being refused. On this occasion however, it seemed as though his father was going to prove an immovable object.

'I am afraid old chap that this is my final word on the matter, I will simply not even consider asking.' Sir Peter sat back in his large chair and offered his open hands in apology to his son. 'I am sorry.'

'I could always ask Mark.' Persisted Barry despite the fact that he knew that he had lost his case.

'Do that if you like, but it would be against my wishes.' Barry knew that it was all quite simple; his father was not and never would be a man to ask for favours from anyone.

'You win father although the final chapter of my book will not have the same degree of authenticity to it as I would like.'

'I am sure that you will think of something.' Sir Peter smiled at his son who returned a similar smile and stood up to leave.

'It's a pity that you couldn't make the squash, I am due you a crushing defeat after this.'

'I am sorry about that. This seems to be my day for saying sorry.' Laughed the distinguished Member of Parliament.

'Don't worry about it father, I appreciate that the nation must come first.'

Barry reached the door and opened it slightly 'I'll call you next week, give my love to Elizabeth.' And he was gone, winking to his father's secretary Sally Gray as he left.

Piers sat for a few seconds with his elbows on his desk, his head in his hands and his son's words ringing in his ears. Shrugging his shoulders, he lifted the brass receiver from the heavy antique telephone on his desk and began dialing the number he was certain that his secretary had recorded earlier. As he waited for the connection to be made, he told himself to remember and get the number from Sally before he left the office.

'Lamont residence.' Came the enthusiastic reply.

'Gosh you sound terribly cheerful today.' He knew that he should have felt guilty about his affair with Susan and his son's words about love to Elizabeth had stunned him momentarily. However, he had not felt this way about any woman for a number of years and was not about to lose out on this occasion just because he was involved in a dull and almost sexless marriage. Of course he knew that it could ruin his political career, but he had no real ambition left in that sphere anyway and a scandal might not do his stuffy image all that much harm, after all, it was what the public suspected all cabinet ministers and Members of Parliament get up to anyway. Thoughts of scandals made him chuckle within himself as he thought of the ridiculous lengths he went to avoid detection.

'I have every right to sound cheerful if I wish.' argued Susan mildly.

'I must admit that I share your feelings and would be even more cheerful if I was with you instead of stuck in this old palace.'

'What have you got on today?' she asked quietly.

'Oh, a navy suit, white shirt and that lovely silk tie you bought me.' He replied knowing full well that she was referring to his office commitment.

'Superbly funny.'

'Seriously, I have a meeting to attend at one-thirty.'

'It's one-fifteen now, you will be late.' Susan sounded disappointed that their banter was about to end.

'Yes, I am afraid that I must go.' Concluded Piers noticing the red light on the intercom, which was his secretary's way of reminding him of the meeting.

'When will I see you?' She asked slightly anxious.

'Got to be Monday I am afraid. I promised Elizabeth that I would take her to her sisters tomorrow.' He realized that he was apologizing for the third time in a few minutes. He would have to stop it before it became habitual.

'Can you stay the night?' She continued and not failing to sound hopeful.

'I think I could force myself.'

'Good, I will see you Monday then. Take care.'

'You too, goodbye.'

Smiling, he rose and lifted his attaché case and slipped some documents inside. Pulling on his coat, he felt in excellent spirits and as he left his office he told his secretary that she could take an extended lunch, as he did not expect to be back that afternoon.

Tidying her desk, Sally Gray threw her scrap pad into an untidy bottom drawer and put the cover over her typewriter. Slipping on her jacket she followed her boss from the office. Bright early afternoon sunshine was beginning to shine over the Thames and the Palace of Westminster as she walked briskly towards the tube station. A couple of hours of retail therapy were just what she needed.

Raymond O'Grady had already received one very distressing call from his wife and now sat with Anna crying in his arms awaiting another. He found great difficulty in comprehending what was happening. He was not a wealthy man by any standards and although he was close to the Irish Prime Minister in his work, he was not an important public figure. He was sure that a mistake had been made. Anna was very distressed and had started the process of blaming herself for her daughter's abduction and in reality needed a doctor. That, however, was not a risk that Ray O'Grady could afford at this time, he had to assume that the people who had taken Patricia were either watching or bugging their home. The very thought made shivers run up and down his spine. As they waited, he and Anna began to recite a Decade of the Holy Rosary in the hope that God would intervene and return their poor daughter to their midst.

What did intervene however, was the shrill of the telephone which gave both of them a start. Anna sat up bravely and wiped her eyes, she had been crying for almost an hour and tried to pull herself together. Ray rose and walked across the sitting room and plunged himself into a soft chair beside the telephone and lifted the receiver.

'Raymond O'Grady?' asked a mysterious voice.

'Yes.' replied Ray nervously.

'I must say that I'm very pleased that you and your wife have been wise enough to follow my instructions this far. I would really hate to have to harm your lovely wee girl.'

'That's very comforting.' commented O'Grady trying to steel himself for what was to follow.

'Sarcasm, as they say, is the lowest form of wit O'Grady and it will not help you get your daughter back.'

'What will?' demanded O'Grady firmly.

'I will get to that in a moment. Firstly, you should know that each day that Patricia is away from home, you will receive a photograph of your daughter holding a copy of one of that day's newspaper. That should put your tiny civil service mind at rest should it not?' To O'Grady the man at the other end of the line sounded very calm with no sound of panic and this he found strangely comforting.

'Yes it will.' he finally conceded.

'Good. Of course it would have been just as easy with a tape recording, but your wee Patricia is not too good with microphones. Is she?' The voice broke into a gentle chuckle, the laughter of the mentally insane thought O'Grady, losing any sense of comfort instantly.

'Yes, you have a point.' Ray stated quietly, fighting back his temper.

'Now, you are a friend and confidant of our beloved Prime Minister are you not?'

'I work for the Prime Minister yes.' O'Grady was beginning to see why they, whoever they were, had picked on him and his family.

'Good, now all I want for the safe return of your daughter, is information.'

'What kind of information?' Asked Ray quietly.

'Well, you will be going in a few days or so with the Prime Minister to meet with the Brits Prime Minister.'

'That's not for over a fortnight yet.' Stated O'Grady nervously.

'Oh, I am not referring to the Anglo-Irish summit, this will be for something far more urgent.'

'I've heard nothing of this trip.' stated Ray honestly, now he was getting really worried, it was beginning to look as though his little girl's life was being put on the line and dependent on conjecture.

'Perhaps I can see into the future, but that does not matter. What does is that you understand the role you have to play. You will be my eyes and ears at the meeting when it takes place. You will pass this information to me via your good wife who in turn will receive a call daily from me at one pm. Understand?'

'Yes.' surrendered O'Grady.

'Good. If you do as you are told, then your daughter will be returned to you unharmed.'

'You have my word that my daughter's life will not be put at risk by me.'

'I am so glad to hear it' and with that the telephone conversation was abruptly ended.

At five fifty-five that evening, O'Neil descended the stairs from his rented flat, walked to the end of the busy street, crossed at a pelican crossing and entered an underground train station.

Finding an unoccupied telephone booth, he pulled shut the antiquated wooden door and began dialing the first number from his memorized list. It was undoubtedly the Frenchman who answered.
'Give me the address.' demanded O'Neil. DeVille quickly gave the address of the house in Kenton and hung up without further discussion. O'Neil left the booth and walked back to the flat, it was beginning to rain.

Back in the flat, he checked the address in his London street map and decided that he would have to risk going ahead with the first meeting. DeVille could surely be trusted with finding a venue.

Later, at the pre-arranged times, O'Neil telephoned Miller and Spencer and gave them the address of the Kenton house and told them to be there at precisely seven pm the following evening. He then re-dialed DeVille and confirmed the arrangements to him.

Hanging up, he returned to the flat and settled in for the night. The real action was about to begin.

Sunday 25 October 1981

6

O'Neil paid the taxicab driver and entered Wembley Park station. Paying for a Metropolitan Line ticket to Northwick Park, he strolled past the newspaper stand, through the ticket barrier and descended a flight of stairs to the platform. The station was surprisingly busy for a Sunday with people heading for destinations unknown. O'Neil's attention was particularly drawn to a large afro-haired black youth who stood with his girlfriend beside a machine dispensing Cadbury's chocolate and listening to reggae music being blasted at them from an enormous cassette player. Despite the number of people, thought O'Neil, not too many would be on their way to plot an assassination. The idea made him laugh quietly.

An Uxbridge bound train rolled into the station and O'Neil selected a no-smoking compartment and boarded the train. Finding a seat, he sat down opposite a uniformed police officer who eyed O'Neil carefully. The gaze disturbed O'Neil unnecessarily to the point of forcing him to stare out of the window as the train slowly left the station. The train driver hardly needed to pick up speed before the train began to decelerate into Preston Road. Standing to get off, O'Neil imagined that the policeman was still watching him.

Forgetting the policeman, O'Neil climbed the steps to discover to his amusement that there was no one to collect his ticket. He would have to be more careful with his expenses in future and again he laughed, a nervous laugh that he forced from his face, it was time to be deadly serious.

As he left the station, he pulled up the collar of his navy blue jacket as protection against the cold and odd speck of cold rain. He walked his memorized street map to the house and reached his destination in just under ten minutes.

Noticing a light on in one of the downstairs rooms, he walked passed the house and continued up the street. Finding a large house with no lights on and a large secluded garden, he skipped over the perimeter fence and found a spot in the corner of the garden where, on his knees, he had an uninterrupted view of the main entrance to DeVille's rented house. It was six-thirty and he would be able to watch the others arrive knowing that if anyone was early, he would want to know why. O'Neil was hardly likely to let those three killers have any time together in which to dream up an escape plan for themselves.

Hearing footsteps coming his way, he held his breath. They drew closer and seemed to stop directly above him. O'Neil lifted his eyes and was just in time to prevent a large sleepy looking Labrador from pissing on his head. Its territorial mark made, the dog led its owner off down the street. O'Neil smiled wryly at this narrow miss thanking God that he did not have to depend on such an efficient guard dog for his safety.

DeVille poured himself a large brandy and settled into a soft sofa. Looking at the carriage clock on the mantelpiece, he noted that they were not due for another half an hour. Leaning forward, he pulled a coffee table in front of him and spread the four photographs of the Cabinet Ministers he had chosen earlier that day into a semi-circle before him.

His decision had not been very difficult, according to the information provided by Blaney and the recent newspapers, they were the only four who spent their weekends in and around London. From his own vast experience, he considered weekends the best times for political killing since most politicians were to be found slightly more relaxed during those couple of days. As for the specific choice of the London area as the hunting ground, DeVille had assumed that the others would have based themselves within that densely populated area.

Gathering up the photographs, he put them carefully into an envelope and stood, brandy in hand, and began to arrange the chairs in the room around the coffee table. Satisfied, he climbed the staircase to the bathroom where he carefully replaced his jet-black wig and combed it into place in preparation for the arrival of the others.

Downstairs again, he took three glasses from the dining room and placed them on the coffee table beside the bottle of best French brandy he had already sampled.

Kathy Drinkwater had left the hotel at lunchtime to return to her flat in London and prepare for her weeks studies. Before her departure Spencer informed her that he would be in London on business and would like to buy her a drink one evening. Delighted, she had scribbled her address and telephone number on a sheet of paper before zooming off in her car.

Spencer enjoyed lunch at the hotel before vacating his room, paying his bill and being driven to the local main line train station by Kathy's father. There, he bought a ticket to London Waterloo and awaited the arrival of the train.

Despite the fact that Spencer had always considered himself to be something of a loner, foreign assignments often made him require friendship and this he found rather disarming, forcing him to try and put Kathy Drinkwater and her superb body out of his mind. Sitting on the relatively quiet train as it sped through the beautiful autumnal English countryside, he felt under threat and began to imagine that everyone on the train was watching him. Panic began to take him over, what if his mission was to fail? What if he was arrested? Such thoughts had never really occurred to him before, why had they started now in an old English railway carriage? The feeling made Spencer feel considerably uncomfortable and gave him the desire for action, movement and perhaps even a little risk.

Feeling the train slow as it approached yet another station, he made the decision to disembark and make his way to the London rendezvous by some other means. Precisely what those other means would be, he did not know. All he did know was that he quite simply had to get away from the train and its prying eyes.

Outside the train station and thankful for the fact that it was not raining, Spencer made his way towards a modern housing scheme he had noticed from the train. He had seen developments like it before and his predatory instincts led him towards a group of lock-up garages.

The first group of lock-ups were disappointing by the fact that one of the overhead doors was open and from the inside came the constant tinkering of tools onto the concrete floor of the garage. Half a mile or so further into the scheme and he found himself in luck. He stood inconspicuously and watched as a rather fat middle-aged man pulled closed the door of his garage and walked towards his house with a small lunchbox under his arm without even locking the garage door behind him. Spencer shook his head in wonder at the thought of the lifestyle that dictated the need to work on a Sunday. Then again, here he was, away from home and working.

With the man carefully out of sight, Spencer slipped into the garage and using his infamous expertise, started the car and reversed the Ford out into the grey afternoon. With nerves now twanging, he got out of the car and closed the lock-up door smiling as he thought of the likely expression on the old man's face the next time he opened his garage door.

Outside the town, Spencer found a self-service filling station and filled the tank with gas before checking the tyres, oil and water. Moments later, he was speeding towards London and his meeting with his fellow assassins, his thoughts lifted away from the depression he had suffered on the train.

The car was in excellent condition and ate up the miles with ease and consequently he found himself in Harrow an hour earlier than he had planned. Stopping at a small café, he telephoned Kathy and arranged to have a drink with her later that evening. Walking back towards his stolen car he thought proudly that he probably found himself a bed for the night.

At six fifty eight he parked the car one hundred yards from the house and walked to the meeting, arriving at exactly seven pm.

Miller had spent most of the day reading through a host of Sunday newspapers, taking mental notes of the recorded actions of members of the Cabinet. Later, he had gone for his daily run in the woods near his mobile home before cooking himself an unimaginative Sunday lunch of pie, beans and chipped potatoes.

Solitude was something that he particularly enjoyed and something that he was well used to. What he did detest however, was the continuous feeling of being unclean. Miller was the sort of man the legendary recluse Howard Hughes must have been in his younger years, would spend hours cleaning his home, his clothes, his fingernails, his toenails, his hair, his teeth. Indeed, the list was endless. Miller had hired and fired six cleaning women at home in Surrey after discovering such major crimes as speckles of dust on the Wedgewood or streaks on a bathroom mirror.

Despite his exactingly high standards of personal hygiene, Miller had more worrying thoughts on his mind as he sat in the cold caravan. He had always considered groups too risky to be involved with. The trip to the farm in Ulster had also concerned him and the meeting arranged for later that evening annoyed him even more. All it took was a nosey neighbour, a passing policeman, somebody walking their dog, indeed any of an immeasurable number of variables. He would argue against further such meetings when he confronted O'Neil although he had doubts about the outcome of such an argument.

Dressed in the army surplus store clothing he left for Kenton at six pm after watching and enjoying Match of the Day on the small portable television, his one luxury from home.

Assuming that there was nothing yet to fear from the police, he parked his hired car near the house and sat and watched the tall figure of Spencer enter the building.

Leaving the car, he walked towards the house in no doubt that he was being watched by the Irishman. Of the three others, Miller felt that he had most in common with O'Neil and he considered it something of a pity that he would have to kill the Irishman to survive. Walking up the garden path, he rang the doorbell and waited for DeVille to let him in.

It is strange how differently people react in the face of adversity. Anna O'Grady had taken two sleeping tablets and retreated to her bed while her husband was left to busy himself about the house doing those little odd jobs he had been promising to do for months.

After the telephone call, Ray had been so nervous that he had actually gone to the toilet and vomited. As time went by however, a numb sense of awareness of what was actually happening began to creep over him leaving him in no doubt about what actions to take, he quite simply had to obey their orders. His daughter would always come first although the strong patriot within him constantly nagged at his innermost thoughts. Once he had come to accept what his line was to be, he felt happier within himself and simply contented himself to sit back and wait and hope.

Dipping a small paintbrush into a jar of turpentine substitute, he carried it to the garage where he stored it carefully in an old grey filing cabinet. As he left the garage he noticed the space normally occupied by Patricia's bicycle. Christ, he cried quietly, why was this happening to him?

Entering the house, he quietly and deliberately ascended the stairs and popped his head into the bedroom he shared with his wife.

Despite the sleeping pills, he was surprised to see Anna still asleep, her unlined face looking without a worry in the world. Pulling the bedroom door shut, he returned downstairs and made himself a cup of black coffee before taking a seat in the sitting room with its views overlooking the garden and hills further to the south.

Tomorrow, he thought, would be very difficult . To carry out his duties, as if nothing was wrong, while leaving Anna on her own at home. The game however, had to be played, a game over which he had no control of the rules and that had his daughter's life as its stake. The priest at Mass had asked where Patricia was and Ray had lied that the girl had the 'flu.

Picking up a Sunday newspaper he avoided the political columns, which would normally have been given top priority in preference to the less formidable sports pages. After a short time he gave up with the newspaper unable to settle and went to refill his coffee cup.

Thinking that he heard a knock at the main door, he put down his drink and strode rather apprehensively towards the door. On the hall floor lay a plain brown envelope and he picked it up noticing that there was nothing written on it. Impulsively he dropped the envelope back onto the floor, opened the door and rushed out into the drive. There was nothing or no one to be seen and as he ran to the end of the driveway he was just in time to see a Volvo turn the corner some two hundred yards from his house. With his daughter's life at stake he decided against giving chase and walked slowly back to the house and the envelope.

Back in the hallway he closed the door and carried the small package into the sitting room and sat down again beside the telephone. Carefully he tore the envelope open and extracted a single Polaroid photograph at which he stared in horror.

In the picture his daughter sat apparently naked holding a copy of the Sunday newspaper he had been unable to read a few minutes earlier. Hearing his wife coming down the stairs, O'Grady slipped the photograph into his pocket and tried to act as if nothing had happened. When Anna entered the room, her face had lost the unlined tranquility of induced sleep and Ray let his heart open to her.

'Who was at the door Ray?' she asked sleepily.

O'Grady had never lied to his wife and found it impossible to start doing so now although he felt sure that under the circumstances a white lie would have been justifiable. Pulling the photograph from his pocket, he handed it to Anna without a word. Anna took it and studied it carefully before speaking.

'At least she is still alive.' Ray O'Grady smiled and took his wife in his arms delighted at her recovering inner strength.

The three men hardly had time to nod to one another in recognition before the doorbell rang again and DeVille left them to let O'Neil into the house. Moments later they were all seated in the chairs and formation set out earlier by the Frenchman. The atmosphere could have been cut in slices with a sharp knife and it was Miller who broke the silence with considerable hostility.

'Let me say right at the start that I am less than fucking pleased about having to come here tonight for a fucking meeting, this is not a bloody trades union we are organizing.' He leaned forward and poured himself two fingers of the brandy provided by DeVille.

'Now, now Miller, surely the company is not that bad.' Laughed O'Neil trying to calm things down.

'Not the point O'Neil as I am sure you appreciate.' The Irishman merely nodded and leaning forward, poured himself a drink before continuing.

'Miller, you have accepted this contract and under the terms of that contract, you are bound to follow my instructions. Whilst I can appreciate your concern, until I give instructions to the contrary, this group will continue to meet in this house. Is that clear?'

'Looks like I do not have an option, but I am still not happy.' Concluded Miller.

'Good, we've wasted enough very precious time, so if we could get on with the business in hand.' O'Neil looked at the others who had so far remained silent and DeVille playing his part like a veteran actor knew that this was his cue. Opening the envelope before him, he extracted four photographs and passed one to each of the others, retaining the fourth one for himself.

'These are my proposed initial targets.' he began as the others familiarized themselves with the photographs provided.

'Any questions?'

After a few moments it was Miller who spoke.

'What sort of fucking choice is this DeVille?' The Frenchman shifted in his seat obviously extremely annoyed at Miller's attitude.

'Please explain.' requested DeVille through gritted white teeth.

'Well, is it fair for me to assume you chose these four targets because they are likely to be living in the London area?'

'Nearly always at weekends yes.' conceded DeVille

'That would appear to be a good enough reason for me.' Interjected Spencer for the first time 'What's wrong with that logic?'

'The bloody point is this Spencer.' began Miller collecting all four photographs together and placing them onto the table one at a time making brief comments on the demerits of each choice as he did so.

'Ewan McEwan the Scottish Secretary will be in Scotland all next week and I presume this lot is next week's work?' DeVille nodded.

'Don Sutherland is due in Brussels until Friday, then he flies on to Bonn, West Germany for three days. John Archer is in the South of France recovering from an automobile accident, and Sir Peter Piers? Well, that might make some sense and he is a close friend of the Prime Minister. So one out of the four is not too bad. What are you trying to do DeVille, test our stupidity?'

'If you feel that such targets are not good enough, what can I do, I thought I was dealing with men not boys.' DeVille spat his response to Miller who simply shook his head in desperation.

'What I am saying you stupid French bastard is that we can make our mark in this assignment without travelling all over bloody Europe.'

'If you think that this assignment is too much for you Miller, I will inform my superiors.' O'Neil interrupted the argument growing impatient with Miller's ill temper.

'Don't be so obtuse O'Neil, you know very well that the initial impact in this crusade of yours can be made with consummate ease.' Continued Miller.

'Have you ever thought that we might want to prove our ability to strike all over Europe?' Quizzed O'Neil.

'Pointless gesture.' Snapped Miller taking a sip of his brandy without really tasting it.

For a few moments a silence spread around the room, generating tension causing all eyes to be turned to O'Neil for leadership. The Irishman had been in similar situations before, was used to getting his timing right and did not fail on this occasion.

'I concede that we can forget Sutherland. However, Piers is your man, Miller can take McEwan and I shall have Archer which leaves DeVille as back up on this occasion.' DeVille motioned a protest but O'Neil waved him down before continuing. 'Your brief is to investigate the expedient liquidation of these people and to report back here to this group at nine pm on Thursday evening. At that meeting, I will make the decision about which two targets we shall hit. DeVille, between now and Thursday, you will supply the necessary hardware for the executions, so I suggest you inform him now of your favoured weapons. Is everything clear?' They nodded in agreement although Miller was still unhappy.

'I've already expressed my feelings about meeting again.' He near shouted.

'I don't really care Miller, just do your homework and report back, if we successfully complete this part of the mission you will earn rather a lot of money. Surely that is worth a risk or two?' O'Neil finished his brandy. The meeting was over.

Miller stood and left without another word and was followed by Spencer and O'Neil thus leaving DeVille to wonder where he was going to collect an arsenal from in the centre of London in four days.

That evening as the British Prime Minister and her entire family enjoyed a rare meal together at 10 Downing Street, Sir Peter and Lady Piers were driving home from Elizabeth's sister's in their Rolls

Royce while Commander John Birbeck and his wife Sara enjoyed a quiet post dinner drink in their Walton-on-Thames home.

It was, to all intents and purposes, the calm before the storm.

Monday 26 October 1981

7

The Cote de Azur was basking in a warm glow of autumn sunshine as the British Airways Boeing 707 from Heathrow airport circled over the green Mediterranean before beginning its descent on to the strip of reclaimed land that helps constitute Nice airport.

A large sign welcoming tourists to the Cote de Azur amused O'Neil as he stepped from the half empty airplane on to the still damp tarmac of the runway. Having spent a summer vacation in Cannes some three years earlier, O'Neil had fallen in love with the area and it had therefore been so easy for him to make the decision that it would be he and none of the others who would enjoy the task of hunting down John Archer in beautiful southern France.

From the meeting with the others in Kenton, he had gone directly to Heathrow where he had booked his flight for the following morning at nine am. Later, he had checked into the airport hotel and prepared for his journey, ensuring that his appearance matched that on his false passport.

Passing through the typically glass terminal building with only the slightest delay at passport control, O'Neil strolled through the milling throng, through the mandatory automatic doors and back into the welcome sunshine to a nearby taxi rank. Opening the rear door of a white Mercedes Benz, he told the driver in fluent French to take him to Nice railway station.

Exactly seven minutes later, the French enjoyed living up to their reputation as maniac drivers, he was paying the driver outside the railway station. Walking into the terminal building, he purchased a ticket to Antibes from an insolent man luckily protected from the public by a plastic partition.

Descending into a subway, O'Neil walked slowly to the other end, admiring as he walked the French beauties on large advertising boards. He quickly climbed the stairs from the subway to find himself on a platform he knew from previous trips, to be the one from which to catch the Antibes train.

As he stood on the platform he could not help but notice the immaculate dress of the French railway workers who were a stark contrast to their scruffy British counterparts. A loud horn sounded and a large green train rolled into the station and along the platform. O'Neil boarded at once, finding a no smoking compartment and sat down in a window seat. The train was almost deserted which was very different from the hazy summer days recalled by O'Neil when the trains were always packed with sun loving people, bronzed and smelling of that joyous mixture of salt water, sand and suntan oil.

As the train meandered its way westward along the coast, O'Neil thought of the deserted beaches as they were in the summer, packed with the lovely topless female creatures he adored so much.

It was, he decided as the train continued its slow progress, where he would live when he retired. That, however, was future fancy, so he cleared his mind totally and thought of his task, which was the expedient demise of John Archer MP.

Miller had picked him up by surprise as he drove from the underground car park at the Houses of Parliament. Luckily, the traffic had been heavy enough to enable him to reach his Ford and soon be on McEwan's tail.

Just why he had gone to the Commons in the first place he

was not quite sure, perhaps it had simply been to sniff the political atmosphere, indulge in the political environment he was becoming involved in. Concluding that he did not know why, and that it was really irrelevant as it so far had turned out to his obvious advantage, he guided his car expertly in gentle pursuit of the Scottish Secretary of State. After half an hour, it was obvious to Miller that McEwan was being driven to Heathrow airport. It was there that we would encounter most problems in finding out which flight McEwan was to catch, Glasgow or Edinburgh, and getting booked on to the same flight.

Confident in his own powers of deduction, Miller decided to forget the tailing of McEwan and get to Heathrow fast in order to solve his immediate problems. Quickly finding a place in one of the large car parks for his car, he entered the terminal building and found the main airline ticket counter. The girl at the desk looked bored but responded as Miller turned on his charm.

'Good morning, how can I help you?' she asked, straight out of the television advertisements.

'I certainly hope so.' began Miller scratching his head. 'But it's a little tricky.' He continued scratching his head as if confused.

'My sister and I were due to be flying to Edinburgh this morning, but I've got a terrible feeling that I am an hour late.' As he had hoped, the girl scanned a passenger list from a plastic folder in front of her.

'Were you booked to travel together and in what name?' she asked studying the list.

'Booked, I think.' replied Miller trying to remain plausible.

'Name?'

'McGovern.' he replied and watched the girl run a beautifully manicured finger down the passenger list.

'Yes, there was a McGovern on the earlier flight.' Announced the girl to the total amazement of a rattled Miller. He soon gathered his composure however and continued to weave his fiction.

'Sorry.' he began laughing. My name's McGovern, my sister's name is McEwan now, I keep forgetting. Could you check again?' The girl smiled patiently and returned to her lists.

'Sorry, no McEwan on the earlier flight and the only one on the next flight is a VIP and I do not think that he can be your sister.'

'Oh I don't know.' Miller laughed with her 'the way that lot behave in Parliament, the entire country must have its doubts.' Miller could have kicked himself for the lapse, scratched his head again and told the girl that he would go and make some telephone calls to try and unravel the confusion.

Returning from the telephone booths, he told the girl that his sister had in fact flown on a rival airline and after some more charm, he purchased a ticket on McEwan's flight, went through to the departure lounge, bought a newspaper and waited for his flight to be called.

When he eventually entered the plane, he was pleased to see McEwan sitting up front with a young man in a sober grey suit that Miller took to be McEwan's Personal Secretary as they were already working on some papers. Finding his seat on the half empty airplane, Miller sat down and relaxed. There would be transport problems in Edinburgh, but McEwan would probably have official transport, which would not be difficult to follow. Fastening his seatbelt, Miller hardly noticed the take-off, so intent was he with his reading.

As the London-Edinburgh shuttle left the runway at Heathrow airport, Crawford Spencer awoke in a state of considerable discomfort in Kathy Drinkwater's London flat. His long frame was obviously not constructed for sleeping on two sofas. Swinging his legs round and on to the floor, he sat up, his feet prickly with pins and needles. Listening intently for a moment as the circulation returned to his feet, he tried to discern whether or not Kathy was still at home. Looking at his watch, he decided in the silence that she had probably gone to university. Walking into the tiny kitchen, he found his conclusion supported by a note, which read:

Crawford,

You looked dreadfully comfortable so I didn't want to disturb you. There's plenty of food etc, please help yourself.

Kathy

PS You're welcome to stay again tonight if you wish.

Opening the small refrigerator, Spencer helped himself to a carton of yoghurt and poured some semi-skimmed milk into a glass. Strolling back into the sitting room, he sat down on the sofa-come-bed and began slowly eating his breakfast. It had not been the bed he had hoped for, but it was somewhere to lay low, with the minimum of risks. What he needed to concentrate on was Kathy's loyalty because he could never be certain that some minute error in any project would not lead to disaster. He would, he concluded, need to get into the girl's bed, nothing could generate more loyalty from a decent woman than being her lover.

Recalling the fact that he had left the car he had stolen nearby, he considered going to move it. He concluded that such an action was too risky since the car would have undoubtedly been reported missing already. Nevertheless, he mentally reprimanded himself. Careless mistakes needed to be avoided and he knew full well that he often got over confident in his ability. Looking at his watch, he had also overslept. An anger slowly crept over him, an anger at his so far unprofessional approach to this task. Finishing his light breakfast, he strode purposefully to the bathroom for a shower, trying to clear another annoyance from his mind, the fact that he had been kept from Kathy's bed the previous evening.

When he left the flat an hour later, it was not the stolen car or the lack of sexual activity which was predominant in his mind, those extraneous matters having been replaced by thoughts of how to kill Sir Peter Piers.

The car was totally out of control. Suddenly it began to spin violently before jumping off the road, through an inept attempt at a crash barrier, tumbled twice, before finally coming to rest with a bump in a wet field full of potatoes. John Archer was aware of the excruciating pain in his legs, the hot flow of blood down his forehead and then of absolutely nothing.

It was six days later when he eventually regained consciousness in a private hospital room deep in the heart of Devonshire. The first face he was aware of belonged to his young wife Jean, who had looked tired and had smiled and had told him that he had been a very lucky man and that had he died she would have killed him. The silliness of the welcome over, she then relayed to him in the nicest possible way, that he had sustained two broken legs, fractured collar bone and oh yes, there was the small matter of the forty odd stitches in his head. In other words, she concluded, he had gotten off rather lightly.

They had come to their holiday villa in the pine-clad hills overlooking the castle and harbour of Antibes some ten days later. Archer had tried desperately to convince Jean that he did not need a period of convalescence in France but had eventually lost his battle when even the Prime Minister had added her considerable powers of persuasion to the argument. Against his wishes, he had surrendered, but only for four weeks.

He was still in a wheelchair two weeks later as Jean pushed him from the villa, down the slight incline to the poolside. Archer was in a heavy woolen cardigan despite the warm sunshine and carried a book on his lap. Jean leaned over her beloved husband and kissed him on the lips before driving from the villa in her small Fiat to do her daily shopping in Antibes.

O'Neil sat amidst the pines above the villa taking in the scene through newly acquired field glasses. It looked to be such an easy killing that he tried to convince himself that there had in fact got to be a catch somewhere. Dropping the binoculars to his chest, he rubbed his unshaven chin, jumped to his feet and dusted down his trousers before beginning his descent.

Arriving outside the Archer villa, O'Neil carefully perused the perimeter wall undetected, finding it totally incomprehensible that such an important political figure would consider setting up home so close to the kidnapping world of the Italian border, without taking any apparent security precautions.

Later, having watched Jean Archer arrive back from her shopping, he made his way back to the airport in Nice, totally convinced that he had come up with a satisfactory time, place and method of assassination. What he could not know was that under his chunky cardigan, John Archer always carried a loaded revolver.

'…… *the significance of this theory is that to treat quadratic forms adequately, it is sufficient to consider symmetric bilinear forms. It is indeed fortunate that symmetric bilinear forms and symmetric matrices are very easy to handle. Among many possible bilinear forms corresponding to a given quadratic form a selected bilinear form* …..'

Kathy Drinkwater ran her finger along the metallic top of the cassette recorder and thanked God for the person who had invented the masterpiece. The lecturer continued on his merry uninterrupted way, pronouncing his thoughts on matrix theory to the half empty lecture theatre. Normally, Kathy enjoyed Professor Edwards-Jones at work, but today she could only think of Spencer and the marvelous time they had spent together the previous evening.

She had never actually wanted a man before. Of course, there had been Russell, but that had been because Russell had wanted sex and she in turn had been intrigued and had obliged. She had also never really enjoyed sex with Russell but had felt that there had to be more to the phenomenon than a quick spurt of energetic activity. Spencer, she was confident could confirm her theory and it had taken all her middle-class British morality to prevent her discovering the truth during the previous evening. She wanted to know everything about him, his background, how he made love, what his parents were like, how he made love, where he had studied, and how he made love. She was she concluded, infatuated with the American and perhaps even already in love with him, or was it lust? She decided that if he stayed the night, he would not sleep on the sofa. In fact, she smiled to herself, he would not sleep anywhere.

Lifting her pencil, she nibbled at the end, a filthy habit she deplored and as if she had turned up the volume on the professor, she was at once aware of what he was saying.

'.... the relationship between poles and polars are quite interesting and are explored in great depth in my book on Projective Geometry ....'

Kathy was happy now in her mind, she had made her decision. It was a decision that would almost certainly cost her life.

Miller walked from the elevator satisfied in his mind that this was not the place to hit McEwan, there were too many people about. He pushed through a pair of glass fire doors, passed the two security guards at the reception desk and out through the revolving doors into the cold afternoon.

At Edinburgh airport he had picked up the hire car he had arranged on the airplane. As he had expected, McEwan's rather conspicuous Bentley had been waiting for him and Miller had followed it without difficulty. The first problem he had encountered occurred when the Bentley had rushed through the barriers at the entrance to New St Andrew's House, the architecturally grotesque concrete centre of Scottish Office activity. Miller quickly found a car parking space in a nearby multi-storey and took up inconspicuous monitoring of the comings and goings from the bureaucratic centre of Scotland from a nearby bus station. Within minutes he saw that there was only one point of entry, and to gain access, he required a security pass. However, with lunchtime approaching, he could foresee no real difficulties in obtaining such a pass. From there, his destination was rather obvious. From a simple scrutiny of the outside of the building anyone interested could see that the ministerial suite at New St Andrew's House is on the sixth floor. The designers of the solid ugly towers which stands just off the east end of the city's famous Princes Street, had, in their wisdom, fitted the ministerial suite with totally different windows from the rest of the building. Miller had found it hard to contain his astonishment at such an obvious security blunder.

The pass turned out to be as easy to acquire as the information telling him which floor housed the ministerial suite. Miller had simply picked at random from a number of housewives who worked within New St Andrew's House and who were rushing from the building to do some lunchtime shopping, more concerned with what was for the evening meal than with national security. The civil service was full of such women, women who did not care about career prospects or promotion, but who worked to help with heavy mortgages and pay for three weeks a year in Florida or Spain or the Canary Islands. Miller had decided on his victim when he noticed her drop her pass into the pocket of her standard Marks & Spencer mackintosh. He followed her down a short flight of stairs and into a shopping precinct known as the St James Centre and in a large supermarket he simply extracted the security pass from her raincoat pocket as she continued happily with her shopping.

From one of many gents outfitters in the precinct he bought a navy raincoat and carried his new purchase back to his hired car where he exchanged the army surplus jacket he had been wearing for his more respectful new coat. The heavy corduroy trousers and shoes he was wearing hardly matched his image of a smart civil servant, but not all civil servants could afford smart new suits, so he reckoned his appearance to be satisfactory. Leaving the car with his newly acquired pass in his pocket, he headed back towards New St. Andrew's House.

Whilst the Scottish Office took the precaution of renewing passes on a regular basis, it was their considered opinion that photographs were not necessary and for this Miller was eternally grateful. The larger of the two security guards merely nodded to him as he briefly displayed his pass inside the building some five minutes later. Casually, he walked towards a row of elevators, which stood some fifty yards away through a couple of glass fire doors. Miller could smell food and assumed that there was a staff restaurant nearby on the ground floor. At the doors to the elevators, Miller joined an orderly queue of staff returning from their lunch and busily discussing their lunchtime squash match, the previous evening's television and even more boringly, the previous morning's work.

An elevator arrived and the civil servants jostled with each other in a not-so-civil manner, which Miller found amusing as he took his place inside. Rather surprisingly, the chatter ceased for the duration of the upward journey and the elevator took ages to ascend, stopping at every floor before reaching the sixth of eight floors. At the sixth floor, Miller stepped from the elevator along with a young man who smiled in a friendly manner at Miller who returned the gesture. Miller followed him as he turned left into a corridor which led away from two fire doors which had a sign post stating that this was indeed the ministerial suite, through more fire doors, passed a suite of male and female toilets and left into a further corridor. Reading the names on the oak paneled doors, Miller noticed one, which read in roman script Sebastian Scott. Miller turned and headed back towards the elevators. Pushing open the fire doors to the corridor containing the ministerial suite, Miller stepped inside immediately aware of the finer texture of the carpet underfoot. Sarcastically he wondered why normal civil servants put up with such obvious class discrimination.

Just then, a door opened and Ewan McEwan entered the corridor only yards in front of Miller who almost froze with absolute astonishment. McEwan smiled a patronizing smile at Miller and hurried into another office leaving Miller momentarily confused as to what to do next.

'Can ah help you sir?' came a gruff uneducated voice from behind and Miller spun round to be faced by a small grey haired man wearing a grey uniform with a gold lapel badge.

'Well.' began Miller trying to reassert himself 'I was looking for Sebastian Scott's office.' he offered hopefully.

'Och you're in the wrang corridor. This is the ministers offices, did you no see the sign on the door?' Miller shook his head and the man smiled and gave him directions to Scott's office. Relieved to get away with pushing his luck too far, Miller took refuge in the gent's toilets and waited for ten minutes before heading for the elevators and his exit from the building.

Miller was in no doubt, he had been taken aback by what had happened and as he descended to the ground floor in a busy elevator, he was coming to the conclusion that New St Andrew's House was no place to hit McEwan, there were too many people about, too many risks.

The last of that afternoon's customers, a middle-aged businessman and a young brunette, were leaving the restaurant as Charles Cherrit abandoned his office in search of other, more exciting pursuits. A tall, fat jolly looking man in a navy pin striped suit, Cherrit was on his way back to his flat, his girls from the agency and his afternoon of fun.

He strolled deliberately slower than he would have preferred through the kitchen in an attempt to keep his staff on their toes. No good in letting them think that he would accept less than one hundred percent from them. The idle gossip of the kitchen staff hushed to a silence as he progressed keeping a watchful eye over their work, only to start up again as he left through the rear exit.

Closing the door behind him he chuckled, his large frame vibrating like a jelly as he did so and skipped almost gaily towards his BMW. He did not see the bald black man lurking in an alley behind him in the corner of the yard, had he done so, he would not have been chuckling.

As Cherrit pushed the key into his beloved motorcar, the man stepped from the shadows and greeted the fat man in French.
'Good afternoon Charles.' he announced and with the sound of the familiar voice, Cherrit froze in his tracks. Gathering himself however, he turned to be greeted by the big bald face he had expected.
'Jean-Claude, what a wonderful surprise.' Cherrit walked towards the man hoping that his anxiety did not show as they embraced each other in the cheek-to-cheek French custom. 'What brings you to London my old friend?' He asked also in French as he stood back looking at the man before him.
'Oh, this and that, you know me Charles, always doing this and that.'

The bald man shrugged his shoulders and looked around the yard before continuing 'Well Charles, are we going to stand here all day looking at each other?'

'I am so sorry Jean Claude. Come, come.' Cherrit led the man to his car and they both got in and Cherrit drove them out of the yard.

'I've got the very thing lined up for us this afternoon Jean-Claude, I'd call it entertainment at its very best, interested?' Cherrit could not help feel nervous, Jean-Claude Marnier always meant trouble and he began to sweat profusely as his mind worked overtime in an attempt to work out what it was that he was after this time.

'If it's what I think it is Charles, you know me, I'm always interested in sex.' replied Marnier who had noticed the fat man's anxiety.

'I'm sure that you will not be disappointed.' offered Cherrit as he somehow managed to drive his BMW expertly through the busy London traffic.

As it transpired, the bald black man was not to be disappointed. He had not had a woman for many weeks and had not realized just how much he had missed his sexual pleasures. The first blond had been tall and very chesty and had expertly satisfied him into a deep sleep. The second blond had kept him full of want and desire for almost two hours before forcing his second and third orgasm of the afternoon from his tiring body. Later both girls had joined him in the large golden bath before departing for pastures new. It had in fact been a rather enjoyable afternoon.

Dressed, Marnier joined Cherrit in a large tastefully decorated room with its view over the Thames. The apartment reminded Marnier of his own overlooking the Seine in Paris, but he dismissed such thoughts from his mind and concentrated on the real purpose of looking up his old colleague Charles Cherrit. The two men drank to each other's health from a five star bottle of brandy and discussed fondly the good old days back in Paris. Marnier thought that Cherrit had relaxed considerably after his afternoon of sexual activity and guided the conversation in a less than subtle manner to the real purpose of his visit.

'Well Charles, as you know I'm not the sort of person who makes social calls. So perhaps I should put you out of your misery and tell you what I really looked you up for.' he began.

'Please do.' Insisted Cherrit again beginning to panic.

'Well, I need some firearms, the specification of which is contained in this envelope.' From his jacket pocket, Marnier passed a small brown envelope to Cherrit and as he did so he asked 'I assume that you are still capable of supplying such items.'

'Oh yes Jean-Claude, I can get you guns. However, in London at the present time, it will be very expensive.'

'Money is no object, but I must have these items by tomorrow evening at the latest.' He handed the envelope to the Frenchman who tore it open and began reading the contents, raising an eyebrow occasionally as he read.

'You have my assurance that I can supply these items.' Cherrit concluded 'However, they will cost you five thousand pounds in used notes.' He looked at the bald man hoping that he had not overstepped himself, not pushed his confidence, caused jointly by sexual relief and alcohol, too far.

'I will bring you five thousand pounds in used notes tomorrow in exchange for the firearms, all carefully packed as specified, here at seven pm tomorrow evening.' Cherrit shook his hand to conclude the deal, guns were no problem and with such a fast profit. He began to relax, but Marnier was aware of his change in attitude.

'But let me conclude.' He began 'that if you let me down, I will cut your fat throat and leave you to dry in your golden bath. Understood?'

'I will not let you down Jean-Claude, you can depend on me.'

'For your sake Charles.' Smiled DeVille 'I certainly hope so.'

The icy wind smashed cold rain at some sixty miles an hour into the face of Joseph Blaney as he stood dressed in heavy yellow oilskins watching the slow progress of the ship towards his beloved emerald isle. The dark green sea below the ship looked so uninviting, so frighteningly cold, yet the seagulls, which followed the ship, swooping and diving in the wind, did not seem to find it so.

Lifting himself from the port side rail, he wiped the rain from his face and climbed the steps holding on grimly to the cold, plastic coated mottled handrail, to the upper deck and entered the bridge. Pushing the door shut behind him, he closed out the gale and was instantly glad of the heat.

The captain turned towards him and nodded. A seaman dressed in navy with a think sweater and the symbol of the Blaney Brothers company stitched in silver on his chest crossed the bridge and offered Blaney a mug of steaming hot tea. Blaney accepted it without a word and cupped his hand round the mug for warmth. He then crossed to where the captain stood looking through the spaces provided in the large windows by the massive window wipers that appeared to be struggling to contain the heavy rain.

'Are we on time captain?' Asked Blaney for the umpteenth time. Despite the fact that the captain had heard the question often and would doubtless hear it again, he tried to show considerable restraint when he replied.

'No problems so far sir, estimated time of arrival in Dublin is twenty two hundred hours, with your pick up at nineteen thirty. We remain bang on schedule.' He looked at his employer and understood his panic. If he took Joseph Blaney into Dublin, the authorities would without doubt take the ship apart and they would all be locked up for years. Without him, at worst the Garda would find the secret cargo and put out an alert for Blaney who had seen it all before and would probably survive. As for the captain and his crew, they had simply carried what was in the ship's manifest, which were electric generators and not a secret supply of Russian guns.

'What do you think of the generators?' Asked Blaney rather suddenly.

'They look as safe as houses to me mister Blaney, but who can tell?' The captain shrugged his tired shoulders and remembered that it was dangerous to underestimate the shrewdness and judgment of Joseph Blaney. It may have been said that Joseph depended heavily on his elder brother, but he had been warned that both men were extremely dangerous.

Blaney sipped at his hot tea as he stared out of the windows upon which the wipers were still fighting their battle against the heavy rain. In the hold below them, he was thinking, stood four electric generators, which had been built in Greece. What the innocuous façade failed to show was the fact that all four generators had been hollowed out and stacked to capacity with Kalashnikov rifles with their fold-down stocks that made them perhaps the best rifle available, supplied at considerable cost by the Palestinian Liberation Order. The weapons would prove invaluable to the Provisional IRA as they strode to rid the British from Ireland for once and for all.

He was aware of the fact that he had taken a considerable gamble getting involved with such an ambitious scheme so soon after his trial. He had been held for almost three months and it would have been considerably longer had his brother Liam not managed to knobble the jury into returning a not guilty verdict. Joseph trusted his brother to the point of distraction and it was receiving Liam's approval to the latest venture that had convinced Joseph that all the risks were worth taking.

Finishing his tea, Blaney left the bridge. It was sixteen forty and therefore just under three hours to his rendezvous, so he decided to go to his cabin and sleep for a couple of hours. If only the ship would stop rocking.

As Joseph Blaney was climbing into his bunk on the rocking cargo vessel some sixty miles south of Dublin, Sir Peter Piers was moving his queen to king three on the chequered board in front of him in the members' chess room in the Palace of Westminster. Pausing momentarily, his finger on his queen, he finally lifted his hand clear before announcing rather proudly to his Parliamentary colleague.

'Checkmate, I'm afraid old chap.' Chuckling to himself he turned and looked out of the large window with its leaded squares, across the terrace and the dark river Thames, to the glowing lamps of Jubilee Walk on the opposite embankment. He thought that if he wanted to avoid the heavy rush hour traffic, he should really be making his move although a check with his watch confirmed that he had already left it rather late.

'Yes, you would seem to have me this time Piers.' Admitted his opponent who had been studying the board in the forlorn hope that there could in fact have been some mistake.

'How about another, give me the chance of revenge, what?' requested Piers rather hopeless partner. They played fairly regularly and Piers was still to have revenge exacted upon him and seriously doubted if he ever would.

'Sorry Steven, but one really must be off, got a number of things to get through this evening.' Piers bid his poor opponent farewell and left the chess room. Turning to his right, he walked along by the Commons Library and passed the tearoom on his left. Returning to his office in the ministers' office block under the shadow of the famous clock tower, which contains London's famous landmark known to the world as Big Ben, he collected his cases that contained papers, which required nothing more than his signature. His personal secretary was sitting by her typewriter reading the Evening Standard when Piers popped his head into her small anteroom to say that he was leaving. She merely smiled and said that she would see him in the morning.

Leaving his office, Piers walked through the Star Chamber Court and left the Mother of Parliaments by the portico known as the Members' entrance where the tall policeman on duty touched his cap as he left. From the underground car park he drove his Rolls Royce up the ramp and out through the police guarded wrought iron gates and filtered into the by now dense rush hour traffic.

Big Ben was about to announce to the City of Westminster that it was five pm when Spencer saw the unmistakable PP123 registration plate on the Silver Shadow as it left the confines of the Houses of Parliament. Thankful for the fact that he did not have the problem of following a nondescript vehicle in the heavy traffic, Spencer slipped Kathy's little motorcar into the traffic stream with ease and followed his prey.

Almost an hour later, he sat across a junction and watched with interest as Piers went through the motions of transferring himself, his cases and an overnight bag from the Rolls Royce to a small Mini Metro in a quiet street in the district of Barnet, North London. Spencer's amusement grew as Piers also replaced his lambs' wool overcoat with a sheepskin jacket and donned a tweed hat. Wherever he was going, mused the American, he was covering his tracks and would be a darn sight more difficult to trail. In fact it took nearly another hour of full concentration by Spencer before Piers parked the Metro outside a small block of rather well kept apartments in Northwood.

Spencer drove on passed Piers and pulled the car into the kerb some hundred yards or so along the tree lined lane. Watching in the rear mirror, he saw Piers get out of the Metro and carry his luggage to the glass entrance to the apartments and press the intercom button.

The American arrived at the glass door in time to see the elevator light indicate a stop on the fourth floor. Seeking out the nameplates on the intercom, he found only two on the fourth floor, JD Walcott and S Lamont. Pressing the first brought no reply whilst from the second he was greeted by a hello from a young sounding female. He had struck gold.

Walking back to the car, he decided that there was little more need for further surveillance; he had found a fatal chink he had not hoped of finding in the armour of such a high-ranking Member of Parliament. He decided to donate the remainder of the evening, in celebration, to Kathy Drinkwater.

On hearing the first buzz of the intercom, Susan had hurried to answer and was delighted to hear Sir Peter's voice. The second buzz had merely raised her curiosity and before she went to greet her lover at the door, she paused long enough at the kitchen window to see the tall blond walking across the street and jump into a small car. Moments later she was in Piers' arms and had forgotten the second buzz incident.

As Sir Peter Piers embraced his latest young lover in her flat in Northwood, Middlesex, fifty-eight year old Jack Kane checked with his charts for the third time and concluded that he was indeed at the rendezvous point. Climbing the few steps from the radio room, he turned the ignition key to cut the engines, throwing the boat into considerable silence. Looking at his pocket watch he saw that it was just after seven pm thus leaving him with half an hour until the arrival of his passenger. Walking skillfully to the aft of his boat, he eventually saw the orange marker he had left the previous day bobbing in the stormy sea. Smiling, pleased with his navigational skills, he returned to the small bridge and started the engines, carefully guiding his beloved Blackrock Boy towards the float. In the storm, it took him some twenty-five minutes to get the boat tied up.

It was twenty minutes to eight when Kane was delighted to hear the engines of an obviously large vessel coming in his direction. Another twenty minutes went before the ship came alongside the Blackrock Boy and in the dark, wet night Kane thought for a dreadful minute or so that he was bound to be rammed and sunk without trace. The skipper of the other ship was obviously an expert however, and he guided his ship slowly passed the Blackrock Boy, occasionally only inches away from Kane's starboard side. The small boat rolled violently in the wake of its considerably larger cousin.

For a split second Kane was sure that Blaney was not going to make it. He had a terrible vision of Joseph being crushed between the two vessels and dumped into the cruel sea.

The Blaneys' however, were born survivors and Joseph had timed his leap from the rope ladder to perfection, landing on the deck of the small boat in a cat-like manner. Kane rushed to Blaney's aid, only to find him on his feet and waving to someone holding a torch on the cargo ship. Deciding it best to sever the rope holding the Boy to the float, Kane left Blaney and went about his immediate business.

Later, Kane entered the bridge to be greeted by the wet and

smiling face of Joseph Blaney. The cargo vessel was already ploughing away from them into the wet gloom.

'Welcome aboard the Blackrock Boy Joseph, I hope that you've had a safe and pleasant journey.' Kane greeted Blaney as he started the boats engine and headed for the shore.
'Bloody sight for sore eyes you are Jack, I've been worried all day that you might not turn up.'
'Oh, you know me Joe, loyal patriot to the last.' Replied Kane setting his course as he spoke.
'Almost was the last jump now Jack, thought I was for the old watery grave for a couple of minutes.' and Kane merely smiled at Blaney with a mixture of amusement and relief.
'All's well.' He finally replied 'And welcome back to Ireland.'

The dockyard security, to quote Garda Chief Inspector Paul Brennan, was as tight as a camel's arse in a sandstorm. Turning to one of his officers standing beside him, he looked at his watch before speaking.
'I thought they said this ship was due in at twenty two hundred hours Patsy.'
'So they did Chief, it must be delayed with the terrible weather they've been having out there all week.' Answered his sergeant, a greying fifty-year old nearing retirement.
'Well I'm frigging freezing standing out here, I'll go and sit in the car for a wee while. Give me a shout if anything happens.'

Inside the car he opened a flask of hot soup and poured some into the accompanying plastic lid. He would be fooling himself to suggest that he was anything but nervous. His information had come from a normally reliable source, but there was always doubt and this had promised to be a large coup into which he had received permission to put considerable resources. However, these operations could always go wrong and he could not afford many more errors in connection with the Blaney family, people were already saying that he was riddled with paranoia in their direction. Lifting the walky-talky beside him he spoke into it.
'What's the latest position?'

'The navy have got the ship in contact Chief, they say that it will be docked in just over two hours.'

'Good, keep me posted of any developments.' He snapped the walky-talky shut, finished the last of his soup and decided to check the security once again, not willing to let any cock-up stand between him and nailing Joseph Blaney once and for all.

Having left Anderson at the vantage point at Treeacre, Elliot made his way through the fields and hedgerows to his car which was parked some two miles away in a quiet, seldom used country lane. They were working watch duty on a six hours on six hours off basis and as a result were not getting a great deal of sleep.

It was almost midnight when he drove carefully over the ramps in the road, built to prevent would be bombers making a speedy retreat, and into the heavily protected confines of the red brick Police Headquarters at Lisburn. It was time for his twenty-four hourly briefing with Mac Bradley.

The large outer office, in comparison to the normal daily rabble was near empty with only a few officers typing reports and answering telephone calls from informants and nuisances alike, it being their job to determine which.

Obtaining two coffees from the hot drinks machine, Elliot walked across the room to Bradley's office and managed to negotiate the closed door and entered.

Bradley was talking to his wife on the telephone, his back to Elliot and his feet raised on a small cabinet by his desk. Waving Elliot into a seat he continued to talk to his wife and Colm was aware of the unusual tenderness in his manner as he did so. His conversation over, Bradley turned his attention to Elliot, thanking him for the coffee before continuing.

'Well Colm, any movement?' he enquired tucking his legs under his paper-laden desk.

'Nope, the old shit has been stuck in that farmhouse all day, not even been out for a breath of fresh air.' replied Elliot.

'It's fresh lungs he needs Colm, not fresh air.'

'Anything on the phone tap?' asked Elliot vowing that he would never drink the office coffee again, it would have to be lemon tea next time.

'Not been a single call all day, perhaps he's dead.' They both smiled and Elliot crossed his fingers in mock hope as Bradley continued 'No Colm, we're not going to be that lucky.' He tossed his empty coffee cup into a near full wastepaper basket. It was all he seemed to do, drink coffee, receive information, pass on said information, sleep a few hours, more coffee, all leading to a probable early grave, probable bullet through the head.

'Any further thoughts on what might be going on?' Elliot interrupted his thought process.

'I've told you that's your pigeon Colm. However, you will be pleased to hear that the stolen car spotted at Treeacre the other night has been found in Girvan, Scotland.'

'A ferry crossing, any clues?' Asked Elliot doubtfully.

'Nothing, the thing was as clean as a whistle.'

'Pity, but at least we've got an ID on the driver.' Elliot responded.

'If it was the same person who took the car away from the farm.' Replied Bradley 'Anyway, we've got something cooking right here in our own backyard and it looks to me as if it might be something big, so we better be right on our toes.' The two men stared at each other across the desk, men with great respect for each other, men aware of the difficulties and dangers involved in their every day existence.

Their thoughtful interlude was suddenly interrupted by the shrill of the telephone on Bradley's desk. Reaching out, he answered it in his usual quick and abrupt manner.

'Bradley. Yes. Hi Paul. And? What about Blaney? Christ, how the fuck did he manage that? Shit, that would have nailed the bastard for years. What about the weapons? How many? Jesus. Thanks anyway Paul, I owe you one.' Hanging up, he turned to Elliot letting out a loud whistle. It was Elliot who spoke first.

'Paul Brennan from Dublin?' he asked expecting a quick

rundown.

'Too right Colm. He and a bloody squadron of Garda and the Irish Army raided the Blaney Brothers cargo vessel as it docked in Dublin this evening. Guess what?'

'Weapons?' He had gathered that much from Bradley's end of the telephone conversation.

'Hollowed out electric generators stacked with Kalashnikovs, a load that must have cost the Provos' a small fortune. Biggest haul in the Republic for years.' Enthused Bradley.

'Arrests?' Asked Elliot surprised at the size of the find.

'None as yet, crew are obviously denying all knowledge of the hidden cargo, and bloody Joseph Blaney was not on the ship, despite the fact that he was definitely on board yesterday.' Standing, Bradley walked across the room from his desk.

'Must have jumped ship en route.' Offered Elliot.

'Picked up at sea you mean?' Suggested Bradley, staring through the glass partition to the quiet outer office.

'No other solution, he's a right slippery bastard Blaney, he simply wouldn't risk sailing into Dublin sitting on those pretty Russian guns, he's brighter than that.'

'Of course you're right Colm, but what I would like to know is where and when he got off, and is that shithouse back in Ireland?' Stretching his clasped hands in front of him, he cracked his fingers, a habit that annoyed Elliot a lot.

'I smell a big fat rat Colm, the failure of the H-Block Campaign has stuck in the gullet of some of these maniacs and some of them will be out to revenge the deaths of Bobby Sands and his mates.'

'What do you want Anderson and me to get onto?' Asked Elliot.

'Continue to watch McCormack, but even closer now. I'm more convinced that there will be a link-up and it's for sure that the Blaneys will lie low for a while and let the heat die down on tonight's little fiasco. Perhaps Liam Blaney will contact McCormack, only time will tell.'

Elliot rose and left the office. He needed sleep badly, but decided against it considering that the telecom section might be a better place to spend the remainder of his time off watch. Down there they would be monitoring McCormack's calls and Elliot could feel it in his water that Bradley was right about a call from Blaney. Against his better judgment, he bought some black coffee from the machine and headed for the basement.

Just before midnight it began to rain in Edinburgh. Miller stretched his aching limbs as much as the limited space in the car permitted and watched carefully as the first of the guests began to leave the function suite of the Royal Scot Hotel in the western outskirts of the city.

From Millers point of view the busy car park ensured that nobody would be suspicious of his presence. All day he had been following McEwan, and not for more than those brief few seconds in New St Andrews House, had the man been on his own. The Scottish Secretary of State was either very popular or very cautious, or perhaps both. Rain was now running down the car windows and Miller had to strain to watch those leaving the hotel some fifty yards away. McEwan's car and chauffeur sat near the entrance and Miller did not expect any problems in tailing them when the time came.

It was twelve thirty by the time McEwan, accompanied by his rather attractive wife, left the function. Miller watched as a hotel porter carried a large multi-coloured golf umbrella over the couple as they strode the few yards to their awaiting car. Sitting back in the drivers seat, Miller yawned, before leaning forward and turning the ignition and starting up his own hired car. He allowed McEwan's driver time to get out of the car park, before following some two hundred and fifty yards behind.

The driver in front was not holding back as Miller realised that he was doing well over seventy miles an hour just to keep in touch. They drove through the quiet suburb of Barnton and headed for the Forth Road Bridge and it's crossing into Fife. At the bridge toll booths, Miller struggled in his pockets for fifteen pence and consequently found himself well behind McEwan's car on leaving the bridge.

The road twisted and turned as both cars headed through quiet country places with such distinctive Scottish names as Inverkeithing, Aberdour, Burntisland, Kinghorn, Kirkcadly and Dysart. They then headed north through the small town of Auchterarder and further northwards before McEwan's car finally entered the grounds of his palatial home, which overlooks the picturesque Loch Leven.

Miller drove on before stopping his car on a grass verge some half a mile up the quiet road. Walking back towards the house in the pouring rain, he was of the opinion that the was wasting his time, but decided to continue his surveillance on the basis that he had no place to go at that time of night in the middle of Scotland anyway.

Finding the wall, which he had noticed to surround McEwan's house, he scaled it athletically and headed through the pine trees towards the lighted home. It was a grand Georgian affair, three stories high and with typically small picture windows which were painted a brilliant white. The lawns in front of the house were beautifully cared for, the lush turf giving like soft carpet as Miller strode across it. The house showed no signs of the decay or difficult times one could often associate with those of the so called landed gentry. Members of the government, like assassins, could obviously avoid economic recession, thought Miller sarcastically.

Only two rooms in the house were lit up, one on the third floor and a small room on the ground floor by the garage that Miller took to be the drivers. Miller quickly spotted the large white box near the top of a south-facing wall that indicated the expected security alarm. After surveying the complete expanse of the property and taking mental notes, Miller suddenly had to dive behind a large tree as two Scottish policemen came into view from the rear of the house. They chatted before embarking on another tour of the gardens, leaving Miller to hastily retreat from the grounds and back to his car.

With an outline plan formulated in his mind, Miller started his car and drove off. He would try to talk the others out of the idea of McEwan as a target. Of course he could be killed, but the risks would be high and at this stage of the exercise, risks were to be avoided at all costs.

At the exact moment Miller was entering his car in Fife, Scotland, an extremely tense Liam Blaney was answering the telephone in a safe flat in north Dublin.

The call as he had hoped, was from his brother Joseph as had been pre-arranged. Liam had wasted no time in getting out of his own apartment following his call from his Guarda informant. The police would want to question him, and this was no time for him to get held up on such business. Joseph was also at great risk and as soon as they knew he was in Ireland they would be after him also.

'Joseph, thank God it is you.' Began the elder Blaney with relief.
'How are you big brother?' Came the somewhat bemused reply.
'Ready to get the fuck out of Dublin, Joe, the heat is on up here, they discovered the weapons.' Explained Liam glad the warning could be given to his brother.
'How in God's name did that happen? They must have an informer.' Fumed the younger Blaney.
'He'll be a sorry bastard when I'm finished with him,' stated Liam.
'What do you want me to do?' Asked Joseph aware suddenly that it was of prime importance for Liam to get out of Dublin.
'Get to the island and I'll contact you there.' Dictated Liam, keen not to have to worry about his brother whilst his project with McCormack was running.
'What will you do?' Asked Joseph.
'I'm going underground, but I must stay mobile while our team is in England.' Despite his pretended confidence, he was only too aware of the difficulties that lay ahead.
'I'll go then,' offered Joseph aware of his brother's predicament.
'Look after yourself.'
'You too, Joe.' The line went dead and Liam Blaney turned, ashen faced, away from the telephone.

Joining Frank Cotton in another room, his huge bodyguard was dressed in the uniform of a Garda officer.

'Did you get the Jaguar put away Frank?' He asked and Cotton nodded. Blaney was pleased. He would have to contact McCormack but the telephone at the farm was tapped and he would have to watch what he said.

'Go to the car Frank and I'll be with you in a moment. Blaney then returned to the telephone and dialed McCormack's number, waiting impatiently for a reply.

Unbuttoning the girl's blouse, Spencer slipped his large soft hands inside and cupped Kathy's perfectly shaped breasts. He continued fondling as Kathy's fingers fumbled at the belt on his trousers.

'How about us getting ourselves undressed and into bed?' She whispered, suddenly desperate to get his tanned body between her legs.

'Sounds like a very good idea to me honey.' Laughed Spencer as they disentangled themselves and began to undress. He felt slightly silly standing there with his penis sticking out from his trousers as he admired the girl's excellent body as it was revealed to him.

Kicking off her tiny panties she was first into bed, and was followed immediately by Spencer who reached to switch off the bedside lamp.

'Leave it' whispered Kathy 'I like to see what I'm getting.'

Spencer smiled and responded by putting his head below the sheets, his lips glossing over her superb breasts, down her taught tummy and onto her delightful mound of silky soft pubic hair. Better give her something worth watching he thought.

It was perhaps thirty minutes later when Elliot entered Bradley's office carrying a taped cassette and two sheets of freshly typed transcript. Bradley took the cassette from him and slipped it into an ancient cassette player on his desk.

'You look like death warmed up Colm.' he commented before pressing the play button.

'You don't look too hot yourself.' replied Elliot jocularly. The tape recording started to run and they sat down to listen whilst they read the following transcript:

'Hello,' the voice of John McCormack.
'John, its Liam.' the voice of Liam Blaney.
'What the hell are you doing phoning at this time of the night.'
'I had to let you know that one or two things have changed from tonight..'
'What?'
'Well, for a kick off, one of my company's cargo ships was apparently carrying arms when it docked in Dublin at midnight.'
'And you've not been arrested yet?'
'Took evasive action John, you know me.'
'What about that brother of yours?'
'Oh, he's safe enough. He was picked up okay and will stay offshore.'
'That's something I suppose. Now tell me what your immediate plans are.'
'I'm going underground for the moment, I'll be okay if I can get out of Dublin and that is well in hand.'
'Good. Everything is quiet up in this neck of the woods by the way.'
'That's always something, what about Fox?'
'Oh, he'll be awake soon enough.'
'Good. Listen, I must get going. You know where to contact me?'
'Indeed I do Liam. See you soon.'
'Goodnight John, sorry I got you out of bed.'
'Huh, I don't sleep much these days anyway.'

Bradley stopped the tape and turned to Elliot.

'Not much there that we didn't know already.' but Elliot did not entirely agree.

'I thought that there were one or two interesting points.'

'You referring to Fox?' Asked Bradley rubbing his tired eyes with both hands.

'Yeah that and Joseph Blaney is not in Eire.' Replied Colm.

'But where Colm?' Bradley sounded tired and irritated.

'Off the Irish coast somewhere?' Elliot smiled and they both knew that there are hundreds of such places, islands off the ragged Irish coastline.

'You know what bothers me the most Colm?' Began Bradley not really anticipating any interruption, 'It's the fact that those two smart arse's know that the telephone at Treeacre is tapped. All that shit about his ship apparently' Bradley emphasized the apparently 'Carrying weapons. Who in Christ's name are they trying to fool?'

Bradley extracted the cassette from the machine and handed it to Elliot.

'They are extracting the urine Colm, taking the bloody piss. Go and find out why.' Elliot rose and walked to the door where he stopped and turned to his boss.

'What about Fox?' he asked.

'Still asleep according to that.' He pointed to the tape 'Make sure it stays that way.'

Elliot left and headed back towards the farm. Bradley watched him go before lifting the telephone receiver and calling Paul Brennan in Dublin. It was the least he could do to let Brennan know that Liam Blaney was still in Dublin.

As Colm Elliot drove away from Lisburn police headquarters, four men sat down around a kitchen table in the back of a small house in a republican area of north Belfast.

For almost an hour, the four men fumed at the fact that their latest attempt to get arms into Ireland had failed miserably and at great expense to their movement.

Having finally concluded that they were more or less powerless to retrieve the situation, one of the four suggested that Liam Blaney be called before them to give a detailed account of the fiasco. The group leader however, the IRA's Chief of Staff, denied the request on the basis that Liam Blaney was involved in a highly important and top secret operation. When quizzed by his colleagues, the Chief of Staff eventually informed them that Blaney was leading an active service unit in England. When pushed further, he informed the group that the objective of Blaney's unit was the expedient demise of the British Prime Minister.

Despite the heavy loss of the arms shipment, the meeting broke up on a positive note, all four of the Provisional IRA leadership team, happy at the thought of the revenge that Blaney and his team would bring.

Tuesday 27 October 1981

8

The physical pains of his daily five-mile run came at different times, but invariably always came. The first mile was always the worst, as his calf muscles became used to the hard roads while his heart and lungs seemed unaware that he was in fact running.

After the first mile however, things always got better. The occasional stitch in his side, or would it be his collarbone? Today, it was in fact his collarbone. Sweat began streaming in large blobs from his short hair, flooding over his eyebrows, down his nose and face to drip from his pointed chin. The towel around his neck and tucked into his jogging suit absorbed his body sweat effectively.

The stitch was beginning to go as he reached the second mile marker; making good time; now feeling aglow; keeping up his strong pace. Down below he felt his bowels twitch slightly, forcing his pace down until they settled again. His leg muscles were becoming accustomed to the running now, but his breathing had become less regular.

He knew that his heart would be beating at some ninety-five pumps per minute now, a considerable contrast to its normal fifty-five beats. Well into his third mile now, he was finding difficulty concentrating his effort; another stitch; but that would pass quickly. The fourth mile marker was in sight but he knew that the hill would test him before he reached it.

Head down, teeth gritted, into the hill, running on the balls of his feet. Up, up, up the one in eight incline, legs pumping, legs tired. He never got the better of the hill, and today was proving no different. Then he was up and over the brow and into the final mile.

Wanting to look at his stopwatch, he did not dare for fear of breaking his rhythm or concentration. His pace increased, half a mile to go.

Seeing his apartment was the spur he needed to launch him into his final sprint, his throat sore, as he pushed on hoping to do his fastest time ever over the route he now knew so well.

Then he was stopped, the jelly legs, the heavy breathing, the sudden awareness of the wet sweat on his back and shoulders. Checking his watch, he was delighted with his time, his best ever time for the run.

Climbing the steps in front of the house, after stretching his run out of his body, he entered the dark and dingy stairwell with its fading yellow walls and near threadbare brown carpet. Up the damp smelling stairs to his studio, it was still dark outside although the London streets were fast coming to life.

Pushing his door open, the postman had been, three letters. Picking them up he went to the tap, filled a glass with water and began drinking from it.

The first letter was an electric bill, red and demanding. The second was an advertisement for clothes and the third what he had been praying for. This thrilled him and he soon forgot his end of run tiredness.

At seven-thirty on the morning of Tuesday the 27th of October, the man who would be known as the Fox was awake, and there was nothing Elliot, Bradley or anyone else could do about it.

When in Rome, thought O'Neil later that morning as he left his rented apartment in Soho. All around him, neon signs offered topless massages, topless waitresses, topless barmaids, live sex shows, adult movies from Sweden and a million other attractions of the sexual variety.

Most of the offerings did not appeal to him. A quiet relaxing massage however, was totally different. Walking through the street stalls and markets with a cosmopolitan selection of people selling fruit or clothes or clocks and watches to cheap mementos, he eventually found a quiet side street containing just the sort of place he was looking for.

Being able to blend into the local scenery was the greatest asset of the Active Service Unit operating in enemy territory. That's what they had taught him during his early training in the Wicklows, those beautiful mountains south of Dublin. Special courses they called them, for their very special men. Indeed of those special men he had shared camp with, the class of '75, O'Neil was the only survivor. Of the violent men of the violent death, he was the champion.

He had hardly started to shave when he carried out his first killing, a chosen victim, a stated address and a pre-chosen weapon. A prison officer at the Kesh, forty, fat, and with a wife and three young children.

O'Neil had stalked him for days, watched his every move, had recognized his car despite the regular changing of registration plates. He had learned the little home-coming signs prepared daily by the man's wife, the empty milk bottles at the side door, the bathroom light left on, the one foot gap in the lounge curtains.

The movement had supplied him with an Armalite rifle that O'Neil considered overkill, but he was being tested, and a rifle it had to be. In fact, when it came to the killing, O'Neil could have taken him with his bare hands. Even now, he could not forget the surprise in those piercing blue eyes as O'Neil met him in the hall. Instead of his wife, who was bound and gagged upstairs with the children.

He had been reaching for his gun inside his jacket when O'Neil with one perfect shot had blown his head away to nothing. O'Neil had then casually walked from the house and drove off into the evening gloom.

The media called it a brutal and callous murder, but O'Neil saw it to be less brutal and callous than the murder of his parents and was glad to at last be in pursuit of the revenge of their deaths.

The girl's expert hands ran the full length of his back, easing away any anxiety and tension in his body. At her command, he rolled over on the soft black leather table with only a tiny white towel to cover his groin. The girl was slim, black and naked with the scanty exception of a small white g-string. She had small girlish breasts with nipples like O'Neil had never seen before, and O'Neil had seen some nipples.

'Would you care for the relief massage now?' she asked, taking hold of the towel. O'Neil smiled, there was no need for a verbal reply. The towel was slowly pulled from him as she gently took a hold of him in an expert fashion. O'Neil watched with growing interest as she slowly and expertly applied herself to the job in hand.

Call it animal instinct if you like, but Jonathan Miller knew that there was something far wrong long before he reached the caravan. Stopping the car at the bend before the approach to the caravan, he cut the engine and got out, quietly closing the door behind him.

Having become very familiar with the land around the caravan during his early morning walks, he followed a small track through the trees, which led to the rear of his temporary home. The farmer's tractor was parked on the grass where Miller normally parked his car and the caravan door swung open.

Reaching a side window undetected, Miller peered into the sitting area to see the old man crouching over his notes on the Cabinet members. That alone would have been relatively simple for a writer to explain, but the farmer was also holding Miller's pistol in his left hand. He must have picked the briefcase lock, thought Miller, sudden anger surging through his body.

The farmer heard the floor creak and turned to receive Miller's expert karate blow to the side of his neck. His sudden movement meant that he retained consciousness, but he still fell to the floor with the sheer might of the blow, the pistol falling from his hands. Miller swinging his foot, kicked the man on the face, forcing his dentures from his mouth in a pool of blood.

The man was stronger than Miller had expected, obviously fit from a lifetime working the land, and tried kicking back at Miller who easily avoided the retaliatory blow. Miller then jumped at the man and butted him back to the floor, breaking the farmer's nose in the process. This attack seemed to drain all strength from the old man and Miller swiftly strangled him to death.

Standing, with sweat pouring from his forehead, Miller surveyed the scene. His plans were more than a little upset, the farmer had fucked things up good and proper. He was working out what to do as he walked back down the path to his car, which he drove up to the caravan and parked it beside the farmer's tractor. He then began slowly and meticulously clearing the caravan of his personal belongings, showing no signs of panic despite his unease at the situation.

Happy that he had removed all personal traces from the caravan, he dragged the dead man in front of the gas fire and placed him in a sleeping position with a pillow under his head. Taking one of the old Sunday newspapers, he fitted it through the fire grill and onto the old man's chest, arranging the position of his hands to suggest that he had been reading before falling asleep. He then closed all of the caravan windows and pulled the inadequate drapes.

Almost ready to depart the scene of this most unsatisfactory of his killings, he reversed the car back down the drive only to return and painstakingly use the tractor to remove all the muddy tracks made by his car.

He then returned to the caravan and pressed the fire to life. Almost immediately, the newspaper caught fire and spread to the old man's chest. Miller hesitated to be sure that the farmer's clothes caught fire and was pleased to see them burst into flames.

As he rounded the bend in the track, Miller looked in his rear view mirror to see the caravan erupt in an inferno of flames. Smiling, he drove carefully away from the scene and the farm and headed for London where he would now need to find himself a place to stay.

It had been a great pity having to kill the old man, but he had been faced with no option and he would have to be more careful the next time. At that instant, he knew where he was heading.

'How nice to hear from you again Jean-Claude.' Enthused Charles Cherrit into the telephone in his small office to the rear of his restaurant.
'Don't tell me that you are going to be unable to keep out little engagement for this afternoon, I was so looking forward to it.' he continued with a confidence that was far from justified.
'I am afraid that your perception once again wins the day Charles.' replied DeVille.
'That is a great pity since I had made very special arrangements for this afternoon. I am certain that you would have enjoyed yourself my friend.'

'I shall come to your restaurant at seven pm this evening, when we shall complete our transaction. I am, of course assuming that you have managed to acquire the goods I ordered.' DeVille, who was annoyed at the relaxation of his own rigid standards the previous day, was determined to press on with his business without further side tracking by the loathsome Cherrit.
'I gave you my word.' Replied Cherrit putting his hand on his heart as if Marnier was in the office beside him.

'And the specified attaché case?' Pressed DeVille.

'All your specifications have been met Jean Claude.' Replied the fat Frenchman.

'Good, then I shall be there at seven pm, with my side of the deal and we can simply exchange cases and I shall be on my way.'

Cherrit was desperately trying to evaluate the pros and cons of Marnier's proposed visit to his restaurant and decided that it was after all a safe, public place.

'Listen Jean-Claude, why don't we have dinner together when you are here, my chef really is the best in London.' He finally offered, his confidence growing.

'Just have the case ready Charles and on the conclusion of our transaction, I shall be on my way, I've got no more time for your fucking stupid distractions. Understood?'

'Of course I understand you Jean-Claude, but you are turning down a great treat.'

'Seven pm Charles.' Concluded DeVille breaking the connection.

A sky blue police Ford Escort drew up beside the large red and silver fire fighting appliance and a portly Detective Inspector struggled to remove his bulky frame from the passenger seat. Walking carefully, picking his footing, he eyed the black charred remains of the caravan. Even to a battle-hardened policeman, the thought of somebody dying such a death sent cold shivers down his spine. Looking around him, he saw the familiar face of the local Fire Chief standing beside his motorcar, talking into the radio transmitter. The Inspector walked across to where the Fire Chief was, and while waiting for him to finish his conversation, took a king size from a packet and lit it, drawing heavily. The Fire Chief turned to him after finishing his conversation on the radio.

'Bit of a nasty business I'm afraid Bill. Old geezer in there burned to a cinder.' He nodded almost casually towards the ruin. He had seen it all before, and would see it all again before his retirement in eight years time.

'Circumstances?' Asked the Inspector, drawing heavily again at the cigarette.

'That's for your man to say Bill, seems to me as if he'd been reading a newspaper by the fire and fallen asleep', guessed the fireman.

'Probably the answer, no doubt our pathologist will confirm your theory.' He looked around at the firemen busy repacking their equipment in the expectation of another emergency, all in a day's work.

'Who raised the alarm Tom?' Asked the policeman suddenly.

'Don't rightly know, some guy in a pay phone, I think some of the lads expected it to be another of the bloody hoaxes we seem to be getting these days', replied the fireman.

'Any idea who the dead geezer might be?' Asked the policeman, puffing again at the cigarette. It was a filthy habit that his kids were trying to get him to quit, but on jobs like this it settled his nerves.

'That old tractor over there belongs to the owner of the land, we've spoken to his wife and she's pretty convinced it's her husband.'

'Poor cow,' thought the detective loudly.

'Yeah, it's a tough old world sometimes Bill, but that's life.'

They were both turning to see another police car arrive up the track, it contained the forensic expert assigned to the division fresh out of college and raring to go.

'That's bloody death Tom,' replied the detective after a few moments, 'not bloody life.' The big fireman smiled sadly at the sarcasm, it affected him in the same way too.

The detective watched his pathologist, dressed in wellingtons and a duffle coat approach, the silly beggar looked like a Paddington Bear he thought, and now he can prove how good he is at pathology.

Miller reached forward his left hand and turned up the radio, he was surprised that the story had reached the regional news, but it was a quiet day on the news front.

'*...A sixty one year old man, Albert Sime, has died in a caravan blaze at his farm in Surrey. It appears that the man had fallen asleep by a gas fire and his clothes had caught fire. A spokesman for the police said tonight* *that there were no suspicious circumstances surrounding the blaze. And now tomorrow's weather ....'*

Switching off the radio, Miller drove on. It had worked like a dream, and he would be at his boat in about ten minutes. He drove slowly down the hill and into the town of Henley on Thames, turning off the main road and into the car park of the small Boating Club. The place was almost in total darkness, only the light from the car headlamps illuminating the trees and small wooden ramp to which six cruisers were tethered.

Miller got out of the car and from the boot took the torch he had bought for use around the farm. Walking carefully, he found the Tapworth Star, and clambered aboard. He had owned the boat for three years yet had very rarely used it, preferring to rent it out to tourists in the summer months. Finding a key from a key ring in his jacket pocket, he climbed inside. It was surprisingly dry and warm, and would give him some place to rest his head. He had thought about using it before seeing the caravan advertised, but had ruled it out because he did not like to use his own belongings, risk losing any part of his lifestyle by involving it in his work. The little adventure at the farm however had convinced him that the privacy of his own boat, in whatever location he chose, was worth the small risk.

Thursday 29 October 1981

9

It was four o'clock in the afternoon two days later when Detective Inspector Bill Turnbull arrived at his office for his usual afternoon and evening shift, carrying his plastic box of sandwiches. Tossing the small yellow container into the bottom right hand drawer of his desk, he took off his anorak and hung it on a standard Government Issue coat hanger and sat down at his desk. As usual it looked as if a bomb had hit it, with papers and documents all over the place. Neatness was not his strongest point. Because of this peculiarity in his nature, his attention was drawn to an immaculately typed document sitting, like a snow peak on the top of a mountain, on top of his in-tray. Leaning across his desk, he picked the thin manuscript up, the front copy of which merely read:

PATHOLOGIST REPORT: 29 OCTOBER
RE: ALBERT SIME
DIED: 27 OCTOBER
LOCATION: CARAVAN FIRE, HIGHFIELD FARM, SURREY
REPORTING OFFICER: DR JUSTIN WILKIE

Turnbull dropped the report onto his desk and felt in his pocket for his cigarettes. Finding them, he opened the report, lit a cigarette and began to read. It took him all of twenty minutes to get through the full document, the young Wilkie had certainly proved his worth as a pathologist. In particular, Turnbull's attention was drawn to the facts that the man had recently broken his nose, and that his dentures were discovered under his torso and therefore relatively undamaged by the inferno. Lifting the telephone on his desk, he dialed the Pathology Laboratory extension, puffing steadily on his cigarette as he waited for the reply.

'Bill Turnbull here, could I speak to young Wilkie?' he waited for him to come to the phone.
'Justin Wilkie.' Came the tentative reply.
'Bill Turnbull here Justin, do you think that you could pop up and see me?'
'Give me two minutes Bill.' Replacing the receiver, Turnbull started to re-read part of the report while waiting for the young doctor.

With a swift knock on the door, and a sudden burst of fresh air into the tiny smoke filled office, Wilkie arrived. It had taken him considerably less than his requested two minutes. Bill Turnbull admired his enthusiasm.

'Take a seat Justin', offered the Inspector, holding up the report in his right hand. 'It's regarding this old man's death at the farm.' with his left hand he stubbed out the cigarette.
'Ah yes, I thought that it might be.' Wilkie was obviously aware of the fact that he was about to be asked for an opinion, a speculative guess even, and was slightly nervous at the prospect. He was employed to give professional information, not to make speculative guesses, but this was in fact what he had joined the police Forensic Team for.
'Well man, what do you think?' asked Turnbull, tossing the report onto the desk and folding his arms.
'Tricky question Bill, as you know all my professional advice is in the report.'
'But, off the record?' asked Turnbull.
'Only sheer speculation mind.' He was savouring the moment.
'Yeah yeah.' Turnbull urged him on.
'Well I think it is very likely that the man was involved in a scuffle, and perhaps even knocked unconscious before the fire began.' He was quite surprised at Turnbull's cool reaction to his statement.

'Go on,' requested the Inspector, his opinion of the young man continuing to be enhanced.

'It's difficult to pinpoint my reasons for it; perhaps the whole thing was too stage managed, too cut and dry. All I can say is that I have my doubts about actual cause of death. Nothing substantial of course, the body was too far gone for anything like that, but just a doubt.' He had the feeling that Turnbull was just having his own theories confirmed, and that deflated his ego a little.

'It's what I hoped you were going to say Justin, what I hoped for. I think that we have got ourselves a little murder enquiry.' Turnbull stood up and put on his anorak.

'Are you busy this afternoon?' he asked the young man who had been about to leave.

'Not particularly, why?'

'Thought you might like to visit the scene of the crime.' he smiled, pleased with the young man.

'Why not?' Smiled Wilkie, his enthusiasm for his new employment returning.

The old lady was dressed in black and led them into the sitting room. Around her eyes were red from obvious lack of sleep since her husband's death. A young woman, perhaps thirty, was sitting in a rocking chair with a china cup and saucer in her hand. She too was dressed in black. Turnbull was aware of the feeling of death that hung over the house. The old lady directed them to take a seat on the sofa.

'This is my daughter Pauline, she's come up from London to stay until after the funeral', the girl nodded to both men without speaking.

'We're sorry to be bothering you at such a sad time Mrs. Sime, but we would just like to ask you a few details about your husband's activities on the day of the fire.' Turnbull had been through the whole scene many times, but the young doctor was just beginning to realize that he had led a particularly sheltered life until now, he felt like a crude intruder.

The old lady however, nodded to Turnbull that she understood. Sitting down in an armchair she was about to speak when her daughter stood up.

'Would you gentlemen like a cup of tea?', she asked.

'That would be lovely, two sugars for me please', replied Turnbull and Wilkie nodded agreement but indicated no sugar.

When the daughter had gone, the old lady began to speak.

'As always, he had gone out on the tractor after milking. He was always pottering about on the tractor, mending fences and the like, just keeping the place ticking over, the wolves from the door he would say.' her speech withered away.

'How did he cope with the chores?' asked Wilkie, speaking purposefully for the first time.

'For his age you mean?' asked the old lady in reply.

'Yeah, you know was he getting accident prone or anything?' persisted the doctor.

'Not that you would notice. Always had black fingernails with the hammer and things like that, but nothing serious.' Her tears had dried.

'Tell me about the caravan Mrs. Sime, what did you use it for?' Turnbull took over the questioning again.

'Oh that was one of Albert's bright ideas to bring in some money, rent it out to families in the summer, make a few extra bob he reckoned.'

'Did you get many customers?'

'Hardly the French Rivera up here I told him, but we got one or two families.'

'But nobody was in the caravan this week?' The daughter returned with two cups of tea and a plate of digestive biscuits.

'Nobody been up here for a couple of months now.' Answered the old lady. Turnbull and Wilkie thanked the daughter for the tea and spent a few minutes saying how sorry they were that the old man had died, and with the tea finished said that they would have to be going. The old lady showed them out, and as they were about to leave, Turnbull turned and asked her.

'By the way Mrs. Sime, how did your husband break his nose?' She seemed bemused by the question.

'My Albert never had no broken nose Inspector, always real handsome he was.' Tears were again welling in her eyes as the two men drove off, up the track in the direction of the burned out caravan.

It looked even worse in the approaching darkness, the black charred frame where the old man had perished standing against the dark skyline. They spent a few minutes looking around for clues, but there was nothing worth talking about. It was Wilkie who discovered the gas cylinder. He was standing over the blue canister when Turnbull came up beside him.

'Penny for your thoughts doctor.' He said gently, they were fast becoming friends.
'That cylinder is half full, it would be interesting to find out who bought it.' Turnbull smiled, and took down the serial number on the cylinder. It was a start.

At nine o'clock that evening in the house in Kenton, it was O'Neil who was conducting the proceedings. As was fast becoming the pattern, he had watched the others arrive and had entered the house last.
'Well gentlemen it's nice to see you all again', he began, before continuing, 'I hope that you've all got your reports ready and that they make interesting listening'. He was rubbing his hands together in mock anticipation. Miller moved in his chair.
'For Christ's sake O'Neil you're beginning to sound like Blaney, get on with it.' O'Neil looked at the Englishman and smiled, he was such an impatient bugger he thought.
'Okay Miller, let's have your report first. McEwan was it not?'
The others, listening to the now familiar exchanges between the two, sat attentively in their seats as Miller began.

'Well, he's a bloody cautious man is Ewan McEwan. He also, as that bloody folder prepared by McCormack and Blaney states, does not spend all, or nearly all, of his time in London. He does in fact commute regularly between London, Edinburgh and his Fife home.

He is driven everywhere he goes, and is very rarely on his own which makes him an extremely difficult target indeed.'

'Does that rule him out?' interrupted De Ville. Miller shook his blond head.

'No it does not. I can kill him all right but it would probably mean killing his wife and driver as well. Would that be acceptable?' He looked to O'Neil for an answer.

'Only if we have no other options.' Considering what Miller had said, he looked at the tall American.

'What about Piers?' The others now turned their attention to Spencer.

'A certain hit!' He announced confidently, smiling before continuing, 'As it happens the extremely overworked Sir Peter, and that is a newspaper quote and not mine, has a little honey tucked away in an apartment in Northwood,' the others smiled with him.

'What about security?' Asked Miller.

'Changes cars and some clothes in Barnet, but that's all.' offered Spencer.

'Jesus Christ, what a bloody fool.' Said O'Neil incredulously.

'No fool like a dead fool.' Laughed Spencer in response.

'When can you take him out?' Asked Miller.

'Tomorrow.' Spencer shrugged his shoulders, 'It's such a cake-walk, no problems whatsoever.'

'How do you know that he'll be in Northwood tomorrow?' asked De Ville, who, having no report to make, was spending the evening in relative silence.

'When he's due to visit his piece of fanny, and I use your British usage of the word, she leaves her child at her mothers the night before. Tonight before coming here, I checked her out.' Replied the American.

'And the kid's at her Granny's?' asked O'Neil.

'Right first time my boy.' O'Neil didn't know why, but he was beginning to hate the smug American bastard. The place fell into silence for a few moments after that as the others watched Spencer enjoying the limelight. It was Miller who continued the meeting.

'That seems to take care of one of our two targets, what about the other?' They all looked towards O'Neil who stood and walked towards the large fireplace. Turning to face the group he placed his hands behind him to prevent the fire from burning his backside.

'Archer is quite literally a sitting duck'. He quietly announced.

'Details?' asked De Ville.

'Not many to give. He spends most of his time sitting beside a swimming pool at a villa in Antibes, up to his neck in plaster cast.' He smiled, shaking his head as if he still did not believe it.

'No security?' asked De Ville doubtfully.

'None. His wife is with him of course, but she's out quite a lot.' The others nodded, with Miller particularly happy that he wouldn't have to kill McEwan's wife after all.

'Where do we go from here then?' asked Spencer. It was O'Neil who answered the question.

'If we are all happy, I take Archer and Spencer takes Piers.' He looked around for a response. The others merely nodded in unison, the committee decision had been made.

'Good. Tomorrow it is then.' Announced the Irishman.

'The day the shit hits the fan.' Laughed Miller, and they all laughed with him. O'Neil turned his attention to the Frenchman.

'Did you get the weapons De Ville?' He asked, and Jacque De Ville stood and walked to a cabinet where, from a drawer, he extracted an attaché case. Carrying the black leather case, he placed it on the coffee table in front of the others and snapped it open. They all admired the tools of their trade like an artist would admire a Turner or a Constable. De Ville spoke, breaking the spell.

'Obviously all the weapons will not be required tomorrow, so I suggest that O'Neil and Spencer take what they need, and I shall hold onto the remainder.'

The American reached out and extracted a Walther with silencer attachment, weighing it in his right hand.

'This little beauty will do me nicely thank you. What about you O'Neil?' The Irishman pushed the case shut.

'Don't be so frigging stupid Spencer, how would I get through airport security with a gun in my bloody suitcase?' The others nodded and Spencer felt like smashing the Walther in his hand into the face of the little Irish bastard.

Miller rose and headed for the door. On reaching it, he turned to the others and said.

'No point in me arguing against another meeting I suppose?' He concentrated his attention on Paul O'Neil.

' Meet back here at five pm on Thursday. Assuming everything goes to plan. See you then.' With that Miller was gone, followed closely by the tall American.

O'Neil as usual was last in, last out.

Standing in front of the full-length mirror, Fox lifted the dumb-bell in his right hand to his shoulder, holding it for ten seconds before dropping it to his side. With the left hand dumb-bell he did the same; then the right; then the left; then the right again. Sweat was now running down his bare body and he began to enjoy the physical plain of his body exertion.

He heard the telephone ring on the landing outside, but he paid no attention to it. Only one person ever called him on that number and there was a ring code that he used. Placing the weights onto the floor, he fell forward into the classic push-up position. He was ten push-ups into his daily two hundred when a knock at the door interrupted him.

Standing, he grabbed a towel and wrapped it around his neck, walked to the door and opened it. It was one of the girls from the flat opposite his own, and she was obviously taken aback at the sight of his superb body in only tennis shorts. Letting her eyes run the full length of his body, she finally spoke.

'Oh I'm sorry, but there's a telephone call for you,' she pointed towards the phone without taking her eyes off him.

'Thank you,' he replied walking to the telephone aware of the fact that the girl's eyes were watching his every move.

'Hello.' He spoke into the receiver as the girl smiled and disappeared into her flat.

'Up the Republic!' Came the familiar voice he been expecting.

'Yeah.' He replied, as pre-arranged.

'Envelope number one to the Yard this evening.' The telephone clicked.

Walking back to his studio, he heard the sound of female laughter come from the girl's flat. The girl was obviously relating her experience to her flat mate. Kicking the door shut, he returned to his push-ups.

Ray O'Grady stepped from the shower, picked up a towel and began to dry himself vigorously. Anna was in bed, not that it was very likely that she would be asleep, she hadn't done so without pills since Patricia had been taken. He had tried to convince her that if they, whoever they happened to be, had intended killing the girl, then she would certainly have been dead by now. Anna had looked at him suspiciously, doubting that he was telling the truth, her doubt probably confirmed by his own lack of belief in what he was saying. Lying was certainly not his strongest point.

Pulling on his bathrobe, he quietly descended the stairs and entered the sitting room. Taking the top from a cut glass Waterford crystal decanter, he poured himself a glass of his favourite Irish whiskey, before sitting on the settee and pulling his feet up and stretching them in front of him.

It was getting to him now as well, the constant daily photographs of Patricia, the constant waiting, the growing difficulty in trying to act normally at the office. Christ he was feeling drained. Finishing his drink, he rose to replenish his glass and had his hand on the decanter when the telephone rang. He froze momentarily, his heart missing a beat or two, before reaching out and answering it. The voice was, by now, sickeningly familiar. It came like a blow to the crutch.

'Good evening Mister O'Grady'.

'What have you got to say this time you bastard,' roared Ray, with a newfound courage, perhaps helped by the whiskey.

'Now, now, that's not the attitude of a man wanting his wee girl back. Now is it?'

O'Grady forced himself to be calm.

'I am sorry,' he said pathetically, regretting immediately his apologetic tone to this sick shithouse, who had taken his daughter. Jesus! If only he could get his hands on the bastard.

'That's better, no need to be getting yourself all uptight now is there?'

'Get to the fucking point,' pleaded O'Grady, gritting his teeth in an attempt to control his surging anger.

'I just thought that I would phone to put your mind at ease, keep you up to date.'

'You've got to be frigging joking!' exclaimed O'Grady. He was a placid man by nature and very rarely lost his temper, but by God he had lost it now.

'It won't be long now, perhaps a day or two and you will fully understand the role that you must play. After you have played that role, you can have your wee lassie back, untouched by human hands.'

'I've only got your bloody word for that haven't I?' he suggested quietly.

'That's right O'Grady, you have.'

'How can I trust you?' he asked.

'You can't O'Grady, that's why you will do as we say, you don't have an option.'

'How much longer?' but his question went unheard, and the phone went dead. Ray O'Grady walked to the whiskey decanter and poured himself another drink.

The bastard was right, he did not have an option.

Making sure that his grey uniform was suitably buttoned; he began to whistle as he pushed open the rubber flaps, which acted as doors to the entry of the Post Office sorting area. The sound of a radio blasted out from a far corner and he surveyed the scene, watching carefully as many fellow whistlers went about their business, happy to pay no attention to their fellow postmen, the newcomer being no exception. Knowing exactly where to go, he moved slowly and deliberately along a row of grey aluminum trolleys. Each trolley supported a large grey sack and was headed by a piece of cardboard depicting the final destination of the contents. Seeing the sack he was looking for, he took from his pocket a small nondescript brown envelope with a typed address and dropped is casually into the sack simply marked in heavy black felt pen 'New Scot Yard.'

Turning, he walked back towards the rubber doors. Again, nobody seemed to notice him. Trying to continue with his whistling, moments later he was out of the sorting depot and into the crisp evening air.

Reaching his van some five minutes later, he unlocked the door and slipped into the driving seat. It was a brown van with the golden insignia of the Property Services Agency at the foot of all the doors. Pulling the door shut, he pulled off the grey woolen gloves he had been wearing and stuffed them in an untidy manner into his jacket pockets, before turning the ignition key and heading back towards his studio flat.

As requested, the letter was on its way. Undoubtedly it would be in the in-tray on Commander John Birbeck's desk first delivery in the morning.

Friday 30 October 1981

10

After sitting outside Waterloo for the best part of ten minutes, the train moved forward with a sudden jolt before moving slowly alongside the station platform. It was two minutes to ten am on Friday 30 October, and John Birbeck was about as cheerful as a bear with a sore head. Walking along the platform towards the ticket barrier, his mind was a mixed bag of joyful holiday thoughts coupled with a feeling of woe at the thought of what might be waiting for him back at the office. He had hoped for a peaceful break with his wife and kids, and his wishes had been granted, but now it was back to work, and on a Friday.

Joining a small queue of people offering their tickets for inspection, he saw his driver at the barrier. Smiling, he nodded at the big man, not particularly glad to see him, or indeed to be back in London.

'Good morning Sir,' began his driver, offering also to carry his superior officer's attaché case. Birbeck waved a refusal, not bothering to reply to the man's greeting.

'How's business been then Jordan?' he eventually asked as they reached the car.
'Apart from the Oxford Street incident, relatively quiet on the western front Sir.' came the reply.
'Good, good', murmured Birbeck to himself, getting into the back seat, reflecting on the sad death of another Metropolitan police

officer at the hands of the IRA.

The majority of his staff were out of the office when he arrived. In a way, he was glad, it would give him time to get into anything that needed urgent attention; attend to his mail, see what was worth answering; acting upon; or simply filing in the bin.

His assistant, a young Oxbridge Sergeant, confirmed what Jordan had so explicitly told him in twelve words. His Deputy Ian Maitland was handling the bomb blast in Oxford Street; another team was liaising with Westminster on The State Opening; the rest however, had been mostly quiet and routine stuff, nothing much, the quietest he could remember since joining the Anti-Terrorist Squad. With continued post-holiday blues, Birbeck dismissed his assistant.

Going to a large bulletproof window, he stood overlooking London's heavy traffic, his hands clasped behind him in a ridiculously policeman-like manner.

After standing there for a few minutes, not really thinking about anything in particular, just feeling generally pissed off at being back, he turned his attention to a large calendar on the wall behind his huge mahogany desk. Christ, he thought, studying the areas marked with red stick-on stars, it was less than three months until he retired, let's hope it remains quiet.

His persistent assistant returned, God how his wife had laughed when he had first used that phrase at home, carrying a tray containing tea and biscuits. Sitting at his desk to drink his tea, Birbeck's attention was drawn to a small brown envelope lying in the side of his in-tray. Lifting it, he inspected it casually before sighing and dropping it back on top of the rest of the mail. It was no good however, his curiosity had been aroused, and he lifted the envelope again and slit it open with the aid of a silver letter opener, a gift from his father. He read the letter while sipping his tea, then putting his cup down, he re-read it. The quiet spell, he was certain, was over.

Lifting his telephone, he told his assistant to get the Prime Minister's office on the line.

Spencer sat in Kathy's car and watched the man with growing interest. Firstly there had been the tired yawning as he parked the car, a large Vauxhall saloon, into the small parking lot some way from his house. Then, from the boot had come the expected suitcase, giving all the signs of a businessman returning home for the weekend after a tired week on the road. Eventually, the man left the car, not even taking the precaution of locking it, and walked the fifty yards or so to his house before disappearing from Spencer's view.

The car, to Spencer's delight, was an extremely comfortable model, with an unexpected bonus being the ample legroom. It was one thing about the British that really bugged him, their preoccupation with small motorcars, the horrific Mini being the prize example. It was difficult to imagine that the Rolls Royce and the Mini had been created by the same nation.

Feeling inside his anorak pocket, he fondled the gun reassuringly. With a gun in his possession, he was unstoppable, uncatchable, the very best that there had ever been. It was a comforting thought for him to know that with his superior intellect that nobody could ever get near to stopping him once he had his prey in his sights. The top man in his field.

Although only lunch time, the traffic was already flowing quite thick and fast, with people obviously eager to get away from London for the weekend. Despite this, he knew that he would be in Northwood in plenty of time to put his operation into top gear. It was so easy. He would simply kill him and dump the body in his pre-planned location, to hide it long enough to get him safely back in Kathy's arms. No need to be too particular about where he put the body, McCormack needed it found, it was all part of the master plan.

He felt a sudden upsurge in his spirits, to him it was like having a good woman. No, better than that, it was like loving a good woman. Considering that thought for a moment, he realized that killing was his surrogate Linda, he had replaced her lost love with killing. It was the first time that he had been able to really accept the fact, his current and past operations were merely ways of returning to those giddy heights gained at Harvard.

Incredibly, his hands were shaking with uncontrolled excitement; he could not wait to see the look on Piers face when he realized he was about to die. At that moment he decided that perhaps a slow, methodical death was perhaps the best way to get maximum enjoyment from the moment. If it was possible, that was how it would be.

Realizing that he was driving too fast, and that sweat was running from his forehead, he slowed the Vauxhall down to a reasonable speed. After all, there was no point in getting a ticket for speeding now. Despite this, he could not help but realize that fact that he was excited like he had never been before. God, it was the weirdest kick of them all.

Having arrived at the rear entrance to number 10 Downing Street at exactly ten minutes to one that afternoon, Commander John Birbeck was ushered by a large police guard from his car to the nearby doorway and into the main building. There, another security guard led him towards the elevators, and moments later he was being shown into the Prime Minister's private study.

Looking up from a large folder of papers on her desk, did she never stop working? Thought Birbeck, she smiled at the large man in front of her. They had indeed met on many occasions during her time in office, the various crises ensuring that it had become standard procedure for the head of the British Government to be kept absolutely in touch with all matters of terrorism relating to national security.

'Commander, it is so good to see you again,' the Prime Minister stood, offering her immaculately manicured right hand and speaking in that much imitated voice that was now so instantly recognized.

'I hope that what you bring me is not too bad, I've got quite enough on my plate at the moment.' Birbeck smiled at the hint of humour, a quality so rarely seen in public, or appreciated by the media.

'I am afraid Prime Minister that it's a very unfortunate side of my job, the fact that you only tend to see me as the bearer of bad news.' Smiled Birbeck, unbuttoning his large overcoat.

'Indeed, indeed', she waved him to a chair in front of her desk, and they both sat down in near unison.

'Well, you better let me have it then.' For the first time in the years that Birbeck had known the woman, he thought that Britain's first lady leader of Parliament was showing an unexpected trace of defeatism in her manner. Taking the letter from inside his jacket, he handed it across the desk to the Prime Minister.

'I received this note this morning, and I have every reason to believe that it is more than just an idle threat from some crank'.

Taking the note from him, she read it slowly, growing concern showing on her face as she digested the content. Birbeck could not help recall that, just before her election as Prime Minister, she had lost a close friend and colleague to the terrorists, something that had strengthened her resolve in her many confrontations with, in particular, the IRA. Hunger striker after hunger striker had died in the Maze Prison during her office, and she had not once weakened from her stance that they did not deserve political status. His admiration of her continued strength in such matters, if not her political leanings, was great, yet perhaps the greatest test of that resolve was about to begin. He wondered if she had the stamina left to meet the new challenge.

Folding the letter she handed it back to her Commander of the best Anti-Terrorist Squad in the world, remaining silent for a few moments. Suddenly, she was refilled with that familiar old fighting enthusiasm, and Birbeck's doubts were banished.

'You say that you believe it is genuine, and I will not doubt your word. What do you propose that we do about it?' It was a directive not a question.

Birbeck, with care and precision, outlined the pre-agreed measures being taken to secure all Cabinet Ministers with immediate effect. His only caveat being that, with the weekend upon them, it may take longer than normal to contact and secure the group.

'Do you really believe that the threat to kill two of my Cabinet is genuine?' This time the Prime Minister was asking a question.

'Yes,' replied Birbeck categorically 'I believe this to be a significant threat. If not, why make it?' he continued.

'Indeed,' mused the Prime Minister 'It seems that we have stirred a hornets nest Commander. I will call an emergency Cabinet meeting for 3pm, let's hope we can get them all here.'

'We shall do our best,' offered Birbeck, standing to leave, further conversation was doing nothing but wasting their valuable time 'I'll see you again at 3pm Prime Minister.'

'Indeed you shall Commander. Let's get our staff on this straight away and please keep me informed.' They walked together towards the study door.

'Whatever next Commander, whatever next?' Pondered the Prime Minister heading for her private quarters as Birbeck waited for the elevator realizing that she was talking to herself as much as she was to him.

The mid-afternoon south of France sun was warming the back of Paul O'Neil as he safely negotiated the garden wall and let himself into the house via a sliding French window. Looking around, he decided that the best place to leave the note was under the cushion on a sofa, it was sure to be found there. Two large three-seater sofas sat opposite one another in a large sitting room, a leopard skin rug between them. O'Neil chose one of the settees, lifted a cushion and dropped the small brown envelope beneath, replacing the cushion. In all ways the envelope was like the one received by Birbeck earlier, even down to the address.

Walking quietly through the house to a large window, he looked down the garden to the pool. He was shocked not to see Archer where he had been sitting minutes earlier. His heart pounding, he moved to another window and was relieved to see him in his wheelchair some yards away. Archer had obviously moved to avoid the shadows now being cast by some large trees that lined one side of the garden.

Looking at his watch, O'Neil worked out that he had forty minutes before Archer's wife would be back from her shopping, and nearly three hours until his flight back to London. It was time for him to act.

Before leaving the house, O'Neil slipped off his shoes, jeans and sweat shirt and folded them tidily in a bundle with a towel he had taken from the car. Carrying his bundle of clothes, and dressed only in swim shorts, he walked quietly and carefully from the house and along the side of the garden lined by trees. Behind some thick bushes he stopped and lowered his clothes to the ground. A dog barked in a garden nearby, but O'Neil ignored it.

The slouched plaster cast figure of Archer came into full view, his back facing O'Neil. Looking around, O'Neil made a final check that the coast was clear. It was.

Archer must have heard his approach at the very last minute because he looked up from his book, sudden horror in his cold blue eyes. O'Neil caught him expertly around the neck, his left hand covering the MPs mouth. Reaching down the side of the chair with his spare right hand, he released the brake holding Archer in position. Archer and the chair rolled towards the pool with constant acceleration, O'Neil still hanging on and holding Archer's mouth, saw the pistol late but just in time to punch it from Archer's grip before it could be used.

They plunged together into the pool, O'Neil immediately at home in the cold water, Archer splashing in a nervous frenzy. O'Neil grabbed him by the hair and forced his head under the water as Archer tried to fight him off. The heavy plaster cast however, was not ideal for underwater combat. The killer watched as bubbles began rising from below the surface, this made him hold Archer's head even tighter.

A few minutes later, O'Neil climbed the steps from the pool and stood for a moment to survey the scene. It was perfect, Archer, his wheelchair beneath him, and his book, floated on the water.

O'Neil walked back up the garden to where he had left his clothes, dried himself and dressed. A couple of minutes later he left the scene by the same way as he had entered, over the garden wall. He headed for the car he had hired and the airport. Part one of his mission complete.

Sir Peter Piers died exactly three hours later than John Archer. Spencer had arrived outside the neat little block of flats in Northwood sometime after four o'clock, and it was already beginning to get dark. He tried to make himself as comfortable as possible in the car, ready for what he expected would be a long wait. His plan was well formulated in his mind. He would pounce as soon as he saw Piers, take him to the car and kill him, drive to nearby woods and dump the body. There, he hoped, someone would find the body relatively quickly.

He positioned the rear view mirror to enable him to watch all cars approaching the flats from a corner some hundred yards away. From an anorak pocked he produced a paperback thriller and began to read, applying his amazing power of concentration upon the incompatible tasks of reading while keeping watch.

The tapping on the car window gave him something of a start. Looking up from the book, he glanced in his rear view mirror before looking to see who was disturbing his surveillance.

She was old, perhaps seventy and maybe even eighty. Spencer thought somewhat jovially for his situation, that her face contained more wrinkles than elephant's foreskin. He waved his left hand to get her to go away, but she was a persistent old beggar and continued tapping. Spencer leaned over and rolled the window down. The old woman's bottom lip quivered as she spoke, and Spencer suppressed a laugh.

'Have you been 'ere long?' she near shouted.
'Not too long,' replied Spencer, aware of his American accent and therefore trying not to do too much talking.
'Well have you seen a pussy then?' Again the American suppressed a laugh, the chance would be a fine thing, he thought.
'No, I can't say that I have,' he replied, but she did not seem to hear him, or be listening to what he was saying.
'Black and white nose he is,' she continued.
'Who?' questioned Spencer, thinking the situation was getting out of hand, and glancing in the rear view mirror.
'Floyd, my cat,' she explained looking around. Thankfully, thought Spencer, she seemed to have decided that this line of enquiry was not going to get her Floyd back. Whoever called a cat Floyd?
'Sorry, I haven't seen your cat old lady,' Spencer began to roll the window up, and she gave him a final glance before heading off down the street. He noticed how she shuffled her feet, and then that she was wearing her slippers. Laughing to himself, he turned his attention back towards the street corner.

Jumping up in his seat, Spencer saw the Mini Metro pull up opposite the flats, Piers was certainly having a long weekend. Dropping the paperback onto one of the rear seats, Spencer pushed open the car door and got out into the street. Zipping up his anorak he walked casually towards the entrance to the flats, Piers, his hat covering his head and most of his face, paid no attention to Spencer and headed in the same direction. When they were only six feet apart, the tall American pulled the Walther from his anorak pocket and pointed it directly at the heart of the MP.

Piers reacted in a totally unexpected manner. He quite simply turned on his heels and headed off down the street like a greyhound released from a trap. Spencer could hardly believe the pace as he followed, especially for a man of Piers age.

As he raced after him, the American's mind was full of the possible consequences, luckily the quiet street was deserted, but he could only follow so far before he would have to shoot him in the street.

Piers however, did not seem too aware of his bearings, and turned up a long quiet bushy lane, the tall blond killer in close pursuit. Spencer quickly decided that this was both the time and the place. Stopping, he put both hands on the Walther, spread his weight evenly by standing feet apart before stretching his arms in front of him in the perfect shooting position.

The Walther spat three, near silent, thudding bullets into the body of Sir Peter Piers, throwing him forward, he landed head first on the path. Dead.

Spencer walked the forty yards to where he lay and lifted the dead man by his feet and dragged him into some nearby bushes. He would be found all right, but that was all part of the plan.

Casually, he walked back to the car, and drove off towards the Metropolitan Line that would take him back to the safety of London and Kathy's flat in under an hour. Despite the fact that it had after all been a quick and painless killing, it had gone well, and he had thoroughly enjoyed himself.

The staff working furiously in the Prime Minister's office had, somewhat worryingly, been unable to make contact with five Cabinet Ministers in time for the meeting that was taking place some ninety minutes later in the Cabinet office at 10 Downing Street.

John Birbeck watched with growing interest the expressions on the faces of the Cabinet Ministers as he outlined the precautions he intended taking with regard to their safety. Initially, it had taken him a few moments to get into his stride, not too many people got the opportunity to follow the British Prime Minister in briefing her cabinet, and it was a well-known fact that she invariably got the last word. Of her ministers, five were missing from the meeting. One, they knew, was recuperating in the South of France, one was on government business in the USA, leaving the whereabouts of three still to be determined.

When he had finished outlining his proposals, Birbeck declared himself available for any questioning. However, before the expected bombardment was able to get under way, there was a strong knock at the Cabinet room door and the mighty figure of Ian Maitland, Birbeck's second in command at the Anti-Terrorist Squad entered the room. Of course, the senior politicians in the room knew Maitland, but Birbeck hoped that the intrusion was a necessary one.

Maitland requested a brief conversation with his boss in private and the Commander made his excuses to the esteemed gathering and followed his colleague from the room. Birbeck was immediately aware of the fact that Maitland looked very disturbed. They faced one another in a large carpeted hallway and it was Birbeck who spoke first.

'Now Ian, what's all this about?' he asked, obviously intrigued.
'I've just had a call from the French police. John Archer has been found dead at his villa in Antibes.' A silence fell between them for a few seconds.
'What's the initial verdict?' asked Birbeck finally.
'At first they thought it had been an accident, but the French police have found a note inside the villa, and without a doubt it's an assassination.' explained Maitland.
'What sort of note?'
'From what I can gather, it is very similar to the one you received this morning.'
'Who was it addressed to? For heaven's sake.'
'You John.'
'And what did the note contain?' Birbeck was aware of

international procedure when it came to terrorism, and the French would have been very careful not to open the letter unless instructed to.

'I asked them to open it John, I hope you don't mind.' offered Maitland.

'Of course not, you did the right thing, but what did it say for Christ's sake?' he sounded anxious.

'Basically, that this was the beginning of the campaign, that another death would be discovered within twelve hours, and that the killings would continue unless ...'

'Unless the government carry out the demands of the first letter.' interjected Birbeck.

'In a nutshell.' conceded Maitland.

'Christ Ian, what can I tell that lot in there?' asked Birbeck nodding his head in the direction of the Cabinet room.

'That's why you get paid bigger bucks than me John.' replied Maitland, a slight sympathetic smile escaping from his lips.

'I suppose so,' muttered Birbeck, turning back towards the Cabinet room.

'Do you want me to wait?' asked Maitland.

'Please, that will be helpful. Besides, I doubt if I will be very long now. They'll want us out searching for these bastards, it might help them sleep tonight.'

The sea of anxious faces that greeted him inside the Cabinet room meant that he relished what he had to tell them even less. Birbeck walked to the centre of the table where he stood beside the Prime Minister and almost robot-like passed on the news. He thought, very briefly, that only the day before he had been on a happy family holiday.

The reaction was of nothing but disbelieving shock.

'How could such a thing happen?'

'Where had the security people been?'

'What about his wife?'

'Had the press been informed?'

Birbeck answered all the questions as well as he could, but had to admit that he was not totally aware of all the details and that he would be better placed to answer their questions in the morning.

The Prime Minister, pale with shock, stood to address the meeting. The panic and enormity of what she had just discovered, was being forcefully erased from her demeanor as she presented herself in the usual calm and controlled manner that she was world renowned for. Birbeck thought that the Iron Lady name given to her by the Soviet media had been far closer than even they could every have imagined.

'I know that you are all shocked and deeply saddened by this awful news, but I feel that we must make a few decisions immediately in order to enable Commander Birbeck to get on with the search for these detestable people.' There was a general rumble of 'here, here,' from within the room before the Prime Minister continued.
'One thing that I would like to get your agreement on, and I would like this to be a unanimous decision,' she turned her attention to Birbeck, 'Commander, how many people know of this dreadful murder?'
'The French police and a couple of my most senior colleagues in the Anti-Terrorist Squad,' he replied.
'Good. I would like it decided that none of this is released to the press. I will not allow Her Majesty's Government to be party to cheap publicity for these people.'
'But Prime Minister, I may depend on the public for help with this enquiry.' interrupted Birbeck bravely and somewhat anxiously.
'Perhaps later Commander, but just now I do not believe that it is in the best interests of the British people to know that their government is being held to ransom by terrorists.' There was a deathly hush around the room. What the Prime Minister was saying was perfectly true, but Birbeck had never thought he would hear her make such an admission.

Despite Birbeck's protests, the Cabinet decided unanimously that there should be a press embargo on the story. It annoyed him, but it was not his job to get the Conservatives re-elected.

He left Downing Street with Maitland and they headed back towards New Scotland Yard to try and cover up one death, prevent another, and generally go some way to solving the mystery before his 10am meeting with the Cabinet the following morning. It was, as they knew only too well, a mammoth task.

Saturday 31 October 1981

11

A slight wind was blowing as the newspaper delivery boy tried in vain to get the flapping newspaper under control. He was walking along Wood Lane towards the apartment blocks that heralded the start of his paper round, and it was just after seven-thirty on the last day of October. He always liked to read the latest news on his favourite football team Arsenal especially as his father would be taking him up to London to see his heroes play later that day.

But for the gusty wind, it is very likely that he would not have noticed the feet protruding from beneath some bushes some twenty yards from the footpath. Dropping his newspaper bag, he ran towards the protruding feet, before heading off in panic towards the local police station.

John Birbeck was standing in front of the mirror in the shower room adjacent to his office scraping the last of the shaving soap from his face with a hastily purchased disposable Gillette razor.

It had been something of an uneventful and frustrating night all round, since they had found nothing to help him with the Archer killing and with one of the Cabinet still unaccounted for. They were still out looking for Sir Peter Piers, and Birbeck prayed to God that nothing had happened to him.

In the mirror he saw the familiar face of Ian Maitland as he blocked the door leading to the shower room. Birbeck new instantly that he was not going to like what Maitland had to tell him, they had been friends and colleagues for far too long.

'Bad news I am afraid,' he began in a mood that was nothing but somber.

'Hit me with it Ian, it seems that you are destined to be my messenger of doom this week.' He lifted a large white towel and cleaned the remains of the shaving soap from his face.

'We think that we've found Piers with a few bullets in him in Northwood.'

'Jesus. The shit hits the fan,' Birbeck pulled on a clean shirt and quickly knotted up one of his large supply of old school ties.

'I suppose that we had better get out there. Where exactly was he found?' he asked, walking into his office, Maitland watching him.

'Under some bushes, to the side of a quiet footpath.'

'Who found the body?'

'A newspaper delivery body.'

'Let's try keeping this one away from the media,' Birbeck had his jacket on and was carrying his heavy coat as they left the office.

'Lady Piers will have to be told,' he began, but Maitland had another idea.

'Don't you think it might be better to inform the son first and then go with him to pass on the bad news to his mother?' proposed Maitland.

'That sounds sensible enough. Get him picked up and taken to number 10 for nine fifteen, we can get to Northwood and back to Downing Street by then and I can brief the PM before the Cabinet meeting at ten.' Maitland nodded, he was used to Birbeck's continual jumping from one subject to another, and it was the way his superb anti-criminal mind worked, like a computer jumping from one storage box to another.

The journey out of London was a general ping-pong match of suggestions and questions that they would turn over in their minds for the next few days. Things went through their minds as they worked together, a perfect partnership, an almost cohesive unit. They both were very much aware of the fact that they depended heavily on one another, years of being a team had formed the most formidable team that Yard had known in decades. Both had a terrible feeling that all their past experience would be called upon this time to produce the goods, already they were well behind. The runners were over the first hurdle and Birbeck and Maitland were stranded for the moment in the starting stalls.

It was just after eight-thirty when they arrived at the scene of the second assassination. Forensic scientists, police photographers and tracker dogs were already at work. Birbeck walked quietly, not really noticed, among his men. Smelling the atmosphere, looking for angles, clues to how it had been carried out, searching for the method, getting to know the man he was looking for, inside his mind. He watched Maitland talking with the scientists, waiting patiently until he rejoined him by the car. Find the method, he thought, and you have the first piece of the jigsaw, some jigsaws unfortunately had thousands of tiny pieces.

'Well?' asked Birbeck, as Maitland came beside him.
'Dead for between twelve and fifteen hours.'
'How?'
'Bullets in the back, hard to say at the moment, but one of the forensic guys thinks that Piers was shot from perhaps sixty or seventy feet,' replied Maitland nodding towards a scientist some yards away.
'What was Piers doing in Northwood?' Birbeck was more thinking aloud than asking a direct question.
'That's what I've been thinking,' conceded Maitland. They had thought at first that Piers had been kidnapped and dumped, but to be shot from a distance? It did not tie in with that theory.
'Local boys know that we're in charge?'
'Yes, and that there is a press embargo,' offered Maitland.
'Perhaps a door to door search will throw some light on the whole thing.'
'Perhaps.' Maitland, like Birbeck, did not sound too hopeful.

They opened the car doors and got in. The press embargo would be blasted to pieces within hours, they had better go and tell the Prime Minister. Birbeck motioned for Maitland to use the radio.

'Better check where they are with young Piers, don't want him arriving at Downing Street ahead of us.'

Maitland lifted the radio and pressed the button on top, as he did so, he turned to Birbeck.

'The Iron Lady is going to be quite upset, their families go back a long way.'

'Not any longer.' murmured Birbeck thinking that his next couple of hours were not going to be pleasant.

Barry Piers stood enjoying his early morning shower. From downstairs, he could smell the inviting aroma of Ann frying him bacon and eggs. As he washed he sang loudly to himself, a loud rendition of a John Lennon classic. It was a big day, he would complete his latest novel and in the evening he and Ann would dine in their favourite little restaurant in the Fulham Road. There, they would have their favourite meal, a meal they reserved exclusively for special occasions.

Hearing his wife call, he dried quickly, red blotches appearing on his skin where he rubbed. Pulling on an old tee shirt and boxers, he descended the pine stairway and entered the equally pine kitchen.

As usual, the food was delicious and he ate as if he had not eaten for a week. As they sat having their breakfast, they read the morning newspapers, looking for comments on Sir Peter, but there was nothing. Downing Street had called last night trying to contact him, but they had not known his whereabouts and had not thought any more about the call.

Breakfast over, he and Ann carried their coffee mugs into the drawing room where they intended to finish reading the papers.

The large windows were still blocked by the blinds and, as a result, neither of them saw the car enter the driveway and pull up outside the front door. A uniformed policeman climbed the few steps onto the porch and rang the doorbell. He was very curious, he and his partner had received the call only twenty minutes earlier and had been surprised by the instructions. Take Mr. Barry Piers directly to Number 10 Downing Street, the rear entrance, where a member of the Prime Minister's security staff would meet him.

Barry answered the door, and as one might expect, was rather taken aback to see a policeman.

'Yes?' he enquired rather pathetically.
'Mr. Barry Piers?' asked the police constable. He did not want to whisk the wrong man off to 10 Downing Street, did he? Wouldn't look too good on his annual report.
'Sorry to bother you Sir, but we have just received an urgent message stating that we were to escort you immediately to 10 Downing Street. Does that sound feasible to you?'
The policeman sounded somewhat doubtful. Barry smiled, his father had obviously changed his mind about asking the Prime Minister, it would very probably mean the re-writing of a chapter, but it would be well worth the extra effort.
'Yes Officer, it sounds perfectly feasible to me. Would you like to come in for a moment while I get dressed?' The policeman declined the offer saying that he would wait in the car.

The stale smell of the shop filtered into Bill Turnbull's nostrils as he entered. A grey haired man in an old brown overall was trying to sell an old lady a large tin of paint, patiently showing her the supposed colour on a large chart.

It had not been difficult to trace the shop, the company who supplied the gas had simply looked up their stock charts and found from the number quoted by Turnbull from the side of the blue tank, the name and address of the retailer. He stood waiting, watching and wondering at the incredible patience of the salesman as the old lady decided, after all, that the 'super colour' on offer was not what she wanted.

The shopkeeper watched her leave, shaking his head in semi-disgust, before turning his attention to Turnbull.

'Good morning Sir, what can I do for you?' he asked. Turnbull produced his identify card and showed it to the man.

'Sorry to bother you Sir, but I believe that you sell Calor Gas cylinders,' he began politely.

'That's right, you'll have seen that by the sign outside,' replied the man nodding towards the door, perhaps rather disappointed that this was to be another non-sale customer.

'Well, I'm interested in a cylinder sold from this shop, as the person who bought it may be able to help me with some enquiries.' Turnbull handed the shopkeeper a note containing the number of the cylinder. Taking the note, the man went to a sales book and flicked through a pile of invoices. After a few moments he finally spoke.

'Here we are, my daughter sold it to a Mr. Smith, no address given, on the 23rd of October, that would be last Friday I think.'

'That's correct,' added Turnbull, 'would it be possible to have a quick word with your daughter?' he continued.

'I'll get her for you,' replied the man and disappeared through a curtained doorway. Seconds later, he reappeared behind a young girl who was perhaps eighteen or nineteen. She was quite tall, and Turnbull could not help but notice her bad complexion. The girl's father pointed out the invoice and asked her if she could remember anything about the sale. She smiled, a broad simple smile, giving Turnbull the feeling that he was wasting his time.

'A real gent was Mr. Smith, and ever so good looking,' she remembered.

'Could you describe him?' asked Turnbull hopefully.

'Well, he was mighty tall, probably six foot, had blond hair and reminded me of that American film star, you know Robert Redford, especially when he smiled.' Turnbull thought rather sarcastically that Robert Redford should not be too difficult to find in the south east of England, but persisted.

'How old would you say that this Mr. Smith was?'

'About thirty, thirty-two, no more,' the girl's attention was drawn towards another customer entering the shop, and Turnbull decided that enough was enough.

'Well thank you very much Miss, you've been very helpful. You too Sir.' and as he turned to leave, he thought of something else. 'Was the cylinder all that he bought?' He tossed the question at the girl over a paintbrush stand.

'Two cylinders, he bought two cylinders.' came the reply, making Turnbull happy that he asked.

As he drove through the driving rain, Barry Piers pondered broken-heartedly on what had happened so far that day, a day that had begun with such high hopes. The drive to Downing Street; the shocking conversation with an obviously distressed Prime Minister and those two senior policemen; the drive to the morgue. He had then driven to pick up Ann, and gone to Piers House to break the news to his stepmother who was obviously devastated. Despite the fact that he should have remained at Piers House to help with the arrangements, he had excused himself on the pretence of having to go to speak to the police.

The rain lashed heavily upon the windscreen of the small sports car and Piers noticed for the first time that tears were rolling down his cheeks. If one thing was certain, he was not going to rest until the person who had killed his father was locked up for life.

The interview at number 10 had thrown up a couple of doubts in his mind, the chief one relating to the fact that the police did not think that his father had been killed someplace else and taken to Northwood to be dumped. Did that mean that his father that gone there of his own accord? If so, why?

Barry let himself into his father's small Kensington flat and was aware of the instant reminders of his never to be seen again father. A lump formed itself in his throat as he tried to busy himself with the task in hand, looking for something that did not quite match, something strange, unusual, any clue would do to start with.

He began with the study and struck luck almost immediately. In the top drawer of his father's desk he found the logbook for a brand new Mini Metro. Why would his father want a Mini when he had a perfectly good Rolls Royce, and an equally elegant Mercedes at home? Perhaps it was for city driving. But why had Sir Peter not told his son? The rest of the study failed to produce anything quite as startling as the Mini, so Piers adjourned to the sitting room. Despite a careful search, he found nothing of any interest there. The bedroom was equally non-fruitful.

Suddenly feeling very hungry, he realized that he had not eaten since breakfast; Piers walked to the kitchen and pulled open the fridge door. It was discovery number two. Despite the fact that his father had told Elizabeth that he would be staying overnight at the flat, he had bought no food, nothing, not even a pint of milk. What the hell had his father been playing at?

From his jacket pocket, Piers pulled the small notebook he always carried with him, and began jotting down all that he had discovered. If he could get the pieces together, then perhaps he at least could begin on the puzzle. He pondered over what to do next, before lifting the telephone to call Sally Gray his Dad's assistant. Despite the fact that it was Saturday, she answered first ring and sounded very distressed. She had heard the news on the radio, the Prime Minister's embargo obviously now gone, and asked what she could do to help. Piers told her that he would like to meet her at his father's office, and she agreed to see him there in half an hour. Barry replaced the receiver, had one final quick look around the apartment, before leaving and heading for Westminster on foot.

It was exactly three pm when he entered Sally Gray's little outer office. The secretary looked in a hell of a state, she had obviously been crying a lot and her mascara had run down her face. Piers tried to pull her together by asking her to make some coffee while he looked through his father's things.

Half an hour and two cups of coffee later Piers re-entered the outer office and slumped into a seat, feeling exhausted. Looking at the pathetically frail girl in front of him he felt sympathy for her. Christ, he thought suddenly, it's me who should be getting the sympathy, I've just lost the best friend I ever had. The girl spoke quietly to him.

'Did you find what you were looking for?' she asked, and Piers noticed that her nose had gone red to match her eyes.

'No,' he replied rather abruptly.

'What exactly were you looking for?' now that she had someone to talk to, she seemed to be recovering some composure. Piers sighed and shrugged his shoulders.

'I don't really know,' he began honestly 'something out of place perhaps, something that might tell me why my father went to Northwood last night.' He looked at the girl and noticed a slight change in her posture. He doubted for a moment that he was imagining things before asking.

'You don't happen to have any idea, do you Sally?'

'Not really,' she replied weakly.

'What is that supposed to mean, for Christ's sake?' He stood and walked towards her desk, and putting two clenched fists on her desktop, he leaned on them causing the knuckles to go white, as he stared at her over the typewriter.

'Well it might be nothing really, but Sir Peter kept getting telephone calls from what sounded to be a young woman.' she began, emphasizing the young.

'Go on,' urged Piers, he heart beating faster.

'Well, he instructed me to inform him every time she called, and only on very rare occasions, such as meetings, did he not take her call. As soon as the meeting or whatever was over, he would then ask me for an outside line, and I could hear him laughing on the phone,' she paused and inspected her immaculate fingernails before continuing, 'I must admit, I was very curious, but it was none of my business was it?' She looked at Piers as if for support.

'No, I don't suppose it was,' Piers replied in a state of semi-shock. The idea of his father having another affair had not even crossed his mind. But, it made sense and perhaps that explained the Mini Metro. He thought of something else.

'What made you tell me all this now? he asked.

'Don't suppose that it really matters now, and when you mentioned Northwood …'

'Yes?' Barry hoped that there was more.

'Well, your father had a call from the girl the other day, and as usual I put it through. He was with you at the time and the funny thing was he asked me to take the number and tell the caller he would phone back. I did, and of course after you had left he simply asked for an outside line, never bothered asking for the number.' Piers was suddenly listening very intently to what she was saying. He remembered the conversation vividly and recalled the telephone interruption.

'Go on,' he requested pleasantly.

'Well, the other morning I was having my coffee when I came across my pad with this number on the back.'

'And?' asked Piers, getting impatient.

'I was slightly curious, I knew what the number was, so I looked up the code, 09274, it was, and it turned out to be the code for Northwood. I remember being quite impressed. Smart area is Northwood.' Piers allowed himself a large mental cry of Eureka, before asking the girl if she still had the pad with the number on it. Sally reached in her drawer and took out the pad, tore off the back page and handed it to Barry.

'I will use my father's desk Sally, would you give me an outside line?'

The girl nodded, and he walked through to the inner office, sat down behind the large mahogany desk, picked up the receiver and dialed the number. He noticed a gilt framed photograph of Elizabeth and hoped that his first assumption had been wrong; perhaps there was another reason. Realizing that his hands were shaking, he composed himself as he waited for the reply. When it came he simply said.

'Hello, this is Barry Piers, I believe you knew my father.'

It was just ten minutes later when the stolen Vauxhall was discovered. Police Constable William Smart and his colleague Steve Thomas were on their usual patrol. They both were a little disappointed at having missed out on the earlier action. The whole bloody station was buzzing about the discovery of the Minister's body. A special briefing had even been held for all officers about to go on duty, where they had all been told in no uncertain terms to be on their toes all day, no stone was to go unturned, especially with the Scotland Yard pratts around. All weekend leave had been cancelled in an attempt to get the door-to-door questioning completed that day, and that had upset a lot of family weekends. And, with no breakthrough so far, the Chief Constable was beginning to look pretty pissed off.

Billy Smart was doing the watching while his partner concentrated on the driving, and they were travelling up a short leafy lane, which was fairly typical for the area, when he noticed the car. The odd thing about it was the fact that it was parked well away from any of the driveway entrances to the large houses. Smart thought that there would very probably be a simple explanation, but it was not worth his life if it had something to do with the crime, and he had driven passed it.

Having reported the car to headquarters they waited, while the computer checked the details. A few minutes later, they were both delighted to hear that the car had been reported stolen in central London the day before. It was not the only clue to be found that day, but it would be the beginning of an incredible chain of events.

As the kettle began to boil before switching itself off, Susan Lamont stood, walked across the kitchen and poured the boiling water into a teapot. It had been the worst day of her life so far, and she was in no doubt that with the upcoming visit from Barry Piers, that things were unlikely to get any better.

The police had been at her door on three occasions, yet she had ignored them, she would have found telling them lies very difficult indeed. The phone call from young Piers had taken her by complete surprise. How had he found out? Had Peter told his son that he was having an affair? No, she was certain that Peter would not have done that. How then? Thinking about it, it had to be via Peter's secretary. Yes, that was more like it, what was her name? Miss Gray. Yes, Barry must have found out through the office. It was coming back to her now, the day the girl had asked her for her number when Peter was busy. It was odd, she had thought at the time, but she had given the secretary the number. That was it.

Pouring some piping hot tea into a rather large white mug, she carried it through to the lounge and sat down on the settee. How she desperately needed to talk with somebody, but she had no one to turn to. Her parents would never understand. Jesus, what could she do? The blasphemy reminded her of her childhood upbringing in the church. Perhaps she should pray? She remembered Sunday evenings with her parents at Benediction, the Latin, the incense, the sore knees, and the boredom. No, she concluded, prayer was not the answer. Tears ran down her checks, poor, poor, Peter. She thought, who could have done such a thing? Suddenly she realized that she would not even be able to attend his funeral, pay her last respects to the man she had loved like no man before. The man who had made her believe in herself again. God, what a nightmare! She hoped that somehow that's what it was, and she would wake up to discover that it had all been a bad dream.

The door buzzer sounded and made her jump. Perhaps it was the police back again. Walking to the kitchen she went to the window and looked out at the main door. God, how like his father he was. Walking to the hallway, she pressed the door release mechanism and let Barry Piers into the block of flats. Back in the lounge, she picked up her tea and took a sip. Peter had spoken very highly of his son, but she had no idea of what to expect, people often spoke highly of their children. Walking mechanically towards the door, she opened it and led the young man through to the lounge. He was taller than his father, yet the resemblance was striking. For a few moments they just stood and stared at each other. It was Piers who finally broke the silence. Susan was instantly put at ease by his manner.

'You look about as bad as I feel,' he offered as an opening, smiling gently. Susan burst into a flood of tears and Barry closed the gap between them, took her in his arms to comfort her, aware of what the poor woman was going through.

During the drive to Northwood, he had experienced some really strange emotions. Why had his father needed to take a lover? She had to be some horrible young tart out for what she could get. Yet no, he had concluded, he had known and respected his father too much to believe that such a thing could happen. Finally he had resigned himself to the fact that his father had very probably loved the girl and no doubt she him. Elizabeth had always been a cold, unaffectionate woman, not like his mother, or at least not like the distant memories that he still had of his mother. Having come to this conclusion, he had visions of the woman sitting alone in her flat, heartbroken, with nobody to turn to. For the second time in a few hours, he felt pity for someone other than himself.

She was much prettier than he had expected, and obviously highly intelligent if the books in the place were anything to go by. Why had he thought anything else possible? His father had always taught him that nothing but the very best of everything was sufficient if one was to enjoy life to the full. Even in his choice of lover, his father would have picked someone special. Susan broke away from their embrace and walked towards the kitchen.

'Would you like some tea?' she asked, surprised that she was not at all uncomfortable by their embrace. He was indeed very like his father, that powerful ability to put people at their ease.

Both held mugs of tea similarly cupped in their hands as they sat facing each other in the kitchen.

'I hope you don't mind me barging in on you like this, but I just had to find out why my father had come to Northwood,' Barry began.
'Not at all, it's good it's you, he had such a lot to say about you,' tears refilled in her eyes ' but I assumed that we'd never meet.'
'I suppose that it would've been kinda difficult.' he replied, handing her a paper tissue from a pack he had bought earlier.
'Yeah, I suppose,' she said reaching for the Handy Andy.
'Hong long ....?'

'Six months,' she anticipated his question.

'And you don't have anyone to confide in do you?' he asked gently.

'Nope.'

'Pity, at a time like this, we all need somebody,' he offered, 'it's so hard.'

'You're being very kind about all this, why?' Piers looked at her for a moment. Perhaps he would wonder about it later, but he could only tell her what he had figured out during the drive.

'Well, I reckon that if you loved him as much, or even half as much as I did, then you must be going through hell. I'm not God, so I can't judge whether or not what you had going was right or wrong. So I am here to talk, help if you like, and perhaps we can work something out about who the hell would be evil enough to kill him.' He shrugged his shoulders as if to let her know that this was the best he could do at the moment by way of an explanation.

'I've been thinking about that, but so far all I keep doing is coming up with blanks.' she sipped her tea carefully, not taking her large eyes away from him.

'I take it that nobody knew that he came here?'

'No, he even bought a new car to enable him to keep a low profile when he arrived,' Barry remembered the Metro he had seen parked across the road from the flats.

'Somebody must have known.' he concluded, looking out the kitchen window.

'Yeah I suppose so, but who?' Tears began streaming down her face, and Piers decided that perhaps it was being too cruel to carry on questioning her. She looked, and sounded exhausted and he guessed that it was very unlikely that she had got much sleep since the previous night. After all, she had been expecting her lover and he had not arrived, she must have been out of her mind with worry.

Piers reckoned that the police were very likely to come to the same conclusions as him. They were bound to have traced his father as the owner of the Metro, especially since it had been parked only a few hundred yards from the murder scene. Again he thought of this very attractive woman sitting in her flat awaiting her lover, his father, to arrive. He realized that his thought patterns were behaving in a peculiar manner. Ideas were jumping around in his head like jumping beans on a tray, like when he had an idea for an article or a book, before they settled down into an orderly solution, the problem solved. He hoped to God that he would be able to solve this particular problem.

'Did you ever watch for my father arriving?' he asked, returning from his soul searching. 'I mean you can see the street from the kitchen window.' He nodded towards the window.

'Oh yes, if I was preparing a meal or something, I would sometimes sit on a stool and watch for his little car to come into the street. I don't suppose that you can really understand this, but I was very much in love with your father, and I believe he was with me.' She held back the tears before continuing, 'he made me believe in myself, made me relax and take life as it came. I can't believe, simply cannot comprehend that he won't be coming again.' Piers offered her a comforting smile.

'Yes I loved him in the very same way, he was a great man and that is why I must get the person who murdered him.' Susan nodded that she understood, but she could not really understand why this young man was not at home sharing his grief with his family.

'That's why it is important that you think back, and try to remember anything that, in retrospect, may seem unusual. Anything that you noticed while sitting in this room waiting for him.' He was aware of the fact that he was rushing her, perhaps pushing her beyond her endurance limits. But he had to keep on the move, get on the trail while it was still hot. Otherwise, the self-pity and grief that he was storing inside himself, was likely to explode and engulf him.

Susan was trying very hard to concentrate, and for perhaps five minutes they sat in silence. After a while he noticed her eyes begin to sparkle ever so slightly, and it was not through tears. She had thought of something, what?

'You remember something?' he asked enthusiastically, putting his cup of cold tea down and leaning towards her.

'There was something,' she began, 'about a week ago. I was here in the kitchen waiting for Peter. The door buzzer went, and I let him in.'

'And?' Piers interrupted.

'Moments later the buzzer went again and I answered but nobody replied. I was obviously curious and went to the kitchen window and saw a man walking away from the main door.'

'What did he look like?' asked delighted Piers.

'Tall, with very blond hair, it was quite dark.'

'How tall?' he continued.

'It's difficult to say from this height above the ground, but he must have been quite big for me to notice.' She was rolling the dry tealeaves in the bottom of her cup.

'Why?'

'Well you are tall, but when I saw you from the window, I never thought so, so I guess he must have been taller than you,' she explained.

'But I'm six foot, surely he couldn't be much taller than me?' he sounded doubtful.

'He was, considerably, and slim too.'

'Did you notice where he went?' he quizzed hopefully.

'Yes, towards a sports car, an MG I think, but I wouldn't bet on it.'

'Anything else?'

'No, your father came in, and I forgot about the incident completely,' she put the cup down and stood up.

'Do you think that it could have been him?' she asked, putting the empty mugs into a washing up bowl.

'Who knows.' answered Piers honestly, but it was a start.

He left Susan Lamont ten minutes later after promising her that he would come and visit her the following day. Perhaps he could persuade Ann to come with him, Susan needed somebody of her own sex to talk to. Ann would surely agree.

Smiling, pleased with his detective work so far, he drove off at speed towards his pre-arranged meeting with Commander Birbeck at New Scotland Yard.

Meanwhile, the images of the Archer killing were etching themselves on the mind of John Birbeck as he sat in his large leather chair behind his desk at New Scotland Yard. On his blotting pad in front of him lay the note left behind in the French villa by the killer and sent hurriedly by messenger to London. There was nothing of any real significance in the note itself, no new leads. It simply stated that if the British and Irish governments did not meet urgently to discuss the immediate unification of Ireland ….

Birbeck was happy in his mind that his forces were now deployed to their maximum effectiveness and that it was unlikely that the killings would continue in the near future. However, what did disturb him was the fact that he had no idea as to how much time he had at his disposal. They had threatened to kill two, and had achieved that threat with shocking ease. But, what next? What would the next demand be? How long did the Prime Minister have to comply? A thousand questions required answers, and so far none had come forward. He knew from experience that results would come given time. But, that said, he also had no fucking idea who was doing the killing.

The intercom brought him back from his thinking. Leaning across his desk, he pressed the button and spoke sleepily.
'Yes.'
'Barry Piers is here Sir. Shall I send him in?' asked his assistant.
'Of course, right away.' He stood to welcome the young author who was showing great character in the way in which he was carrying such a heavy burden on his young shoulders.

Piers entered and took the seat proffered, opposite Birbeck.

'Well Barry, how is your mother?'
'As well as can be expected thanks Commander, but as you well know, I am not here to discuss anything but the business in hand this time.' He was drained, totally exhausted mentally by what had happened, and now knew that he could face nothing until his father's killers were captured.

'And what do you have for me, my boy?' asked Birbeck, at once annoyed by the patronizing tone in his voice.

'Well, I think that I am now in a position to throw some light on the entire Northwood business, where would you like me to start?'

'At the beginning please.'

Piers relayed the entire story of his discoveries to Birbeck, who gradually became more and more interested in what he was hearing. When Piers had finished, Birbeck sat quiet for several moments as if collating the facts in his computer-like brain.

Picking up his pencil, be began jotting down a few points on a small pad. Finished, he dropped the pencil on the pad and looked at Piers. His hands were raised in front of him, his fingers tapping against each other in a pose not uncommon in a doctor contemplating a prescription for a patient.

'Obviously I am very grateful for your help Barry, However, as you can imagine I am also very disappointed in my own staff for failing to come up with such good results. Especially one or two points.'

'Such as?' interrupted Piers.

'Well there is your father's car for example, you are sure that it is still parked in the same street?' Birbeck sounded disappointed, only minutes earlier he had been sure that his staff was deployed to their full efficiency. Now he had his doubts, and what a time to have doubts in his team! Turning back to Piers, he said.

'Well Barry, I shouldn't keep you from your family any longer, is there anything I can do for you?' Piers stood and began heading for the door, Birbeck now by his side.

'No Commander, there is nothing. But thanks anyway.' Birbeck offered his hand.

'Well if there is anything you want, just call,' he admired Piers considerably and hoped inwardly that his own boys would grow into such fine young men. Piers opened the door, but before leaving turned back and spoke again.

'There is one thing Commander.'

'As I said Barry, anything you want.'

'Well, I'd like to be in on the operation to find these people.' He looked hopefully at Birbeck who rubbed his jaw hesitantly before answering.

'It's against all procedure to have emotionally involved civilians working on our cases, but I think that today you have earned your wings,' again he shook Piers hand before finishing with a simple 'welcome aboard.'

Having updated Maitland and before his deputy left for Northwood some ten minutes later, Birbeck received the news that an old lady in the area had reported speaking to a rather rude, blond American yesterday afternoon. It was the second breakthrough in less than an hour, and with spirits lifted he let Maitland travel out to Northwood to rally their troops. Birbeck then returned to his office, phoned his wife and decided to get a couple of hours sleep before his arranged meeting with the Prime Minister at Downing Street.

Despite the fact that the camp bed in an anteroom near his office had not been designed with such a large man in mind, he found no difficulty in getting to sleep.

The small portable television was playing up and once again the picture disappeared into a snowy haze. Spencer stood, a towel wrapped around his waist and began to fiddle with the fragile aerial perched on a shelf above the TV. The picture gave a fuzzy response and gradually normal service was resumed. Kathy, in a short dressing gown smiled at him as he sat down beside her on the sofa, and they both turned their attention to the evening news as broadcast by the BBC.

Had the picture not gone from the screen at that moment, they would have been listening to the police description of a tall American who had been seen driving an MG sports car in the Northwood area a few days earlier and who was wanted for questioning in connection with the death of Sir Peter Piers. It would surely have been too much to expect a budding mathematician, like Kathy Drinkwater, to be given so many variables and not solve the problem.

As it was, with the news and their hot drinks finished, Spencer led the girl through to the bedroom where she made love to him as if sex was about to go out of fashion.

Commander John Birbeck's unmarked car arrived at the rear entrance to number 10 Downing Street less than an hour later. The Commander rushed to the door and was ushered to the large Cabinet room to make his daily report to the Prime Minister.

As expected, two other men were sitting waiting for him to arrive and the PM arrived a few moments later. Birbeck knew both of them fairly well as he had often worked with them on major security matters. They were, Major General Peter Rowe, Supreme Commander of the Special Air Service and Commander Jim Townsend of the Special Branch.

The Prime Minister sat herself at the head of the long table with the Heads of her security forces around her. With them all seated, she announced that Birbeck would give them a full briefing on progress to date, and for the next twenty-five minutes they discussed and explored the options available to them before finalizing on their joint plan.

With the plan outlined, the Prime Minister informed the group that she was intending to make immediate contact with her Irish counterpart with the aim of inviting him to London to bring up to speed with developments and to agree an Anglo-Irish response. Despite the fact that formal talks were due to be held on the sixth of November, the Prime Minister and her cabinet had agreed earlier that day that it made good sense to fully engage with the Irish Republic on this matter.

Finally, and satisfied that things were, at last, in hand, the Prime Minister called the meeting to a close and left the room, leaving her security chiefs to go over the plan again before departing. They were agreed, Rowe would make himself and his teams available to Birbeck as required, whilst Townsend would coordinate an uplift in the protection of the Royal Family in the lead up to the State Opening of Parliament on the Fourth of November. An event certain to attract even greater public interest than usual due to the fact that Prince Charles and his popular new bride Princess Diana were planning to attend the ceremony.

Before leaving Downing Street, Peter Rowe who had been fairly quiet during the meeting announced that he intended to go to Northern Ireland immediately and brief his senior people on the matter. At over six feet tall, he was what could be classified as a handsome man. Educated at Harrow and then Oxford, he had gone through Law School before joining the Army. He had been Commander in Chief of the SAS for four years and was held in high regard by John Birbeck who thought that having him on the ground in Ulster would be no bad thing.

Just as they were leaving the Cabinet room, the Prime Minister re-appeared to announce that the Irish Premier would be arriving in London with his Private Secretary and Head of Security in the morning. Birbeck and the others were surprised by how quickly she had got this organized and noticed, as they left, a renewed vigor and resolve in their political boss. Birbeck made a mental note never to underestimate her again.

As Birbeck climbed into his car, he could not help but feel that inviting the Irish PM to Britain was clearly calculated to give the impression that credence was being given to the terrorist demands. This, in turn, could buy more time. That said, it could just as easily have the opposite effect. It could give the terrorists the feeling of being in the driving seat and that could result in them putting their foot down on the accelerator. He hoped to God that he was wrong.

It was perhaps thirty minutes later when the telephone rang in Ray O'Grady's Dublin office. He was not surprised to hear the voice of the Irish Prime Minister, but what did surprise him was what he was hearing him say. He was suddenly aware of the fact that what he was being told was so importantly relevant to whether or not his daughter would live or die. The nights without sleep, the torment with Anna, the daily photographs showing that his daughter was alive, they all seemed to be given a purpose. At that instant, he decided through the pain, to betray his position, his employer and his country. Yet, even more important to him was the fact that he was betraying his own very high moral standards and he hoped that afterwards, despite the outcome, that he would be able to live with his conscience.

Mechanically he listened and replied, even took notes on what his Prime Minister was telling him. They would be leaving early in the morning for London by Air Force jet. Before the call was over, the Prime Minister stressed that the proposed journey was top secret.

When the PM had finished giving his instructions, O'Grady telephoned the local Air Force base and spoke to the Commander. He then telephoned his wife and asked her to prepare an overnight bag, just in case he might be required to stay in London. Next, he arranged for Anna's mother to come and stay with her, she would be no good on her own.

Afterwards, he telephoned the number supplied by his daughter's abductors and passed on the required information. Inwardly, he hoped that this was the beginning of the end of the terrible nightmare that he and his family were going through.

Just before midnight as McCormack sat in his study with the customary glass of Cragganmore whisky in front of him, the telephone rang. As pre-arranged he did not move to answer the call, counting the number of times that it rang.

After five rings it stopped and he relaxed, knowing that the contact between the two governments had been made. His ploy was working very nicely indeed. Lifting his glass he drank the contents and walked to the drinks tray for a refill. He chuckled to himself, thinking of the panic that would be taking place in New Scotland Yard. The British police, he thought, would be running about like blue arsed flies. Lifting his glass again, he murmured softly.

'Up the Republic,' and drank the lot in one gulp.

He then climbed the stairs towards his bedroom, hoping that he would survive to see his dream come true. Not even the whisky on top of the pills could reduce the pain now, only determination could see him through.

Meanwhile back in London, the British police were rushing about like blue arsed flies in a desperate attempt to ensure that the surviving members of the Cabinet could rest assured in their homes.

However, despite the significant extra police presence, not many members of the Cabinet would have been able to admit to a good nights sleep the following morning.

Sunday 1 November 1981

12

As a rule, Elliot did not particularly like driving. Bradley however, had said over the radio that he was to get himself back to HQ in a hurry. Anderson had not been too pleased at being left on watch without a car, but Elliot had simply pulled rank and promised a relief driver as soon as he reached HQ. Slowing the car down to something approaching the legal limit, he bumped over the sudden ramps across the road and approached the security post, which guarded the entrance to the HQ car park. The young soldier recognized him and waved him through. Elliot took a mental note to pin the young man's ears to the wall for not checking his car thoroughly, you could never tell when a terrorist might be in the back with an Armalite up the drivers arse.

Bradley was in his office with a strip of telex paper in front of him on his desk. Elliot offered him one of two cups of coffee and sat down opposite.

'What's up Mac?' he asked sipping the hot coffee. Their working life seemed to revolve around hundreds of such meetings.

'This telex and the info issued to the press by New Scotland Yard in connection with the Piers killing,' began Bradley, taking his coffee.

'The American geezer?'

'Yeah,' replied Bradley somewhat deliberately.

'What about it?' Elliot was annoyed that somewhere along the line he had missed something, he had worked with Bradley too long not to realize where he was leading.

'Well it's just struck me that his ID just about fits one of those snapshots that you and David Bailey Anderson took out at McCormack's place a couple of weeks back.' Elliot, on his feet, was suddenly on the same wavelength.

'I'll nip down to my office and get the file.' Why, he thought as he left the room, had he not made this connection earlier? He had become far too subjective, with the watch on McCormack, he had concentrated all his energies on the old bastard and left the rest of the work to others, his objectivity becoming cloudy. God he felt fucking stupid.

A few minutes later he was back, and they looked at the photograph in conjunction with the description and details issued by the Anti-Terrorist Squad. To both men, there was no doubt, this was a photograph of perhaps the most wanted man in Britain at that moment in time. Silently, they finished their coffee and it was Elliot who spoke first.

'Well, what do you think?'

'It's him all right, I can feel it in my piss.' Elliot shook his head, Bradley certainly had a way with words.

'I suppose we better get in touch with London then.'

'Yeah, but you get all the information that we've got on this operation. Tapes, photographs, transcripts etc.'

'It's mostly all in my office,' offered Elliot.

'Good. And I would nip home and get a bag ready. I'll get you booked on the first flight to London. Those bastards at the Yard will reckon we've been sleeping on the job for the last fortnight, so we can't afford any more slip-ups. You'll be needed to advise them on everything we know.'

Bradley lifted his telephone and Elliot left the office, remembering to arrange a car to pick up Anderson before heading for home, his tiredness evaporating with the prospect of the trip.

At that same moment, the jet carrying the Irish Prime Minister lowered its under-carriage and began its descent into RAF Northolt on the outskirts of northwest London. The early morning light was about to break through but the truck drivers and early Sunday travelers heading into town along an already busy A40 paid little attention to the screeching jet as it hovered over the carriageway with its peculiar cut-down lampposts and down onto the damp tarmac of the runway.

The Irish Prime Minister, his Private Secretary Ray O'Grady and Nick Glynn his Head of Security, were met by a member of the British Prime Minister's private team of Civil Servants and led, escorted by two officers assigned from the Special Branch, to an awaiting black Rover 3500.

O'Grady smiled to himself as he saw the blacked out windows. It made him feel more secure than he had done for weeks, and climbed in beside his boss. As the car drove off, he noticed a police car following behind as a police motorcyclist took up position in front of the two cars. Gradually the tension began to flow out of O'Grady and he relaxed to enjoy the drive to 10 Downing Street where he knew he would be unable to afford such luxury.

Replacing the receiver, Birbeck rubbed his chin, deep in thought. Was this the break through that he had been praying for? Rising from behind his desk, he left his room and walked slowly and mechanically through the small anteroom and out into the corridor.

The beaverish activity of the last few days was not yet totally evident, but with every new day came re-charged batteries, fresh ideas, and the place was beginning to come alive again. The Commander's pace quickened and he reached the end of the corridor and entered the Special Operations room set up especially to cope with the latest in a long line of security problems.

The room was not dissimilar to an Operations Room in an old World War II movie, only the equipment was more modern, more complex, to meet the demands of a more complex enemy.

Maitland stood to meet him and Barry Piers finished a cup of tea and walked from where he had been standing beside a large map of London and the southeast, with red markers showing the current whereabouts of all surviving members of the British Cabinet.

The three of them grouped around Maitland's somewhat cluttered desk, and Birbeck relayed to them the details of the conversation that he had just had with Bradley.

'If that's the case, then we could be looking for three assassins at the least,' stated Maitland, his mind instantly aware of the difficulty in such a task. 'Jesus, it could even be a dozen or two,' he mused.
'No use speculating Ian, we should be content in the knowledge that there may be three,' he stressed the may be.
'Could it simply be an ASU?' asked Piers.

Both men looked at him. Active Service Units had long since been the body and soul of IRA bombing campaigns, so the question was not so silly. However, both men, with their years of experience, were on the same wavelength. This was different. Why, or in what way it was different they were not quite sure, but the overall pattern was odd and that was the most dangerous point to bear in mind. Birbeck nodded and said that it could be. He looked around the room, and then at his watch before speaking to them both.
'I want you two to go to the airport and meet Bradley's man. His name is Elliot and by all accounts he's one of their bright and highly respected young intelligence men. Take two cars with you and I want you, Ian, to come back here with Elliot; Barry I want you to take a copy of the photo of this American over to our little friend in Northwood and see if we can get a positive ID from her. We can then get the ball rolling on the others.'

Maitland and Piers lifted their jackets from a grey, Government Issue coat hanger, and Birbeck followed them towards the door. Birbeck seemed to have a last minute thought.
'Oh, before you go Ian, I've been thinking and reckon that it's about time we had another note from these people, so would you

please initiate a search. You know the sort of thing we are looking for, so get some men on it.'

'Will do John.' and Maitland went to fix it. Birbeck turned to Piers.

'You sure that you're not neglecting your family?' he asked, more friendly than reproachful.

'Yes, there are more people at Piers House than watched the FA Cup Final, they won't miss little old me.'

'Good. I hope the Lamont girl comes up trumps with this face, make life a good deal easier to have a photograph to go on.' He patted Piers on the shoulder and said that he was off to tidy himself up before going to Downing Street. The PM wanted him there at nine-thirty.

The British Airways flight from Belfast arrived ten minutes late. Elliot, in a hurry to leave the plane, was one of the first people to disembarking. He knew that, as usual, there would be a considerable delay before the baggage would come through but, with his stuff in a small overnight bag, he had no such delay. As he headed for the exit, he heard an announcement over the tannoy system asking for a Mr. Elliot from Ulster to go to the enquiry desk. Five minutes later, his hand luggage strapped with the white tape used by security at the airport in Antrim, he jogged through the exit and rushed to the enquiry desk. If anyone noticed him, they would probably have mistaken the scruffy longhaired guy in denims as an aging student or lorry driver.

At the desk, he was met by Maitland and Piers. Brief introductions over, Maitland outlined the immediate plans and Elliot, in turn, handed Piers a brown envelope containing a 5 x 7 inch photograph of the tall American. Piers said that he would call them as soon as he had shown the photograph to Susan, whatever her reaction, and left along with his Special Branch driver, for Northwood.

As they drove back to New Scotland Yard, Maitland, sitting next to Elliot in the rear seats of the Ford Granada, studied the photographs carefully, committing them to memory.

'Where were these photographs taken?' he asked suddenly without looking up.

'At John McCormack's farm, he's been under constant surveillance for quite some time now,' explained Elliot.

'Why?'

'Well, he's a known associate of Joseph and Liam Blaney, both of whom ....'

'Yes, I know all about the Blaney brothers,' interrupted Maitland who lifted the photograph of Liam and showed it to Elliot.

'Liam Blaney,' he stated, and Elliot simply nodded. He was not at his most comfortable in the large policeman's presence.

'And what have you put together in connection with McCormack, the Blaneys and these other three faces?' he asked, again rather abruptly.

'Well, we know from our tape recordings of telephone conversations that Blaney, or rather both Blaneys are still somewhere in Ireland, and that they are working with McCormack on something that they consider big enough to risk staying to see through. What they are actually working on, we have not yet uncovered, they are clever men.' Elliot was aware of the fact that the latter part of his statement may have sounded like an apology.

'Too bloody clever by half,' scorned Maitland. 'How those Blaney bastards have avoided prison in the past amazes me, does it not you?'

'Sure.' Elliot replied with a shrug of his shoulders, aware of the point that Maitland was referring to. The fact that it was thought in many circles that the Blaney family had influential friends within the Dublin government, although to date, no connection had ever been found.

'The tapes that you talked about, you've brought copies with you?' asked Maitland putting the photographs away and staring ahead along the motorway.

'Of course,' replied Elliot.

'Good. Perhaps they will give us a clue or two.'

Susan Lamont wore a dark grey tracksuit when she let Barry Piers into her flat in Northwood some twenty minutes later. Although personally tired and depressed, Piers could not help feeling great sympathy for the woman.

'Would you like some coffee?' she asked, leading him into the lounge.

'Yes please,' he replied, still stunned by her beauty. The last time they had met he had thought her attractive, but the beauty that was now so obvious had previously been hidden by a sleepless night and the agony of suffering death alone. Now, after a couple of visits from Ann Piers she had gained some, if not all, of her natural beauty and composure.

Returning from the kitchen, she handed Piers a mug of hot coffee before sitting down opposite him on a two-seater settee and tucking her legs up underneath her. For an instant Piers experienced a feeling that was not forgiveness for his father for wanting this woman, but more of jealousy that he had not been the one to bed her.

'To what do I owe this unexpected visit?' She asked bringing him back to reality.

'Oh,' said Piers, somewhat startled, 'I've brought a photograph of a man the police believe may be our American friend.'

He fished the envelope from his pocket, took out the photograph and handed it over. Susan looked at the photograph for all of five seconds before stating categorically that this was indeed the man.

'You're sure?' asked Piers, retrieving the photograph and looking at it, he was overcome with a renewed surge of hatred for the bastard who had killed his father.

'One hundred per cent positive.'

Piers returned the photograph to the envelope and put it back into his pocket. Smiling, he looked at Susan.

'Thanks again for your help.' he began.
'It's nothing. You should know that this means as much to me

as it does to anyone, I loved your father very much.' Tears began to well in her eyes and Piers closed the gap between them and took her in his arms.

'I know Susan, and I am very sorry to keep coming back to upset you again.'

'Don't be silly, just help the police find that bastard. Promise me that.'

'I promise.' said Piers, offering her a reassuring smile, knowing that he meant it with all his heart.

'Then go to it cowboy.' She smiled back and Piers stood and walked towards the door, Susan followed and as he left the flat she kissed him gently on the cheek.

'You know Barry, you and Ann are very lucky having one another, you should make the most of it. Life has a nasty habit of being far too bloody short.' She did not wait for a reply, simply closing the door on Piers. And on the outside world, he thought as he awaited the elevator.

'Mother of God, do you really think that they will carry this out?'

'Believe me Prime Minister, I do. Two very dear friends of mine are already dead.' The British Prime Minister looked, and sounded, extremely distressed, yet Birbeck was wondering just how much of her appeal to her Irish counterpart was just the old political warhorse striding into action.

The Irish Prime Minister rose from the table and walked to the windows and looked out over the rear gardens of 10 Downing Street. He looked shaken by what he had heard, and after a few moments he returned to his seat.

'What do you suggest that we do?'

'Well, there is obviously no way in which we can be seen to capitulate in any way to these demands. That said, it is a very different scenario from the hunger strike. In that instance our resolve, as I had predicted, turned out to be greater than theirs, their losses greater than ours. They have however, discovered that they have lost public face, so our main problem is the fact that I believe that this campaign may be the most ruthless yet.'

The Irish Prime Minister simply nodded and Birbeck who, along with Captain Nick Glynn, was a mere onlooker, wondered what it was that made a man of medicine become a politician. Perhaps he would never understand. The Prime Minister continued to answer the question.

'It is my proposal therefore that we give the impression that we are discussing the Ulster problem together. This may be construed by these murderers as us giving into the first of their demands and may give us, or rather our security people such as Commander Birbeck here, more time to get to the root of the problem and weed them out.'

The British Prime Minister looked at the small Irishman for approval.

'It would appear to me that this is our only possible option. And obviously, I will do anything I can to help, so yes, I will go along with it. But I am not sure we need to go public just yet.' He said, before continuing ' As I believe that I may have a mole in my camp.'
'How convenient, but let's continue with our plan to hold our joint talks next week as previously scheduled.' Responded the British PM showing no surprise to the mole revelation.

Again the Irish leader simply nodded before standing and heading for the door. 'Good, I will speak to my Private Secretary and confirm the arrangement.'

For the few moments that it took the Irish Prime Minister and Glynn to consult Ray O'Grady, the British Prime Minister spoke to Birbeck.

'Well Commander, how do you think I put our case?' She asked, a cunning smile on her face.

'Admirably Prime Minister, quite admirably.'

'Yes, I thought so too.' She smiled again and just then the Irish Prime Minister re-entered the room to announce that the arrangements for his return to London on the 6th of November were confirmed.

While the two Prime Ministers had a late breakfast and discussed other business, Ray O'Grady was considering how soon it would be until he was asked to provide the kidnappers with the outcome of today's meeting and Commander Birbeck was heading back to New Scotland Yard and to the news that the photograph was in fact of the man that they were looking for.

'Another burning question, as far as I am concerned is, who the hell is Fox?' It was Maitland speaking to Piers and Elliot in the Special Operations room in New Scotland Yard as Inspector Paterson extracted the last of the tapes from the cassette machine.

'I've discussed that point with one or two of my colleagues back in Lisburn, but so far it just does not seem to fit into the scheme of things,' offered Elliot in reply.

'Could it be the London based leader of this group?' asked Piers pointing to the photographs of Miller, Spencer and De Ville that were spread out on Maitland's untidy desk.

'It's possible, but why the other three at the farm and not him?' countered Maitland.

'Already set up somewhere in London to keep a watch on the proposed targets?' pitched in Elliot.

'Again a possibility, but we're really just clutching at straws, we need to come up with something more substantial, and fast.'

For a few more minutes they continued to bounce ideas off each other in the hope that something might clarify itself. This procedure was a common enough occurrence in the Special Operations room, ping-pong they called it in the Squad, and the system had a remarkably high success rate.

As they continued their verbal exchanges, Birbeck returned

back from Downing Street and slipped unnoticed into the Special Operations room where he stood, leaning against a government issue grey filing cabinet, listening to the, thus far, fruitless discussion. Suddenly, the others were aware the Commander had joined them.

'Well?' he asked quietly.
'It's him all right.' smiled Maitland in reply.
'Has it been issued to the media?'
'Lunchtime news broadcasts, this evenings newspapers and tomorrows nationals.'
'Good, and the tapes?' Birbeck nodded towards the cassettes.
'We've been through them, but they don't throw any great beams of light on our situation,' replied Maitland, also outlining the mysterious topic of the Fox.

Birbeck raised his right eyebrow and looked at Elliot.

'You must be Colm Elliot,' he offered his hand.
'Pleased to meet you Commander.' he replied accepting the handshake. 'Pity it's not under better circumstances.'
'Indeed.'
'What's the downside of us hauling McCormack in?' asked Maitland to Elliot.
'Hard to say, could frighten off the Blaneys. But I'd love to get my hands on the old bugger before too long, or worse still happens and he dies on us.'
'What do you mean?' asked Birbeck somewhat bemused.
'Lung cancer. Rapid deterioration according to his doctor.'
'In that case,' began Birbeck, 'I think that you should go back and carry out as much questioning as possible. I'll speak to Peter Rowe of the SAS, and your own boss Bradley, get them to get McCormack to Lisburn for your return. Report direct to me.'

Elliot said his goodbyes, and from the outer office took his overnight bag and headed for the airport. Waste of time packing his frigging bags had been.

Back in the Operations room, Birbeck turned to Piers.

'How did our little friend in Northwood react to the photograph?'

'Upset her a little, but made me promise that I would help you nail the bastard.'

'Understandable reaction I suppose. I hope that you were confident enough to promise.'

'Of course,' replied Piers and Birbeck smiled and headed towards his office to phone Rowe and Bradley.

Shortly after two pm a note addressed to Commander Birbeck was discovered in the mailroom of the Daily Express offices in Fleet Street. A special motor cycle messenger carried it to New Scotland Yard, and Birbeck tore it open and was reading the contents at exactly two-twenty.

The information that it held was now less of a mystery, the terrorists had known in advance that the Irish Prime Minister was going to be in London that morning. The mole mentioned by the Irish Prime Minister, was well informed. Such a security leak would normally have made Birbeck furious and put him into a terrible rage, but this time they could make it work to their own advantage.

The interview room was deathly silent when Elliot arrived. McCormack lay spread on the floor having obviously collapsed from his chair. The young policeman who had been on guard while awaiting Elliot's arrival was leaning over the sick old man and he looked up at Elliot, shock obvious on his face.

'What happened for Chris sake?' screamed Elliot.
'He just clutched his chest and fell over Sir.' offered the constable.
'Had he complained of any pains?'
'No Sir.'
'Do you know if the doctor is in the building?' asked Elliot, realising that there was no point venting his anger on the young constable.

'I'll go and see if I can find him.' offered the PC.
'No, you stay here, I'll go.'

Elliot rushed from the interview room in the basement of the building and headed for the elevator.

Moments later, he was in Bradley's office and pulling the door shut with a bang. Bradley looked shocked at Elliot's obvious anger, and the other man in the office, whom Elliot instantly recognized as Rowe the SAS Chief, stood and offered his hand towards Colm.

'Pleased to meet you Elliot,' he began.
'Who brought McCormack in?' stormed Elliot, ignoring the offer of a handshake.
'Two of my men.' announced Rowe, annoyed at the rebuff.
'Did they allow a doctor to see him?'
'Well no, I didn't think that it was necessary at this juncture.'
'Well it's bloody necessary now.' fumed Elliot, looking at Bradley who was still stunned at his young colleague's outburst.
'Explain yourself.' demanded Bradley moving from behind his desk to face Elliot.
'I've come straight from the basement where McCormack has just collapsed and looks to be on his way out.'
'Oh fuck!' groaned Bradley turning to lift his phone. 'I'll get an ambulance here immediately.
'I dare say the press will have another field day of this,' sighed Rowe, 'I mean to say it is a possibility that this man could die in police custody.' he was remaining calm, as he always did under difficult circumstances.
' You should know Sir, surely your men knew just how ill McCormack was before they charged to Treeacre to pick him up?'
'Well, I can only say that they were fully briefed and that he was reported to be okay on arrival, so I would advise some caution in your assumptions Sergeant.'
'Jesus.' Muttered Elliot, leaving the room. Bradley called him back.
'Where are you going Colm?'

'To phone Birbeck, collect Anderson and go over to Treeacre. No use me sitting about here all day on my fanny, now that our man is out for the count.'

'I'll call London. You get over there, but keep in touch.' Elliot nodded and turned again to Rowe.

'Any word on the Blaney boys?' He asked, and when Rowe shook his head, he muttered to himself once more, pulled the door shut with a bang and headed for his office in a terrible fury.

To most of the population of the UK, the remainder of Sunday the 1st of November would pass without much incident. Colour supplements were read; television films watched; love was made; children prepared homework for school the next day; dogs were walked; beer was drunk; the list of domesticity endless.

For a few men however, the situation was getting out of hand. Birbeck, for example, was even angrier than before following the news from Ulster, and due to an automobile breakdown on a remote country road, it was just before midnight when Elliot and Anderson arrived at the gates of Treeacre Farm.

Monday 2 November 1981

13

The dial clicked and Elliot held his breath as Anderson pulled the tubular handle on the small silver door of the safe. It seemed like ages before it opened to reveal the contents.

Anderson lifted out some bundles of five-pound notes and handed them over his shoulder to Elliot. This was followed by some rather expensive looking jewellery in a black velvet lined box, and finally by the folder containing the notes on the killers.

'That's the lot Colm.' stated Anderson turning to look at Elliot who was by this time opening the folder. His expression changed with instant horror as he read.
'Jesus Christ, you should read this,' announced Elliot letting out a long slow whistle.
'What does it say?' asked Anderson now looking over Elliot's shoulder.
'It's a complete biography on each of the three faces, plus one that we have missed so far. And if this is even half accurate, then who we are dealing with here are perhaps four of the most wanted men in the western world.'
Anderson was reading quickly and coming to the same conclusion.
'No bloody wonder the Squad have come up with no leads on these bastards so far, they could hunt them for years.' Added Anderson.
'Only if they know that we know who they are,' began Elliot closing the folder and heading for the door.

'Let's get back to HQ. It's my guess that if this lot are plastered all over tomorrows papers then we'll never see them again.'

'Today's newspapers' corrected Anderson.

'What?'

'Today's newspapers. It's almost one am. The early editions will already be on their way to the distribution points.' He explained and Elliot stopped in his tracks.

'You're right of course. I better ring Birbeck now, he'll reckon that we've wasted enough bloody time already.' Colm crossed the room, picked up the receiver and began dialing London.

'I've always said that bloody British Leyland would be the ruination of this country.' He said without humour while awaiting his connection.

'What?'

'Well if that shitty car hadn't packed in on us, we would have been here two or three hours ago.'

Anderson simply nodded and slumped into a leather chair, remembering that he had wanted to crack the safe days ago. Such was life.

Later that morning, Joseph Blaney lay in the small uncomfortable bed with the feeling that the walls were closing in about him, threatening to squash him to a pulp. The sound of snoring from the farmer who lay in another narrow bed only feet way was also beginning to drive him wild.

The small room in which they lay was the only bedroom in a small cottage on the small L shaped island of Rathlin which lay some eight miles off the coast of County Antrim in Northern Ireland. Liam had promised to get him out of the country as soon as possible, but the bastards were after him too, and that made things a little more difficult to organize.

The sound of the farmer snoring next to him was beginning to drive him mad, it had become unbearable. He had found the man, crude, dirty, illiterate with no powers of conversation at all. Taking all things into consideration, he thought the farmer to be nothing but a boring shithouse and resented having to live under the same roof. Blaney decided to teach him a lesson, and what was to follow could at best be described as farcical and, at worst, as tragic.

Rising quietly from his bed, Blaney crossed the bare wooden floor to an old chest of drawers on which sat a large bowl of icy cold water. Blaney tried lifting the bowl but decided against it, it was too heavy. Instead, he simply lifted a small drinking glass and filled it quietly from the bowl.

Crossing the room he stood over the farmer who was still snoring as loudly and as annoyingly as ever. Raising the glass above the man's head, he poured the water over his sleeping face.

The farmer reacted in a shocking way, drawing a pistol that Blaney had never seen before from under his pillow. Blaney was absolutely speechless as the man took aim and fired directly at Blaney. He wanted to shout and tell him that it had all been a sick joke, but the words would just not come.

He felt the bullet rip into his side and stumbled against the chest of drawers, the farmer was now getting out of bed and coming towards him, his gun at the ready. Suddenly however, he slipped and stumbled and as he fell Blaney saw him take aim. Reaching for the water bowl, Blaney called upon resources of strength he was not sure he had, lifted the bowl and crashed it down upon the head of the falling man.

The crunching sound of the skull being smashed open was sickening and as the farmer fell to the floor the pistol cracked and Blaney felt a second bullet ripping into the top of his right leg.

For a long time he sat slumped against a wall, his blood flowing from his wounded body. As he thought over what had occurred, it brought a smile to his face, it had been that stupid. The horrible sight of the dead man's brain seeping from his smashed skull soon removed his smile. He was, he concluded, in deep shit!

Slowly and painfully he dragged himself to the sitting room. There was only one avenue of hope open to him and that was Liam, but he would not be able to get help to him that quickly, perhaps not quickly enough. Positioning himself beside the telephone, he ribbed off his pyjama trousers and began trying to stop his blood from running away. Even if he did get through to Liam, it was fair to reckon that it could well be too late to stop him bleeding to death. All in all, he thought as he began dialing, he wished that he had left the bastard to snore in peace.

The six o'clock news had many important people listening to it that morning. One of them was the British Prime Minister who was already up and at her desk preparing for her daily business. Renowned as someone who could survive on four hours sleep, she had reduced that by an hour but was still ready for the day.

The news, as it turned out, was to carry nothing of any great significance and it was some five minutes later when what she had been hoping for came through via her first telephone call of the day from New Scotland Yard.

The Prime Minister listened intently to what was being said while drinking her first cup of coffee of the day as Birbeck informed her of the folder discovery and the serious state of McCormack's health. Later in the conversation she was angry to hear that there had been no progress on the hunt for the Blaney brothers and after listening to Birbeck at some length, put a call through to Ulster.

Major General Rowe was then told in no uncertain terms that the Prime Minister wanted the Blaney brothers in custody by the end of the day. It was indeed an order that Rowe did not relish and was, in fact, one that he would be unable to carry out.

Liam Blaney consulted his Rolex. It was just after six but it was too much of a coincidence to ignore the possibility that it may just be an emergency call. Leaning out of bed, he lifted the receiver.
'Liam?' came the weak yet unmistakable voice.

'Joseph, what's the matter?' he asked, alarm bells sounding in his mind.

'I've been shot and I'm not sure that I am going to pull through this one.' Came the painfully quiet reply.

'Jesus, Joseph how did it happen?'

'Can't go into detail now, not got the strength. Wouldn't mind a doctor though.'

'You still on the island?'

'Yeah, tucked up in the safe house.' mocked Joseph.

'I'll be there in a couple to three hours with a doctor, we'll get you patched up and back to the mainland.' announced Liam, hoping that he did not sound as panic stricken as he felt.

'Don't waste any time Liam, I've lost a lot of blood.'

'Don't move Joseph and try to stop the blood flow.'

'I've done all that, just get here for Christ's sake. I'm dying.' It was obviously the plea of a desperate man.

Liam Blaney replaced the receiver, jumped from his bed and ran to the next bedroom to wake Frank Cotton.

Cotton was sent to fetch one of their republican doctors while Blaney ate some breakfast and thought about the journey. It would take the best part of two hours to get to the coast and then he would need a vessel. For the first time in many years he began to utter prayers that had once been so familiar to him. Realising the absolute hypocrisy, he stopped and waited impatiently for the return of Cotton and the doctor.

Half an hour later, they were heading at speed in a nondescript Vauxhall through the beautifully quiet Ulster countryside. As usual Cotton drove while a hung-over, whiskey-loving doctor occupied the second rear seat next to Blaney who was looking in horror at the front page of the Daily Mail. A large photograph of Spencer was emblazoned across the newspaper, followed by a plea for information. A gut wrenching nausea grabbed Blaney, his body was telling him that things were in danger of coming apart.

The car sped through the countryside and just outside a small town with its whitewashed bungalows and ever-present churches and orange hall, Blaney told Cotton to stop by a telephone box.

It was something he had hoped to keep in reserve, but he decided that the mission now depended on fooling Birbeck for as long as possible. From memory, he dialed the Commander's private number at the Yard and when he was finally connected he was silenced momentarily at the surprise of hearing the voice of his long time adversary.

'Commander Birbeck?' he eventually asked.
'Who is this?' demanded the Commander, switching on a recording machine and pressing a button that would ensure a rapid phone tracing effort by back-up staff.
'O'Connell.' Replied Blaney, giving the name with which all the previous notes had been signed.
'What can I do for you?'
'I've got a message for you and I will not repeat it because I am in no doubt that you will be recording this conversation.'
'Suggest that you just get on with the message in that case.' Urged Birbeck, realising that it would have been pointless to deny what was, frankly, so obvious.
'Well I want you to know that your Government has only forty-eight hours to comply with our original demands. Remember, forty-eight hours, no extension will be given. After that, the killings will re-commence. I also know that the Irish Prime Minister was in London yesterday and that he will be back again next week, so this time make sure that there is no delay, no trying to pull the wool over our eyes. You may think that you are clever getting onto that stupid big American bastard, but you had better believe me when I say that we've got far better men than him deployed on this mission.'
'Oh you mean Messrs Miller, O'Neil and De Ville?' interrupted Birbeck, realising that he was taking a risk. Blaney's reaction convinced him that his gamble had achieved the desired effect.
'Remember, forty-eight hours, you smart arsed British bastard!'

Blaney slammed the phone down and headed for the car congratulating himself on his performance, he too convinced that his gamble had paid off.

'Remember, forty-eight hours, you smart arsed British bastard!' Birbeck's assistant walked across the room and switched off the tape machine. John Birbeck looked at Ian Maitland and raised his eyebrows as if to invite comment.

'What do you think then Ian?'

'There is no doubt in my mind that that was Liam Blaney, but why the hell did he bother?' It was a point that was annoying them both. Why indeed had Blaney decided that there was a need to call? Surely he knew that silence could be worse than an ultimatum in circumstances such as these. This ultimatum, experience was telling Birbeck and Maitland, was a sign of desperation.

'It's not the only point about this case that annoys me,' continued Maitland, 'for example, McCormack had a habit of going out to make telephone calls, what does that suggest to you?'

'That he knew that his own telephone was bugged.' concluded Birbeck.

'And if he knew that it was bugged, then he must also have known that he was under surveillance.' he continued.

'Exactly what I've been thinking.' They fell into a thoughtful silence for a few moments, and it was Birbeck who spoke next.

'Anyway Ian, it's no use speculating, we better get these names and their mug shots distributed nationwide. Has Elliot arrived yet?' Maitland looked at his watch.

'He should be here any minute now.'

'Good.'

Just then, the internal phone on Birbeck's desk buzzed and he picked up the receiver. After a series of nothing but 'yes' answers, he made a note on a pad in front of him and hung up.

'The call has been traced to a public telephone booth in north Antrim.'

'The town or the county?'

'The north of the county.'

'Well at least that's something.'

'Indeed, I better call Peter Rowe, he can get some of his men onto it.' He lifted the receiver and Maitland left, heading for the Operations room.

As he passed the elevator, the doors slid open and Elliot stepped out carrying his briefcase and an overnight bag, accompanied by a large uniformed constable.

'Good morning Sir.' he greeted Maitland with a ribald smile.

'Ah, Elliot, just the man.' they walked together towards the Operations room and on the way Maitland told Elliot of the call from Blaney, leaving the constable to return to his duties. Elliot rubbed his unshaven face with two fingers, his mind working overtime. Suddenly something clicked in his mind.

'Sir, I think I know where he is heading.' he suddenly announced.

'What? Or rather where?' asked Maitland surprised, and they stood facing one another at the door of the Ops room.

'Do you remember on one of the tapes we listened to the last time I was in London? Blaney spoke to McCormack of having sent Joseph to the island?'

'Yes, but we all agreed that it could be one of a hundred off the Irish coast.' recalled Maitland.

'Agreed, but off the north Antrim coast there is only Rathlin Island.'

'Rathlin?'

'Yes, local folklore has it that there is a cave on Rathlin where Robert the Bruce watched the spider before returning to Scotland to beat the English Army at the Battle of Bannockburn.'

'If he is there, there could be more than just a passing coincidence.' mused Maitland.

'The island has a small population these days of course, but there are plenty of places for someone to hold up.'

Maitland pushed open the door to the Operations room and led Elliot in.

'Come on, show me the place on the map.'

Barry Piers was in the room and stood to join them by the map.

'Now,' asked Elliot, 'where exactly was the call made from?'

'I don't know the name of the town, but if you wait I'll go and ask the Commander.'

While Maitland was gone, Elliot gave Piers a brief rundown and moments later Maitland returned.

'A town called Ballygowan, just south of Bushmills.' he advised the small group.

Elliot consulted the map, as a member of the Northern Ireland security forces, he knew exactly where Ballygowan was and stuck a red drawing pin into the map over the town.

'It's my bet that he's heading for Ballycastle. From there, he can quite easily get a boat to Rathlin.'

'How long would it take him to get there?' asked Maitland.

'Well some of the roads are pretty narrow but he won't have any problems with security, it's not really a troubled area, so it's my estimate that he could reach Ballycastle in under an hour.'

Maitland looked at this watch before concluding.

' If that's right, he should be there in about half an hour.'

' In that case, I think an army chopper to Ballycastle is called for. ' Elliot went to make the necessary call, leaving Maitland and Piers hoping to God that he was right.

People were scurrying about in the early morning rain as they headed to, or home from, work. Kathy Drinkwater entered the small newsagents where she bought two pints of milk, some bread and a Daily Express, all of which she bundled into her shopping bag.

Spencer was dressed in jeans and a t-shirt when she entered the flat and the kettle was about to boil for the morning coffee. He closed the gap between them and kissed her gently on the lips.

Kathy gave him a loving smile and went into the small kitchen table where she began to empty the contents of her shopping bag. The newspaper spread open in front of her and she stared in horror at the face of her new lover. Spencer came up behind her and slipped his hands under her arms and felt her breasts. He then noticed the article that Kathy was reading and began to panic. Kathy turned towards him and spoke very quietly, her facing having gone a deathly pale.

'It's you isn't it?'

'It sure as hell looks like me honey,' he shrugged, trying to gain control of the situation.

'You bastard.' she screamed, breaking away from him.

'Kathy it must be a mistake,' he followed her, but she had picked up a bread knife and pointed it at him.

'You had better get out of here,' she announced in a tone that was more controlled than she felt.

'It's a mistake.' he pleaded, moving towards her.

'Stay away, I will use this if I have to.' With that she slashed the air between them with the knife, as if to prove her point. 'It's no mistake, the police are even looking for a car like mine and that is too much of a coincidence, wouldn't you say?'

'Kathy please,' he tried again suddenly aware of the sad fact that he was going to have to kill her. The situation however, was not entirely under his control.

'Get out of my flat.' she screamed loudly at the American.

'Okay, okay, I will go, just give me two minutes to get my things together.' As he turned he saw the knife waver in front of her and he sprang cat-like towards her, knocking her off balance. The knife fell to the floor and Kathy Drinkwater gave another scream that was half-stifled by his hand as he covered her mouth.

Spencer's left forearm locked around her neck while his right hand remained over her mouth. In a last gasp attempt to save her young life, Kathy bit his hand with all her might, forcing Spencer to release his grip on her for a fraction of a second. It was just enough to allow her to turn and force her right knee into his groin. Spencer fought to overcome the terrible sickening pain from the blow and struck her across the side of her head in sheer anger with a clenched fist, causing her to fall in a stagger across the floor, bumping her head against the cooker as she fell. Spencer closed the gap between them and wrapped both hands around her throat, holding her down with the aid of a knee in her midriff.

Moments later, Kathy Drinkwater lay dead on the kitchen floor while Spencer looked in amazement at the front page of the Daily Express. How could it be? He then came to the conclusion that all four of them had been set up, perhaps only three of them. But why? What was he to do? To begin with, he had to get out of the flat fast. Kathy's father would no doubt see the picture and the police would come to see the girl.

It was a disaster, but a plan began to formulate in his mind.

Cotton drove the car with his usual effortless ease into Ballycastle, down Market Street, left into Ann Street and down towards the seafront. On a clear day it was possible to see Scotland from Ballycastle, but this was not one of those days.

Blaney looked with some disgust at the empty site where once had stood the fine white building of the Marine Hotel. It has been raised to the ground after a series of bombs had exploded in the bedrooms. The very idea of such an act had made both the insurance company who had paid out the claim and Blaney extremely sceptical. Indeed, he had stayed in the hotel many years ago while enjoying a rare holiday playing the beautifully peaceful local golf courses such as Royal Portrush and Ballycastle. Things had changed quite dramatically since then, and both he and Ballycastle carried the scars to prove it.

On the drive up to the coast Blaney had told Cotton of his need for a boat to take them all to Rathlin and accordingly the large man parked the car in the harbour car park and went in search of a local boat owner willing to rent his craft for the day.

As he and the doctor sat in silence in the car awaiting Cotton's return, Blaney noticed that it was beginning to rain quite heavily and that his cashmere cardigan was hardly ideal clothing for a boat journey. Still, he had no time to spare and thought catching a cold was a fair exchange for saving Joseph's life.

Moments later Cotton came bounding across the car park and jumped into the drivers seat.

'Well?' enquired Blaney.
'We're in luck Mr. Blaney, there is a man down by the harbour who has a small cabin cruiser tied out in the bay, you can just see it from here.' began Cotton, pointing towards a small, white boat that was bobbing up and down in the sea some three or four hundred yards in front of them. Blaney nodded, and Cotton continued.
'He says that we can have it for the day providing that we pay in advance, and give him a returnable deposit.'
'That sounds fair enough, but how do we get out there?'
'He says that he will row us out and go over the controls.'
'Good,' said Blaney, nodding at the ever-silent doctor and pushing open the car door. 'Let's go.'

The telephone call anticipated by Spencer from Kathy Drinkwater's father went through the normal channels at New Scotland Yard, and some fifteen minutes later Maitland, Detective Inspector Paterson and Barry Piers were blazing a trail through the streets of south London towards Kathy's flat.

The back-up team handling incoming calls from the public were expert at picking out those useful messages that so often led to an arrest, from those which came from cranks who had nothing better to do than to make hoax calls to the emergency services. The call from the motel owner had been considered 'hot' on two accounts, namely that the American had signed the motel register in the name of Spencer and that the motel owner's daughter, who had been friendly with the American, happened to drive an MGB.

Two police patrol cars were parked about a hundred yards along the street from the block, which contained the girl's flat, when

Maitland and company arrived. A uniformed Inspector seeing Maitland arrive, walked to the car and informed him that the area had been sealed off and that police marksmen were on their way. Just then, a navy blue Fort Transit pulled up alongside one of the patrol cars and six policemen carrying rifles and wearing protective headgear and bulletproof vests began clambering out.

Within minutes of their arrival, the armed policemen were discreetly in place along the street with excellent views of the two entrances to the block of flats.

It was on old building, a converted town house so common in that part of London, and if Maitland's information was correct, Kathy Drinkwater's home was the only one on the first floor.

Moments later, Maitland and Paterson left the group gathered around the vehicles and began walking slowly along the street towards the block in which the girl lived. Casually, they both ascended the short flight of steps to the main door of the block, which, rather fortunately, stood open. Paterson asked over a discretely placed radio set if there was any sign of movement from within the house and was simply told 'negative' in reply.

Inside the house, the stairs were not carpeted and creaked as they climbed. Paterson led the way, his pistol held firmly in his left hand. Eventually, they reached a white doorway upon which there was sellotaped a hand written note saying 'Drinkwater'. The only lock on the door was a rather innocuous Yale, and Paterson pulled a skeleton key from his pocket and slipped it silently into the keyhole without difficulty.

Seconds later, they were inside the flat and moving with expert efficiency from room to room, covering each other as they ducked through each doorway. In the kitchen, they discovered that they were too late.

Major General Peter Rowe arrived in Ballycastle along with two supporting armoured vehicles only seconds after the boat carrying Blaney, Cotton and the doctor disappeared around the Bay. From Ballygowan, where a local man had told of seeing a man return to a blue Vauxhall Chevette after making a telephone call before being driven through the town at speed, it had taken Rowe and his travelling companions only forty minutes to get to Ballycastle.

In the harbour car park he found the blue Chevette and dispersed some of his men to the harbour to enquire about any recent boat movements. One of them went down a short slope to the narrow boat slip and stood waiting for a man who was rowing a boat in from the Bay.

'Good morning sir,' said the soldier, trying to sound friendly as the man waded ashore, pulling his boat behind him.
'What's good about it?' asked the man, looking up at the misty rain clouds.
'I'm looking for this man,' began the soldier moving onto the wet sand to confront the man with a photograph of Liam Blaney. The man gave the photograph a brief glance and went back to tethering his boat.
'What would you be looking for him for?' asked the man eventually without looking at the soldier.
'He is wanted in connection with a murder, a very serious murder.' stated the soldier.
'Sure I am thinking that all murder is serious to the person who gets killed.' laughed the man, and the soldier had to agree that it had been a bit of a stupid statement.
'Whatever, he is still a wanted criminal.'
'You don't say.' scoffed the man, thinking that he was about to pocket a very hefty returnable deposit.
'Yes, I do say.' countered the soldier who was beginning to run out of patience with the man. It was always the same, no matter what side they were on, they hated the soldiers.
'And what would you be doin' to him when you get him?' asked the man, turning his full attention on the soldier, obviously happy that his boat was secure.

'Take him into custody.' replied the soldier. The man looked at the rifle the soldier was carrying.

'Why?' asked the soldier, losing interest.

'Well I just hope that there will be no shootin'.'

'Why do you say that?'

'Because that there man in the photograph has just hired my friggin' boat.' replied the man raising his voice slightly.

'Jesus Christ, why didn't you say so in the beginning?' The soldier looked up towards the harbour wall and saw Rowe looking down at him. 'What kind of boat is it?'

'A cabin cruiser.'

'Did he say where he was heading?' asked the soldier finally.

'Aye, he did that.'

'Then where is he heading, for fuck sake?'

'The three of them are heading for Rathlin, and in my lovely boat they should be halfway there by now.'

'Don't worry old man, you'll get your boat back.' The soldier turned and began to run up the slope towards the car park, leaving the man as he raised his cap and scratched his head in bemusement.

Rowe took the news quietly and even allowed himself a half-smile. He had not enjoyed his telephone conversation with the Prime Minister that morning, but at least he would now be able to give her what she wanted.

'Okay, re-group back here, there is nothing we can do until the chopper arrives.'

'Yes Sir,' said the soldier, rushing off to follow his orders, and with that the drone of an Army helicopter could be heard in the distance.

As the aircraft hovered above the harbour car park some minutes later, locals, shopkeepers and shoppers alike left their houses and shops to see what was happening. When they saw the uniforms however, they returned to their business, they had seen it all before.

The girl's death brought the tally for the current campaign to three murders, and that was not a fact digested too well by Commander Birbeck. Three terrorist killings within his direct domain, were three too many. The Prime Minister had not been terribly impressed when he had told her the news either. It was on occasions such as these that retirement loomed up as something to look forward to.

There was a tentative knock on his office door, and Ian Maitland entered, looking extremely grim.

'This is becoming a very bad business Ian, we had better come up with something soon, the PM is on my back like never before.' began Birbeck, hardly giving his friend time to reach his desk.
'And I'm afraid that it's getting worse John,' suggested Maitland as he nervously handed a slip of paper to his boss. 'That just came through.'
Birbeck took it and read it, more than once judging by the length of time that it took him to comment on the latest news.
'Jesus.' he said finally, throwing the piece of paper into a wastepaper bin beside his desk.
It had simply stated that John McCormack had died in hospital earlier that morning.

Despite the noise from the engine of the cabin cruiser, Liam Blaney and two traveling companions were fully aware of the sound of the helicopter as it sped over their heads in, what appeared to be, the same direction in which they were heading. Overall visibility had become very poor and, as a consequence, as all three looked skyward, all they got was a brief glimpse of the aircraft.
'Routine chopper,' suggested Cotton less than confidently, but Blaney did not reply, he rarely spoke to Cotton unless to give orders and this was not the time to change the conditions of the big man's employment. Blaney's mind however, was working overtime. Cotton may have been right but, under these grave circumstances, he could not afford to take the risk and instructed Cotton to take the wheel while he lifted a map of the area supplied by the boat owner and found a seat below deck. The living accommodation on the boat was fairly cramped, but it was surprisingly dry and comfortable.

The mist that now enveloped them could lift just as easily as it had arrived, so he decided to act on his intuition while he had the foggy protection. It was highly unlikely, he concluded, that the people in the helicopter would be looking for him. Yet, if they were, he would be sailing into Rathlin Island and into their welcoming arms. From the map, he picked out the exact point at which he would leave the boat. He had always been a strong swimmer and reckoned that, despite the cold and time of year, he could swim ashore fully clothed without difficulty. From his landing point he could reach Joseph in less than half an hour on foot. It was risky, but for his brother's sake, he needed to stay in the game.

Back on deck, he told Cotton of his part in the plan. The doctor and he would go into Church Bay in the boat and if the Army were there they were to head back to the mainland, keeping the Army in pursuit for as long as possible. Losing the doctor was one part of his plan that he regretted, but someone had to be sure of getting to Joseph. Cotton simply nodded his approval, believing that he would see his employer at the cottage.

The helicopter put Rowe and five of his men down in a field just north of Church Bay, Rathlin Island, a few minutes later. If his calculations were correct, Rowe expected the boat to enter the Bay in about five minutes time. He therefore led his men away from the helicopter, hoping that the aircraft was suitably hidden, and towards the Bay to await his prize.

Blaney was shocked at the coldness of the water but managed to pull himself together long enough to wave Cotton on towards the Bay. There was no time for them to hang about because, if the Army were on Rathlin they would become suspicious with any delay in the boats arrival, and that might mean the island being searched. On the other hand, if they were forced to chase the boat, then their attention would be diverted.

Turning his own attention back towards his swim ashore, Blaney was surprised to see that the rocky shore had in fact got further away.

The current was obviously much stronger than he had anticipated. Concentrating all his effort on his freestyle, he began to make slow but positive progress.

Despite the fact that Rowe had positioned himself and his men discreetly about the small harbour, Cotton caught a glimpse of what he thought to be a helicopter rotary blade and his instinct for survival forced him, against his will, to turn the boat in the Bay and accelerate out at full speed. Rowe and his men remained motionless for a few seconds, finding it difficult to comprehend what they had just seen. Moments later however, they were running towards the aircraft, inside which the pilot, seeing them approach, began the engines.

Tiring fast, Blaney was only some fifty yards from the shore when the boat carrying Cotton and the doctor appeared out of nowhere and all but struck him head on. The energy dissipated in avoiding the boat would have been better used in his attempt to reach the shore and when he recovered from his near-miss, he realised that he was just about as far from the shore as when he had started his foolhardy swim. This time however, he was not convinced that he had the strength to make it, and began to panic.

The train began to slow down as it moved through the town of Folkstone towards the docks. Spencer rose from his seat and from an overhead rack grabbed his rucksack. The train had not been too busy and nobody in his carriage took much notice of him. Of his appearance, there was perhaps only one aspect that worried him unduly and that was simply his height. Otherwise, with a small woolen hat covering his hair, steel-rimmed spectacles, anorak, jeans and hiking boots, he looked like a tree-hugging academic.

Getting into France was going to be another story, but he planned to tackle that problem in the morning. The train finally bumped to a stop and he clambered off and began walking towards the ticket barrier. There, a uniformed policeman was busy looking at the arrivals as they presented their tickets. Spencer looked about him and was pleased to see a young student type girl walking behind him dressed in a fashion similar to his own. Slowing down he let her catch him up and spoke to her quietly.

'You a student?' he asked, trying to give the impression to anybody who might be watching that they were together.
'No.' replied the girl curtly.
'Sorry, I just thought,' continued Spencer desperate to conceal his accent whilst indicating the girl's clothing.
'That's all right, I suppose I do look a little 'studentish' today,' she said, 'but I am afraid I just work in Boots, I've been on a trekking holiday in Scotland.' They reached the barrier and Spencer could feel the policeman looking at him, but he fought to stay calm.
'That sounds interesting.' he continued, his ticket was collected and they walked towards the exit.
'Oh it was, the scenery is so beautiful up there.' enthused the girl who seemed to be looking around for someone.
'Well it's been nice talking to you.' said Spencer casting a backward glance at the policeman who had lost interest in him and was surveying a final group of people waiting to surrender their tickets.

It was a cold afternoon as he left the station, but he felt happy at getting over the first hurdle. Of course, the morning would bring the real test, but for now he had to find somewhere to spend the night.

With the visibility becoming increasingly poor, the sea search for Liam Blaney around the north Antrim coast was called off just after four pm that afternoon.

Cotton and the doctor had eventually ran out of fuel and had been towed into Portstewart harbour under arrest.

The land search for Blaney continued however, with Rowe instructing that all the houses on Rathlin Island be searched in the event that he had managed to swim ashore. It was just before six o'clock that evening when the bodies of Joseph Blaney and his host were found in one of the last houses to be searched .

'The search will be stepped up in the morning of course, but at the moment Rowe believes that it may be the case that both the Blaney brothers may have died today.' The Prime Minister looked at Birbeck for a few moments before asking.

'And what has become of this American fellow?'

'We have nothing fresh to go on as yet Prime Minister but there is simply no way through which he can leave the country. All air and sea routes have been closed as tightly as humanly possible.' offered Birbeck less than confidently.

'Mmm' began the Prime Minister standing up and walking to the windows that had attracted the Irish Prime Minister the previous day. Birbeck wondered if this was magical glass where pilgrim Prime Ministers came to clarify their thoughts. It was an interesting theory and he afforded himself a slight smile at the silliness of it.

'I don't like it, not one little bit. How can these people be in England without being seen?' the mere thought seemed totally unreasonable to the Prime Minister.

'These are experts, probably four of the best men in their field in the world. They wouldn't even stand out in a crowd of two.' offered the Commander.

'Then why did they allow themselves to be photographed and plastered over every bleeding newspaper in Europe?' asked the Prime Minister, returning to her seat and looking straight at Birbeck.

'That is something that is confusing me and my colleagues, I must admit that it does not conform to the sort of behaviour that we would expect from such people, they should have known better.'

'Perhaps it is a good job that they did slip up.' interjected the Prime Minister, 'Or we would all be running about silly with worry, wondering if there would be enough Ministers left alive for me to form a Cabinet. And can you imagine how difficult it would have been to trace these people without the photographs?'

'It's proving difficult enough with them.' Birbeck nodded in agreement.

'So we must thank our lucky stars that they have slipped up.

They have done it once, perhaps they will do it again.' concluded the Prime Minister once again rising from her seat.

'We can only hope that they do.' agreed the Commander, realising that their meeting had reached its end.

'Well,' began the Prime Minister, 'I have business to attend to, and a very full schedule tomorrow, but please keep me updated as things progress.'

'I will do Prime Minister.' Replied Birbeck, standing to take his leave. His movement however, was a little slower than usual and the ever-alert Prime Minister noticed this and asked.

'Is there something else Commander?'

'I was just wondering what we shall do with these people when we catch them,' he began, wondering whether it would have been more prudent to say 'if we catch them'.

' I suppose that will depend on the circumstances.' She began, before continuing carefully ' But I personally find it hard to imagine the damage that all the media attention a public trial would cause. Bit of a sticky problem I would say, what about you Commander Birbeck ?'

'Very hard to imagine Prime Minister.' Replied Birbeck, hoping that he had successfully deciphered her encoded answer to his question.

The rain was falling heavily as Birbeck slipped into the rear seat of his waiting car a few minutes later. He felt exhausted, the pressure was really beginning to take its toll on him. His police driver turned to him.

'Where to Sir?'

'Take me home please.'

'To Walton Sir?'

' Please.' snapped Birbeck and as the car pulled away, he looked forward to a good night at home with his wife. Sara had her own ways of making him relax, and the very thought made him feel better already.

Tuesday 3 November 1981

14

It was just after ten past seven the following morning when Bill Turnbull received a call from the father of the girl who had sold the gas cylinder to Miller. At first Turnbull had difficulty in working out what the man was telling him and then it began to make sense. Reaching over his desk, he picked up a copy of the Sun newspaper and opened it at page three. There, to the right of the usual topless beauty, were the photographs of the four men wanted by the Anti-Terrorist Squad in connection with the Piers assassination. Turnbull scratched his head and thought for a few moments before speaking into the phone.

'What you're saying is that one of these men is the Mister Smith that your daughter sold the gas to?' He asked, trying to contain his excitement.

'She is absolutely convinced that it is Miller, the one pictured top right of the group.' Announced the man proudly.

'Well,' said Turnbull finally, 'that is certainly great news, thank you very much for calling.'

'It's a right pleasure Sir.'

'Oh, and by the way, thank your daughter very much for me.'

'I will do.' and the phone went dead.

Turnbull studied the photograph of Miller for a few moments. He did in fact fit the girl's description very closely. It was also perfectly conceivable that these men would have tried to find somewhere as quiet as possible to hide themselves away, and the killing at the farm had been an extremely thorough job.

He considered what to do next. If he contacted the Yard, he would end up with an unsolved murder file, because it was quite unlikely that, even if caught, these people would ever be brought to trial in an open court. It was something of a dilemma for him, and then he remembered his old friend Luke Stevenson, who now worked for the Anti-Terrorist Squad in central London.

Lifting the telephone, he dialed the Yard's number from memory, and asked for Stevenson's extension number when the connection was made.

The Aer Lingus jet taxied to a halt on the runway at Gatwick Airport just after eight o'clock. Ray O'Grady followed the Irish Prime Minister down the steps from the plane and onto the tarmac and headed towards the waiting limousine, half a dozen policemen trying to keep back scores of photographers and journalists who were busy snapping shutters and directing questions at the Irish Premier.
'Martin Shaw the BBC, what is the purpose of your visit?'
'The Times, are you here to discuss possible unification?'
'The Daily Express, has the Hunger Strike altered your government's position?'
'Who called this meeting Prime Minister?'

O'Grady slipped into the back seat beside his employer and friend and the car began to make its way slowly towards the exit, a police escort moving in harmony, front and rear.

The Irish Prime Minister turned to his Private Secretary, and smiled.
'Just the sort of welcome we were hoping for Ray, wouldn't you agree?'
'Yes Doctor.' Replied O'Grady, the Irish Prime Minister had been invited, at the last minute, to attend The State Opening of the British Parliament and they would be staying over for their joint talks on Friday. O'Grady just prayed that matters would be resolved quickly.

Spencer adjusted his tartan bonnet, fiddled with the Nikon around his neck, pulled back the curtain and entered the small photographic booth. Gently he rotated the stool to its lowest point so that his head when he sat was in line with the indicated spot on the glass in front of him. Slotting forty pence into the machine, he smiled when the red warning light came on and waited for the flash.

Afterwards, he stood leaning against the outside of the booth waiting for the developed photographs to appear. His eyes were roving the departure building as he waited and he was comforted to see that there was no obvious police presence.

Photographs in hand, he carried them along with an already complete visitors pass to the desk and handed them over to the bored looking female attendant.

The girl was busy talking to one of her colleagues about a film she had seen the previous night and did not pay much attention to Spencer. The card was completed in the name of James Crawford of 32 Drummond Place, Edinburgh, and the occupation quoted was that of Civil Servant. The girl glued the photograph to the card and stamped it before handing it back to Spencer who said, in a much practiced accent, 'Ta.' The girl smiled and Spencer walked towards the departure lounge.

He had bought his ticket the previous evening and was again pleasantly surprised to see that the police were not represented at the single desk that was the customs post. The old man there glanced briefly at Spencer and said, looking at the twenty-four hour passport,
'What's the purpose of your visit?'
'Goin' over to take some photis,' replied Spencer in his newly acquired Scottish, and the man noticing the Nikon camera nodded and handed Spencer back his pass.

The departure lounge was fairly quiet and Spencer found what he was looking for in the coffee bar. There, two pretty girls sat talking in French and Spencer bought a coffee and walked to their table and asked, in French, if he could join them. The girls smiled and said that it was all right.

'You two been over on holiday?' he began.

'No,' replied one of the girls, 'we've been visiting our father. He lives and works in London for Renault.' and they both laughed at the thought that visiting their father could not be considered a holiday.

Over coffee, they talked randomly about very little although Spencer still managed to discover that the girls were returning to their mother's home in Paris, where they lived. Eventually, they were called for embarkation and Spencer walked with them towards the ticket barrier.

When they turned into a passageway some twenty yards from the ship, Spencer was shocked to see a single policeman, with an unusual pistol belt around his waist, standing by the gangplank watching everyone carefully as they went aboard the ship. For a moment he was shocked rigid and his plan was in doubt when one of the girls gave him an idea for a way out. She was commenting to her sister on how cute British policemen looked in their funny hats.

The policeman was physically checking all the passports and when it was their turn, the girls handed theirs over. Spencer stood unclipping the cover from his camera as the policeman merely glanced at the girls' passport before giving them back and it was at this point that Spencer has to take his chance. He lifted his camera and spoke to the officer who was turning his attention to the American.

'Could you hold it the now Jimmy?' he began 'the lassies would just love tae have their photis taken wi' you.' The policeman, although taken aback, simply took Spencer's pass while he motioned for the girls to strike a pose. This they did, and with the photographs taken, all three went laughing up the gangplank and onto the ship, leaving the policeman holding Spencer's newly acquired 24-hour pass.

The policeman realised that he still had the pass but he could not go running after the daft Scotsman until his partner returned from an unscheduled toilet break, so he slipped it into his pocket meantime.

Spencer and the girls found a seat in the lounge and settled down for the journey. It was a clear morning so the view from the large windows would be good. Spencer sat with what could best be described as a satisfied grin on his face, more than pleased by the way that his gamble had been rewarded. In just over an hour and a half he would be in Boulogne and safely out of the grasp of the British police.

The second policeman opened the passport and looked at the photograph while his partner told him what had happened.
'Just a stupid Scots git, if you ask me,' he concluded.
'Or that's what he wanted you to think,' began the other, taking a photograph of Spencer from an inside pocket, 'how tall was this guy?'
'Pretty tall, what are you getting at?'
'I think that this could be our American friend,' he stated, showing his colleague the similarity between the photographs.
'Jesus, you know, I think you could be right.'

Spencer was late in seeing them coming towards him with pistols drawn. Suddenly though, he was up and running, crashing through the lounge door onto the deck. Without a gun he was helpless and he knew it. He reached the bow of the ship with its nose standing open to allow trucks, cars and coaches access to the ferry. Looking out over the handrail he saw two trucks carrying bales of paper on the dockside some twenty-five feet below. He turned to see the first of the policemen crash through the lounge door, fall to the ground and shout.
'Freeze, or I'll shoot.'

With the second policeman arriving only seconds later Spencer decided that he quite simply had no option and he threw himself over the rail in the direction of the nearest of the two stationary trucks.

The very instant that his hand left the rail he knew that he was not going to make it and crashed to the cobbled ground with such force that he fell backwards and into the gap between the ship and the harbour wall.

As his feet were about to enter the water, a slight swell in the sea caused the ship to move the few feet and bump gently against the wall. The safety rubber on the bottom of the ship trapped Spencer at the bottom of his spine for all of two seconds and when the boat rolled away from the wall on another swell, he fell unconscious into the murky oily water.

The two policemen standing on the deck some fifty feet above, watched his horrible death in silence.

The sun shone on the streets of London for the first time in many days that morning, which made the job facing the large numbers of the Metropolitan Police Force seem considerably more pleasant. These were the members of the force mobilized at the command of the Met Chief Jim Townsend to throw a security blanket over the entire length of the route to be taken by the Royal Family from Buckingham Palace to the Houses of Parliament the following day. Their brief was simple, find and seal up all possible terrorist vantage points or risks within the area.

As a result, hundreds of letter boxes were emptied before being closed off to the public; plain clothes officers settled down to perhaps thirty hours rooftop duty; helicopters hovered above the area; empty houses, offices and shops were opened and checked; sewers were searched; sniffer dogs and their handlers roamed the streets; and many more duties were planned for that day to ensure maximum possible security for the British Royal Family.

Although he thought that it was extremely unlikely that a top class assassin would choose to have his home bordering the famous Wentworth golf course, Luke Stevenson decided that it was the least he could do to inform Bill Turnbull.

From the small telecoms room situated to the rear of the Special Operations room in New Scotland Yard, he walked to his own office on the same floor and dialed his friend's number.

'Bill?' he asked when put through.

'Yes,' came the reply.

'It's Luke, listen I've just taken a call from a guy who works as a barman at a golf clubhouse in Wentworth.'

'And?' asked Turnbull, getting out of his chair to reach for a note pad.

'Well this geezer claims that our friend Miller is a member of the club he works for.'

'That would hardly make sense,' commented Turnbull, 'but you had better give me the address anyway.' And when Turnbull had finished writing down the address he asked.

'How much of a start can you give me on this?'

'Not much more than half an hour I am afraid Bill.'

'That's great Luke. Remember that I owe you one.'

'Don't you worry,' said Stevenson, 'I won't let you forget.'

Turnbull walked from behind his desk and over to a large map of the south east of England. It was reckoned that Miller had never operated in his own country before, so why shouldn't he have a fine home here? Estimating that it should not take him much more than an hour to get to Wentworth, he left his office. All things considered, he should have plenty of time to reach the house before the Squad and perhaps he might even net himself a prize fish.

O'Neil had been expecting something of the sort and stood looking at the silencer barrel of De Ville's Walther. Miller stood well away from them, not saying anything, just taking in what was going on.

The three of them were in the sitting room of the house in Kenton as pre-arranged and, as expected, Spencer had not turned up.

'Well O'Neil, from what I hear on the radio it would seem that there are now only three of us involved in this half-arsed scheme, and I for one do not intend to delay my departure from this country for one minute longer.'

O'Neil stood and listened, hands deep in an oversized greatcoat and aimed the three inch barrel of his Smith and Wesson .32 at the Frenchman. He was glad that he had fitted the silencer but unhappy that he had Miller out of his immediate vision, that could make things a little tricky. Deciding to try and knock the others off their guard, he tried the softly-softly approach.

'Then why did you bother to keep this meeting?' He asked gently, 'You don't think that I am here to hold you both to your contracts?' he continued, giving one of his ice-melting smiles.

'We assumed from our meeting at the farm that you were ordered to do just that.' Miller spoke for the first time.

'That was only Blaney and McCormack making sure that you understood who was boss, but McCormack is now dead and Blaney has gone missing,' explained O'Neil, his finger tightening over the trigger of the Smith and Wesson.

'I have never heard such rubbish,' argued De Ville, and at that moment O'Neil realized that the Frenchman or Miller had no intention whatsoever of allowing him to leave the house alive. He pressed the trigger and the bullet soared through his coat and entered the Frenchman's heart.

Part two of the Irishman's plan was to sweep round and catch Miller off guard, but as he attempted to turn, the lights seemed to go out and he fell headlong onto the coffee table in front of the fire, quite dead.

Miller had to look twice at De Ville's baldhead but, getting over the shock, he headed for the door. It had been like watching two prize gunfighters meeting their exact equal in an old Wild West movie and as a result blowing each other to pieces.

Still, he was out free and nobody knew where he was going. It struck him that he actually didn't even know himself.

Holding the girl had become something of a strain, and now rumors were circulating in Dublin that Liam Blaney, like Joseph, was dead. He opened the telephone booth door and headed for his car. It was three days since he had heard from Blaney and had decided it was time to put an end to the girl's misery.

Parking his car near the woods, he took the bag containing her clothes from the boot and walked at a hurried pace to the shed and unlocked the door. The girl looked dirty and her eyes were red from lack of sleep and on seeing him, cowered deeper into her sleeping bag. It was her normal reaction and usually he would just take a Polaroid snap of her holding an up-to-date newspaper, leave some fresh food, and go.

Today however, he went to her and pulled her, without difficulty, from the small bed and motioned for her to stand in front of him. The girl's naked body caused him to hesitate for a few moments before he opened the bag and began handing her the clothes that she had been wearing when he had taken her.

Slowly and meticulously she dressed, aware of the fact that he was eyeing her body, and hating him much more than she had ever done before.

When the girl was dressed, he locked the shed and led her back through the woods to his Volvo where he bundled her into the front passenger seat, her eleven-day ordeal over.

Just over an hour later Patricia O'Grady was running up the garden path to the front door of her home and frantically ringing the front door bell.

Anna O'Grady could hardly believe her eyes and helped her sobbing daughter into the house, an enormous burden lifted from her frail shoulders. Her first thought was of her husband in London, worrying himself sick. She went to the telephone and dialed the number that Ray had given her earlier that morning.

The House at Wentworth was indeed very grand, set well back from a quiet lane in half an acre of wooded land. Architectural purists may have thought the modern building offensive, but Turnbull considered the dark glass and timber aesthetically delightful. Flicking open a wrought-iron double gate, he walked up a pebbled drive to the front of the house. It looked deserted and he began to think that he had in fact been very fortunate to stumble on something big. From his pocket, he extracted one of the ever-present king size cigarettes and lit it, taking stock of the area surrounding the house while taking heavy draws on the smoke. Climbing the immaculate stairs to the wooden main door of the house, which was painted black gloss within a glass frame, he could see into the hall with its natural brickwork walls and thick pile carpet. Pushing the front door bell, he stood for a few moments not really expecting a reply.

To his surprise however, a small lady, perhaps in her early sixties and wearing an apron, appeared in the hall and opened the door.
'Hello,' she said looking curiously at the portly police Inspector, 'what can I do for you?'
'Oh,' said Turnbull, somewhat taken aback by the human presence in the house, 'I've come to speak to Jonathan Miller. I hope I've got the right house.'
'Yes,' said the lady, 'Mr. Miller does live here.'
'Well, could I possibly have a word with him?'
'Not here I'm afraid.' stated the woman.
'Do you happen to know when he will be back?' asked Turnbull producing his identification card and showing it to the woman who seemed to take ages to read it.
'Gone abroad again I s'pose,' replied the woman, 'I just come to clean the house once a week, not that much needs cleaning in this beautiful house, but Mr. Miller does like it done regular, out of habit I s'pose, and who am I to turn down good money?' The woman stopped talking, watching in obvious disgust as Turnbull stamped out his cigarette on the doorstep. I don't suppose Mister Miller would like that, thought Turnbull sarcastically.
'Well,' he said, pulling a cutting from a newspaper, which contained a photograph of Miller from his jacket pocket. 'Could you tell me if this is your Mr. Miller?' He asked handing the woman the paper. She studied it very carefully for a few moments.

'Could be I s'pose, looks very like him I must admit,' she finally concluded, 'let me go and get my glasses just to make sure.' She turned and Turnbull followed her into the house and into an extremely large lounge with huge French windows overlooking the lush lawns of the garden and out over the fairways of the world famous golf course. White posts at the bottom of the garden indicated 'out of bounds' for wayward golfers and Turnbull speculated on where the money to buy such a beautiful home had come from.

The cleaning lady had found her spectacles and had given the photograph her fullest attention before turning to him.
'Yes, that's definitely Mr. Miller.' she announced proudly.

Turnbull could feel his heart pound. After all his years in the force, he was at last on the threshold of something gigantic.

Just then, Turnbull heard the sound of a car pull up on the pebbles outside the house followed by the slamming of a car door, which was followed by someone climbing the steps and entering the hall through the open door.

Thinking back, Miller thought that it was the most satisfactory outcome. De Ville had told him that he had formulated a plan to get them out of the country, but that Frenchman was a murderous bastard and had probably intended giving him the same treatment he had prescribed for the Irishman.

He had just turned his hire car off the main road and was heading up a private lane towards his home. There, he had all the gear necessary to get himself safely out of the country on his own, and since it could be a while before he would be able to return, he intended to make sure that all his much-loved and treasured belongings were locked safely in his strong-room beneath the swimming pool.

He had thought it very risky to get involved with those mad Irishmen. Previously, he had always insisted on not working in the UK. Greed and possibly arrogance, he decided, were the main reasons for his near-downfall and it was a lesson that he would never forget.

Approaching the house he noticed that the gates had been allowed to swing open and he swerved the car into the drive and up to the house. As he climbed the steps to the door he saw a cigarette butt on the ground, not the sort of thing that Mrs. Jones would normally tolerate. Something told him that there was something seriously wrong and as he entered the lounge, something or somebody rendered him unconscious.

Ian Maitland felt a curious pang of déjá vu as he, Elliot and Harry Paterson arrived outside the house at Wentworth. A blue police patrol car was stationed by the open gates, and another car sat in the driveway by the house. For the second time in two days, he had arrived too late and was not amused by the coincidence.

Getting out of the car, Maitland stretched before walking towards the house, showing his identification card to an unformed constable who was keeping guard at the gates, and walking up the drive towards the open door.

Inside the house, a portly man in plain clothes was talking to another rather overweight Sergeant in the hall and an old lady was sitting in a chair looking extremely shaken. The plain-clothes officer broke from his conversation with the Sergeant and turned his attention on Maitland whom he seemed to recognize.
'Detective Inspector Bill Turnbull Sir.' he began offering his hand to Maitland.
'Pleased to meet you Turnbull,' grunted Maitland, 'do you mind telling me what the hell is going on here. And, it better be good.'
'Well Sir, ' began Turnbull, in no way disturbed by Maitland's attitude, 'I've been investigating a murder on my patch and my enquiries have led me to one Jonathan Miller, whose home address this happens to be.'
'Christ Turnbull, don't play silly buggers with me, you know full well that the Squad are after Miller, you should have contacted

us,' Maitland was not as angry as he may have sounded, it was understandable that a local CID man would want to close a murder case as neatly as possible. 'And where, is your Mister Miller?' he asked finally.

'Oh, he's in the lounge Sir, handcuffed of course, and I took the precaution of binding his feet. Got a bit of a temper has our suspect.'

Maitland allowed himself a slight smile and was followed by Turnbull, Elliot and Paterson into the lounge. There, Miller sat with hands and feet bound, on an expensive looking sofa with bloodstains on his face. Maitland walked over to where Miller sat and leaned over the man and spoke in a voice that was too quiet for the others to pick up.

'Well, well, if it's not the Blond-Anglo.' Whispered Maitland and Miller gave him a cold stare that for a moment, sent shivers down his spine. Turning back to Turnbull he asked.

'What happened to him?' Noticing for the first time fragments of a porcelain vase scattered across the deep pile carpet.

'I am afraid Mr. Miller had the misfortune of walking into a vase before I had time to read him his rights.' Explained Turnbull, with just the traces of a smile on his face, and Maitland's heart lifted to the man who had so obviously been round a few blocks in his police career.

'Okay Turnbull, you've done very well here, but this is where the Anti-Terrorist Squad takes over. This man is wanted in connection with the Piers assassination.' stated Maitland but Turnbull had other ideas.

'Like hell you will, I've got a murder file to close on this bastard so I am not giving him up quite so easy.'

'Come on Turnbull,' said Maitland, putting his hand on Turnbull's shoulder and leading him away from the ears of the others and towards the large windows, 'You'll get your file closed all right, but I am under direct orders from the Prime Minister, so I must take Miller into my custody.' Turnbull knew the score and that it was pointless protesting further.

'Okay Sir, I can accept that. However, can I ask for your personal assurance that you will let me have a written statement regarding the farm murder and Miller.'

'Send me your file and I'll have a statement signed by my Commander added and returned as soon as I can.'

'Very well Sir, he's all yours.' Turnbull gave Miller one last glance before handing the handcuff keys to Maitland and leaving the house. Maitland went into the hall and dismissed the Sergeant and his men. Before returning to the lounge however, he noticed the old lady still on the same chair as when he had arrived.

'Who are you?' he asked patiently.

'Just the cleaner, but not any more I s'pose.' she replied.

'Well, you get your things together and one of the constables will take you home.' He said, before returning to the sitting room where he handed Paterson Turnbull's key.

'Okay Harry, he's all yours. Come on Colm we've got two more to find.'

As they reached his car, the old lady and the other police officers already gone, there was a sudden noise and from the house came the sound of a single gun shot. Maitland and Elliot ran from the car back up to the house where, in the lounge, an untied Miller lay dead on the carpet, leaving Patterson to explain that the prisoner had tried to escape.

Much later that evening a refreshed Commander Birbeck relayed the facts to the Prime Minister at 10 Downing Street. It had, she agreed, been a fairly successful day and she hoped very much that the other two assassins would be caught very soon.

Later, as he was driven back to his makeshift bed in his office at New Scotland Yard, Birbeck's conscience began to eat at him. Even in the dog eat dog world of the international terrorists, he doubted if what had happened that day was in fact justified. His pending retirement had become a great deal more attractive.

It was approaching midnight when John Mayo took some care in parking his Volvo in a side street near his small flat in central Dublin.

Looking at his watch, he concluded that his wife, a nurse at the local hospital, would be well into her night shift. Perhaps, thought Mayo, I have time for a quick pint of Guinness, before bed.

As he stepped away from his car, he caught a sudden glimpse of the uniform badge before the bullet crashed through his rib cage and into his heart.

Wednesday 4 November 1981

15

A cloudless sky indicated that the sun would shine on the good people of London for the second day in a row and this was to the obvious delight of the sightseers who were already beginning to arrive in the city by train, coach, car and even airplane in order to grab the best vantage points for the Royal Parade.

Red, white and blue was very much in evidence with Union Jacks adorned with photographs of members of the Royal Family predominant. Already, the route was a mass of dark blue with policemen and women stationed at intervals of less than ten yards while others mingled with the crowd searching handbags, rucksacks, paper bags, shopping bags and being generally vigilant. Meanwhile, on the rooftops others were keeping themselves awake with black coffee and looking forward to getting home to their beds.

For the policemen and women of London, it was nothing new, they had seen it all before, and they would see it all again.

The man rushed through the 'Nothing to Declare' customs area at Heathrow and out onto the main concourse, looking for a public telephone. Moments later, he found one free in the middle of a row of five and, looking at the newspaper again, dialed the New Scotland Yard number given in the article.

Elliot sat at a makeshift desk in the Special Operations room reading a Daily Mail and drinking coffee from a paper cup when Stevenson came into the room and crossed to where Elliot sat.

'Anything exciting this time Luke?' asked Elliot without looking up from his newspaper.

'Geezer just back from Cyprus this morning, says that he rented his house in Kenton to someone answering De Ville's description about a week ago.' answered Stevenson, dropping a piece of notepaper on top of Elliot's newspaper. 'That's the address for what it's worth.' He continued before returning to his post in the telecommunications room.

Crossing the room to the wall containing various maps, Elliot reckoned that it would not take too long to check it out, perhaps a patrol car would do, he thought. Deciding to check with Maitland, he went to retrieve the big man from the toilet.

Maitland pressed the button on the front of the hot air blower and began rubbing his hands together to dry them. Elliot stood by the door and Ian Maitland was considering what he had just heard. Looking at his watch, it was seven-fifteen and it would only take them half an hour or so to get out to the house. From inside his jacket, he took out a black comb and, in front of a mirror, gave his short hair a few quick delicate stokes.

'Okay Colm, get a driver and let's get out there and take a look. It probably won't come to anything but it sure as hell beats sitting on my arse in this place.'

The so-called Fox lowered his dumb-bells and went to have a shower. Outside, London was beginning to come alive with the morning rush hour and the tens of thousands of extra people arriving in the city for the opening of Parliament by Her Majesty the Queen.

Soaking his body, he thought of the day that lay ahead; the shock that lay ahead; the panic that lay ahead; and even greater than all that, the victory that lay ahead.

Later, dried and dressed in only swim shorts and a tee shirt, he left his studio and went to the pay phone in the corridor outside and began dialing his foreman's number. Just then, one of the girls from the flat opposite opened her door and headed for the stairs. Looking at him, she smiled and said 'Good morning'. The so-called Fox replaced the receiver and blocked the girl against the wall, a look of panic on her face.

'I heard you and your friend having a laugh at my expense the other day,' he began, running his right hand up inside her dress to her pants. The girl looked at him, a mixture of horror and sickening pleasure in her eyes. Reaching the top of her pants he slipped his hand inside and took a gentle grip of her pubic hair.

'Don't ever laugh at me again, do you understand?' The girl nodded and he kissed her gently on the cheek before releasing her and letting her hurry away down the threadbare stairs to work.

Slightly annoyed at his own lack of concentration, he smiled to himself as he telephoned his foreman to say that he was unwell and would be taking the day off work. If his boss sounded in any way surprised it was only because in his seven years working for the Property Services Agency, the man had never previously missed one day.

The PSA is that part of the Department of Environment, with its head offices in Ashdown House, Hastings, East Sussex, responsible as its name suggests for the maintenance and upkeep of all government properties large and small.

The so-called Fox had, in fact, been working as a member of the team that had just completed a series of extensive repairs to buildings within the Palace of Westminster including the House of Lords.

The elevator doors opened and Barry Piers was about to step out when Commander John Birbeck opened the door leading from his office and stepped into the corridor, his large overcoat in his hands.

'Stay where you are Barry and hold the lift.' Piers did as he was asked while waiting for Birbeck who was busy giving instructions to his assistant to 'Tell the Prime Minister.'

On the way down to the ground floor, Birbeck relayed the good news to young Piers who was absolutely delighted.

'Looks like they had an argument and went for their guns,' smiled Birbeck and as they walked across the concrete towards the waiting car, Piers laughed heartily for the first time since his father's death.

'So, are you saying that they simply shot each other?' he asked finally, the bizarre picture of the scene forming in his mind.

'That would seem to be the case. Of course, forensic will have to confirm our theory, but it seems to fit the scene. Ian Maitland and Elliot are there now, and they seem pretty convinced.'

Piers sat in the back of the car and enjoyed the journey, feeling as if a great burden had been lifted from his shoulders. Looking out on the busy streets, he noticed that the sun was beginning to shine and he wondered just how symbolic that was.

Jordan drove with his usual clinical efficiency and it was just before eight o'clock when they arrived outside the house.

Having fought their way through a growing band of journalists, Maitland led them into the sitting room where they briefly looked at the bodies of O'Neil and De Ville.

'Good job this happened,' nodded Maitland at De Ville's bald head, 'or we would never have been able to trace him.'

'Well I'll be.' began Birbeck as Elliot passed him the passport and other documents that had been in the Frenchman's pocket when he had died. 'If it's not the Bald Eagle Jean-Claude Marnier.' He concluded quietly to himself.

In the end, it had been much easier than some campaigns he had known. But, never before had he felt so threatened. And with little wonder, when he was up against people like Marnier, who had eluded arrest on so many occasions in France. He had remained for years the man the French police had most wanted, and now he was dead. Birbeck looked around at his team, their relief was obvious, before instructing that the house be sealed off until forensics arrived.

They all adjourned to the dining room where Elliot and Maitland had been awaiting Birbeck's arrival. Elliot, Maitland and Barry Piers stood without speaking for a few moments, before the Commander broke the silence.

'Well,' said Birbeck, turning to his colleagues 'that would seem to be that.'

'You're assuming that Liam Blaney is dead?' asked Elliot.

'According to Major General Rowe that would seem to be most likely.'

'Well, we can only thank God that they are all out of the way,' began Maitland, before continuing ' tell me Colm, do you really think that they believed that they could pull this crazy plan off?'

Elliot considered the question for a moment.

'Difficult to say, Blaney would have, especially if that con man McCormack had really gone to work on him.' he looked at his shoes as he spoke, something niggling at the back of his mind.

'So McCormack would never have believed that they had a chance?' asked Birbeck.

'I doubt it, and what did it matter to him?' replied Elliot, 'He wasn't going to live long enough to enjoy it anyway, was he?'

'Then why the hell did he bother? These guys wouldn't have come cheap.' Maitland sounded unconvinced, the terrorist was an animal that he would never understand.

'Don't know,' Elliot shrugged his shoulders, 'probably wanted to go out with a bang.' he continued.

'Fairly appropriate choice of phrase given that it's Bonfire Night tomorrow,' smiled Piers and they all joined in light laughter. It was Birbeck who spoke next, his face turning grey.

'Jesus Christ!' he began.

'What is it John?' asked Maitland, realizing that something was wrong.

'McCormack has conned us all, don't you see?' Suddenly they were all aware of the possibilities.

'The Fox, as in Guy Fawkes?' Offered Piers.

'The other four were just a highly expensive smoke screen, sacrificed to get our attention focused on them, while they got on with a more spectacular revenge for the hunger strike deaths?' Speculated Maitland.

Birbeck looked at his watch, the Royal Family would be on their way to the Houses of Parliament in just under two hours time.
'We better get to Westminster.' He announced, leading the others out of the house.

The Palace of Westminster, which houses both the Commons and the Lords, is a vast bewildering complex containing eleven courtyards, a hundred staircases and over eleven hundred rooms. The site covers eight acres. With the exception of Westminster Hall, which dates from the eleventh to the fourteenth centuries, and the Debating Chamber of the Commons, rebuilt in the forties after being destroyed in 1941 by German bombers, virtually the whole of the Palace was built between 1840 and 1870.

The architecture of the buildings is a flamboyant example of neo-gothic, all spires and pinnacles and vaulted arches. It was, in fact, the first significant Gothic revival building other than a handful of churches to be built in England, and it was designed specifically to harmonize with the thirteenth century Gothic style of Westminster Abbey, its near neighbour across the road. Visitors to the palace often have the feeling that they are entering a cathedral rather than a secular building. Members of the public and other visitors normally enter via St Stephen's entrance, but it was through the Members' entrance that Birbeck led his men that morning.

One of the many policemen on duty at the Palace led them through the long corridors to the Housekeepers residence. The Housekeeper, perhaps better known as the Sergeant-at-Arms, was sitting behind his desk getting ready for his part in the ceremony due to begin in a couple of hours. He knew Birbeck well, they had first met when part of the Palace had been bombed by the IRA in 1974 and had worked together on Palace security on many occasions since.
'Commander Birbeck, how nice to see you again,' he began

walking towards Birbeck and his companions from behind his desk, 'but I fear this is not a personal visit, what can I do for you?'

Birbeck looked around at Maitland who was behind him, as if searching for somewhere to begin.

'I am sorry to say that we fear there may be a bomb planted in one of the two Houses.' he explained.

'Why that is impossible Commander, you know how good the security is in this place, and your boys have been very thorough as usual.' began the Housekeeper.

'I know, I know,' Birbeck held up his hands in despair, 'but I must insist that the Palace is searched again and as quickly as possible, a team of experts will be here in minutes.'

'But Commander, the guests are due to begin arriving very shortly, surely you cannot believe that …?' argued the Housekeeper, unable to finish.

'Look, I am not asking for your help, I am simply saying that we are going to search the Palace for a bomb. Do you understand?' Maitland had rarely seen the Commander in such a mood and neither had the Sergeant-at-Arms.

'Very well Commander, but what of the early arrivals?'

'Well, if there is a device it is fair to assume that it will be in the House of Lords or the House of Commons, so why not usher them into the Westminster Hall?' suggested Birbeck.

'Yes that makes sense, I'll go for that.' replied the Housekeeper and Birbeck turned to Maitland.

'Would you see to that Ian?' he asked and Maitland went without a word, while Birbeck turned back to the Housekeeper.

'Now, who has been in either of the Houses over the last couple of weeks, who would not normally be in there?'

The Sergeant-at-Arms scratched his head while thinking.

'Only people who've been in there were a team from the PSA,' he offered.

'What were they doing?' asked Birbeck impatiently.

'The usual preparations, as well as some fairly substantial repairs and replacement of woodwork at the Bar, but these people are scrutinized and checked thoroughly.' he replied.

'How thoroughly?'

'The usual checks. Papers, passes etcetera.'

'Can you assure me that nothing was overlooked?' And Birbeck was aware by the expression on the Housekeepers face that he would not get such an assurance.

He left the Housekeepers residence in a hurry and met Maitland coming towards him.

'Everything arranged John, and the bomb squad have arrived. Where do you want them to begin?' he asked.

'Tell them to begin at the Bar in the House of Lords.' replied Birbeck rushing off to speak to the television and radio people.

Just then, a small brown Property Services Agency van pulled into a private car park beneath a Civil Service office block a few hundred yards from the Palace of Westminster. The so-called Fox stopped the van and reached forward, opening a glove compartment and extracting a small metal box.

Opening the lid, he took out a grey aluminum remote control panel the front of which contained a crude red light with a switch beside it, and a black button. Extending an aerial from the top of the panel he flicked the switch and the light came on, forcing him to smile.

Looking at his watch, he reckoned that he still had another seventy-five minutes to wait, so he switched off the panel, pushed the aerial back into position and put the panel back into its box and put it down on the spare seat beside him.

Broadcasting from the Houses of Parliament had begun permanently in 1978. The head of Parliamentary broadcasting is responsible for ensuring that broadcasts happen on time. On that morning, the job had a lot more attached to it due to the fact that the State Opening of Parliament was one of the few occasions in which live television coverage came from the Houses.

The head of the BBC's Parliamentary Broadcasting unit, Martin Bruce, was sitting in the small BBC radio commentary box, which is situated at the rear end of the chamber of the House of Commons overlooking the benches and facing the chair of the Speaker, when Birbeck found him.

Like most of the staff at Westminster, he recognized Birbeck immediately and left his fellow broadcaster George Coats sitting with his headphones on, to join Birbeck outside the commentary box.

Terrorist threats at Parliament were a common occurrence and the Anti-Terrorist Squad and the broadcasters had a rule of conduct known only to themselves and Martin Bruce agreed that if Birbeck felt the need to apply this rule, then he and his staff would implement it.

It took the bomb disposal experts and their highly trained sniffer dogs the best part of an hour to find and defuse the device. It had been connected to less than ten pounds of Semtex explosive and fitted neatly into a false balustrade in the Bar of the House of Lords, some ten feet from where the Prime Minister was due to stand, surrounded by the Leader of the Opposition and scores of other Members of Parliament, during the reading of the Queen's speech.

Birbeck, relieved with the discovery, insisted that the place be double checked for other similar devices although he was confident that no more would be found.

As he walked back from the House of Lords towards the Central Lobby, he saw Elliot and Piers standing talking to the Sergeant-at-Arms. They stopped their conversation and all three smiled at him as he joined them. It was Piers who spoke first.
'Congratulations Commander, it would appear that you have beaten them again.'
'Thank you Barry, I am just sorry that your father had to be a victim of this elaborate scam.'
' So am I Commander, so am I.' Reflected Piers sadly, before shaking hands with the policemen and turning to head for the exit, glad that it was over.

Elliot and the others watched him go and it was Colm who spoke next.

'I suppose that I should go too, I've still got my war to fight.' But Birbeck shook his head while looking at his watch. It was nine fifty and the Peers, Members of Parliament and their guests really needed to be in their places very soon if the public were to know nothing of this latest near-disaster.

'I am going to call out my men,' he began, turning to the Sergeant-at-Arms, 'but I would like to have a word with the Royal Family when they reach the Robing Room. Can you fix that?' The Housekeeper smiled and said that he would.

'Okay Colm, let's go and meet the Queen.'

The opening of Parliament by the Queen is one of the most spectacular official indoor events of the year. By ten o'clock that morning, the Peers had taken their places in the centre of the chamber of the House of Lords, dressed in their scarlet robes trimmed with ermine. The Archbishops and Bishops were dressed in scarlet velvet too. Also present were foreign politicians, Ambassadors representing their countries, some of them in uniform and others in national costume. The wives and husbands of the Peers were seated on the side benches dressed, even at that early hour, in formal attire.

To the delight of the massive crowds who lined the route, the Queen travelled from Buckingham Palace to the House of Lords in the Irish State coach accompanied by Prince Philip, Prince Charles and his recent bride Princess Diana. The Royal coach was escorted by the Household Cavalry with their shining breastplates and plumed helmets. To those watching at home on television, it was a stunning display of the greatest of British traditions.

On arrival at the House of Lords, the Queen was shown to the Queen's Robing Room, a handsome chamber decorated with scenes from the legend of King Arthur and the Knights of the Round Table. There, unseen by those television viewers, Commander Birbeck and Elliot told the Royal Family of the recent turn of events. When they had finished, Prince Charles turned to Birbeck.

'What odds would you give on another bomb?' he asked, playing with his pinky ring as he spoke, and the question had taken Birbeck slightly by surprise.

'Let me say Sir, that I am ninety-nine per cent certain that the Palace is now safe.' He answered confidently and it was the Queen who spoke next.

'Thank you very much for your on-going efforts and concern gentlemen, but since when did I or members of my family ever go anywhere in the knowledge that a place was going to be completely safe?' And with that, the Queen and her family passed out of the Robing Room, through the Royal Gallery and its immense murals of the battles of Waterloo and Trafalgar, towards the House of Lords.

A few hundred yards away, the so called Fox was one of the millions tuned into the BBC broadcast as the announcer described the Queen's arrival in the House of Lords followed by Black Rod's procession to the House of Commons, and the arrival of the Prime Minister, the Leader of Her Majesty's Opposition and hundreds of other Members of Parliament at the back of the House of Lords, at the Bar, as it is called.

Picking up the grey aluminum panel, he extended the aerial and flicked the switch. To his absolute horror, the red light failed to go on. Frantically, he pressed the black button, but on his car radio, the broadcast continued uninterrupted, the Queen delivering the proposals set out by the Prime Minister and her team in the Cabinet.

Closing the van door he walked towards the Houses of Parliament where, half an hour later, he watched in disgust as the Royal Family were cheered by the crowds as they left the House of Lords on their way back to Buckingham Palace.

Friday 6 November 1981

16

Apprehensively, Ray O'Grady left the elevator and approached the room in which his boss and long-time friend, the Irish Prime Minister, was busy preparing for his meeting with his British counterpart later that morning.

Waving Ray to a chair in front of his desk, the politician finished some amendments to a typed document open in front of him before turning his attention to O'Grady.

'So Ray, what is it that's so urgent?' he asked looking over his reading glasses to his Private Secretary.

'I am here to tender my resignation, for private and personal reasons, to be effective immediately,' began O'Grady.

'Really? And is there any point in me trying to dissuade you Ray?'

'No point at all Prime Minister.'

'Very well, I accept.' concluded the politician, standing and offering O'Grady his hand.

The two stood in silence, shaking hands, before the Prime Minister added

'But you should know Ray, that in your shoes, I would probably have done exactly as you did.'

'You knew?' Asked O'Grady, bemused.

'Of course I knew, I may not be at the same level of risk as my British opposite number. But, as you should know Ray, my own security is pretty tight.'

'I am glad to hear it,' began O'Grady before saying ' I am so sorry Prime Minister.'

'So am I Ray, so am I.' And with that, a stunned Ray O'Grady turned to take his leave and return to his fractured but re-united family.

Later that day, the British and Irish Prime Ministers announced at a joint meeting in London that they had officially re-opened Anglo-Irish talks on the issue of Northern Ireland.

The announcement caused an outcry from Ulster's protestant extremists who claimed that both governments were planning, in secret, the unification of Ireland.

These claims were, of course, categorically denied by both governments.

Friday 22 January 1982

Epilogue

As the train approached the platform at Shepperton station, John Birbeck pulled himself from his champagne induced reverie and stood to put on his heavy overcoat. The Blaney McCormack plan, with its expensive decoys, had undoubtedly been one of the most audacious Republican attacks on mainland Britain and had consequently been the closest he had come to ending his stellar police career in disgrace.

The potential death of many of the UK's leading politicians along with the risk to the Royal Family including the Queen, her heir Prince Charles and Princess Diana, who unbeknown to the public that day, was already carrying her first child, would have been catastrophic.

As it was, eleven people had died as the IRA hardliners had tried to force politicians on both sides to negotiate the re-unification of Ireland by showing their financial strength and military capacity to organize and cause carnage at the very heart of the British establishment. However, thought Birbeck, what if their plan had been successful?

Leaving that thought unanswered, he walked towards Sara, waiting for him in her car, happy in the knowledge that Liam Blaney was dead. But what of the cunning and evil man who had been mistakenly known as the Fox? So far, no trace of him had been found, but Birbeck was in no doubt that the man would return again in the future and attempt to create more havoc for the people of Britain.

By coincidence, at the precise moment that the now ex-Commander John Birbeck was slipping into his wife's car at Shepperton railway station, a man closely answering the description of the so-called Fox, was locking up his small camping equipment shop in his hometown of Hunstanton in north Norfolk.

Known locally as a quiet but helpful man who kept himself to himself, he was enjoying his time away from active service but knew that a call would come soon enough. A call that would require him to put the skills developed, and fine-tuned in the steamy heat of Libya, to use in the ongoing struggle with the British.

About the Author

Gerry Rose grew up in Scotland, graduated in Mathematics & Economics and received his MBA from the University of Edinburgh. He has worked internationally as a management consultant since 1994, working extensively in Europe and the USA. He now spends his time on new business projects and writing, and lives in Buckinghamshire with his wife Lesley and their three children Rebecca, Olivia and Ben.